DEVNEY PERRY

MERIT

Editing:

Elizabeth Nover, Razor Sharp Editing

Proofreading:

Julie Deaton, Deaton Author Services

Judy Zweifel, Judy's Proofreading

Cover:

Sarah Hansen © Okay Creations

OTHER TITLES

The Edens Series

Indigo Ridge

Juniper Hill

Garnet Flats

Jasper Vale

Crimson River

Sable Peak

Christmas in Quincy - Prequel

The Edens: A Legacy Short Story

Treasure State Wildcats Series

Coach

Blitz

Rally

Merit

Haven River Ranch Series

Crossroads

Sunlight

Clifton Forge Series

Steel King

Riven Knight

Stone Princess

Noble Prince

Fallen Jester

Tin Queen

Calamity Montana Series

The Bribe

The Bluff

The Brazen

The Bully

The Brawl

The Brood

Jamison Valley Series

The Coppersmith Farmhouse

The Clover Chapel

The Lucky Heart

The Outpost

The Bitterroot Inn

The Candle Palace

Maysen Jar Series

The Birthday List

Letters to Molly

The Dandelion Diary

Lark Cove Series

Tattered

Timid

Tragic

Tinsel

Timeless

Runaway Series

Runaway Road

Wild Highway

Quarter Miles

Forsaken Trail

Dotted Lines

Holiday Brothers Series

The Naughty, The Nice and The Nanny

Three Bells, Two Bows and One Brother's Best Friend

A Partridge and a Pregnancy

Standalones

CONTENTS

CHAPTER ONE

MAVERICK

The daisy on my mini pumpkin was smudged.

"Damn it." I'd worked hard on that daisy.

I licked my finger, rubbing the white streak, trying to make the petal look like a petal again, but the paint had dried overnight.

This was what I got for doing a craft project at three o'clock in the morning.

At least the red and yellow *Happy Thanksgiving* still looked pretty good. Mom wouldn't care if this pumpkin was less than perfect. She had a plastic tub crammed with my elementary school art projects and loved them to pieces even though most were a hot mess.

With my pumpkin in hand and Mom's favorite prosecco under an arm, I knocked on the door to my parents' house, not waiting for an answer as I pushed inside. "Hello."

The house didn't smell like turkey or rolls or stuffing or pies.

We were eating here, right? Mom had said come over at

noon so we could eat around one. Or were we eating at the Adairs'?

"Maverick?" Mom called from the living room.

"Yeah." I toed off my shoes and walked down the entryway to the living room. Mom was on the couch with a crocheted blanket on her lap.

The sick blanket.

When I was a kid, that was the blanket she'd cover me in whenever I had a sick day. That fucking blanket had been a constant lately.

"Hey." I went to the couch, sitting by her feet. "Not feeling well again?"

"Not the best." She gave me a sad smile.

Her brown hair was pulled into a knot at the base of her neck. She was dressed in a cozy cardigan, and though she'd put on makeup, beneath the blush and foundation, her skin seemed too pallid. She looked too thin.

"For you." I handed over the mini pumpkin. "I fucked up the daisy."

"Maverick," she chided. "Language."

"Sorry. I screwed up the daisy." I set the prosecco bottle on the end table and relaxed into the couch. "Got another bug, huh?"

"Yeah." She lifted a shoulder, smiling at the pumpkin. "This is cute. Thank you."

"Welcome." I lifted her feet into my lap, massaging the arches through her fuzzy *Gobble Gobble* socks.

A gift from my sister, no doubt. Mabel probably had a pair like that in her purse for me too. It wasn't a holiday if we weren't all in matching, themed socks.

Mom sighed as I kept massaging her feet, sinking into the pillow behind her shoulders. "I'm sorry I didn't cook."

"Meh. I don't care. We can order pizza. Hang out. Watch football."

"No pizza," she said. "Your dad is in charge of food. He had to run to the store. He should be back soon."

Which meant we'd probably have deli sandwiches. A ham and turkey sub was about the extent of Dad's culinary expertise. But the man could make a solid hammy sammy, and I wasn't picky.

"Where's Mabel and Bodhi?" My sister's car was out front, and Bodhi's shoes had been by the front door. They were the new pair of Nike LeBrons I'd given my nephew for his eighth birthday.

"Mabel went with your dad. Bodhi is downstairs playing, I'm sure with a ball of some sort. I swear he's worse than you were at that age."

Soccer or basketball or football or baseball. If I'd been awake and not in school, there'd been a ball in my hand.

"I'll go say hi," I said, shoving to my feet, but before I could head downstairs, the doorbell rang.

"That'll be the Adairs." Mom shifted to get up, but I waved her off.

"I'll get it."

It wouldn't be Thanksgiving or Christmas or Easter or Flag Day or the Fourth of July without the Adairs. We hadn't spent a holiday without my parents' best friends since, well . . . ever.

Declan Adair was Dad's best friend. Elle Adair was Mom's.

My parents had moved to Montana from Nebraska before I was born, and though I had a few aunts and uncles in Omaha, we'd never been close and rarely visited. The distance had always made gatherings tough.

The Adairs had filled the role of family.

Declan was an uncle of sorts. Elle was an aunt. And their daughter, Stevie, the bane of my existence.

"Maverick." Mom stopped me before I could leave the living room. "Be nice to Stevie today."

I scoffed. "I'm always nice to Stevie."

Mostly nice.

Mom arched her eyebrows.

"Are you going to tell her to be nice too?"

"You sound like Bodhi. Don't pout. You're too old to pout."

"Fine," I muttered. "I'll be nice."

"Good."

I waited until I was in the entryway, out of sight, before I rolled my eyes.

"And don't roll your eyes at me, young man."

"Sorry, Mom." I opened the door, stepping to the side as I waved in the Adairs. "Happy Thanksgiving."

"Hi, Maverick." Elle's hands were covered in oven mitts as she carried in a silver roasting pan.

"Can I help?" I asked.

"Nope." She winked, then strode through the house for the kitchen, smiling at Mom as she passed the living room. "Hey, Mer."

"Hi, Ellie," Mom said.

"Maverick." Declan clapped me on the shoulder. He had two large totes, one hung from each shoulder, and at a quick glance, both were full of food. "Good to see you."

"You too. I can carry one of those."

"Nah. I've got it." He headed for the kitchen, following his wife.

I didn't bother asking if Stevie wanted help carrying in

the ceramic dish in her hands. The look she shot me was a very plain *get the fuck out of my way.*

Why was I always the one being told to be nice? She started our fights half the time. Why was it always my fault?

"Happy Thanksgiving, Adair," I said, too brightly.

"Houston." She scrunched up her nose as she passed like my breath was bad.

I cupped a hand over my mouth, let out a hot huff and sniffed it. Cinnamon fresh.

Women loved cinnamon, and I loved women. Most of them loved me too.

Except Stevie.

She followed her parents into the house, giving me a shoulder as cold as the winter weather. The skirt of her dress swished at her hips as she walked.

Her dress was long-sleeved and black with a tiny flower print. The fabric was flowy and a tie cinched it around her waist. Her chocolate brown hair was in a loose braid, the end hitting just above her ass. An ass barely covered by the hem of that dress.

Which meant her mile-long legs were almost entirely on display. Or would have been if not for the tan boots that came up past her knees.

Where was her coat? It was freezing outside. There was snow on the ground. Shouldn't she put some fucking pants on? Was it really necessary to flash us all those damn legs?

"Happy Thanksgiving, Meredith," she said, smiling as she passed the living room.

Stevie smiled at everyone. She smiled all the freaking time. Unless she was looking at me. Would it kill her to give *me* a smile?

"Thanks, sweetie. You look pretty today."

Stevie always looked pretty. It made hating her a little bit harder, but I managed.

"So do you. As always," she told Mom.

It was a stretch. Mom looked rough today. But if there was anything that would ensure I'd be *nice* today, it was Stevie's love for Mom.

I closed the door to keep out the cold, then padded into the kitchen. The Adairs were taking over and setting up everything for a traditional Thanksgiving meal.

The roasting pan went into the oven, probably to keep the turkey warm. Elle swapped Mom's empty crockpot dish for the one Stevie had carried in. And from the ingredients Declan was hauling out from his totes, it looked like we'd be having some sort of fruit salad and green bean casserole.

They'd spent enough time in this kitchen that it was as familiar as their own. The reverse was true at their place. Mom had made more than one meal at the Adairs' house.

"Can I help?" I asked.

"No, you kids go relax." Elle shooed Stevie and me out of the kitchen. "Keep Meredith company."

"Okay." I shrugged.

"I can set the table," Stevie said. "Or pour waters. Or make the veggie tray."

"Or do anything other than be around me," I said. "That's what she really wants to say."

Stevie walked over, a smirk on her lips, and tapped me on the nose. "Exactly."

I scowled and batted her hand away.

"You two." Elle sighed. "Not today, okay? Save your bickering for another time. Please just . . . not today."

"Be nice to Maverick," Declan said, giving Stevie a pointed stare.

"Ha," I snickered, covering it with a cough. Then I pounded my fist over my heart. "Frog in my throat."

Stevie's lip curled.

"Go." Elle shooed us again. "Out."

I turned for the hallway as Stevie marched out of the kitchen, crossing her arms over her chest, the heels of her boots clicking on the hardwood floor as we both headed for the living room. "Why are you all dressed up? You know we're just hanging out today."

"Just because you're okay wearing ratty gray sweats and a hoodie that looks"—she leaned over and sniffed my arm—"and smells about five wears past its need for the washing machine doesn't mean the rest of us have given up on hygiene or appearance."

I lifted the front of my sweatshirt, bringing it to my nose. Okay, so it wasn't exactly fresh.

This was my favorite Treasure State University Wildcats hoodie, and I'd had it since freshman year. The sweatpants too. They were a bit frayed at the hems but they were comfortable. Perfect for a day of lounging. Which was why I'd plucked them both off my floor this morning. And because I'd gotten behind on laundry.

They weren't that bad. Were they? I sniffed my sweatshirt again, this time at my armpits.

Maybe I should have worn something else. Not that I'd ever admit that to Stevie.

Before I could come up with a snarky reply, Stevie walked ahead of me and into the living room, taking the end of the love seat that sat perpendicular to the couch. She flicked her braid over her shoulder, all but dismissing me from the room.

"So how was the date?" Mom asked her.

The absolute last thing I wanted to do was listen to her tell Mom about whatever guy she was dating at the moment, so I veered toward the stairs. Downstairs, Bodhi was shooting a rubber ball into his mini hoop.

"Hey, bud. Happy Thanksgiving."

"Hey, Uncle Mav." His cheeks were flushed and a few strands of his wavy, brown hair were sweaty. He had on the same fuzzy socks as Mom.

This kid was my favorite human on the planet. He was funny and smart. He said whatever crossed his mind. And he didn't do anything half-assed.

Kind of like his uncle.

"Watch this." Bodhi backed into the corner, lined up his shot and launched the ball into the air.

It smacked the ceiling and bounced off the floor, not even coming close to touching the rim.

"Dang." His shoulders slumped. "I just made that shot."

"It was a good try." I grabbed the ball from the floor and tossed it over. "You shoot. I'll rebound."

The basement was a large, open room, perfect for sports on cold Montana days. We'd spent plenty of hours down here together, usually with a game on the TV as background noise, doing trick shots or playing foosball.

"'Kay." He shot the ball again, the arch better this time, so the ball hit the rim.

"Nice." I caught it off the bounce and walked it over. "Smell my sweatshirt. Does it stink?"

He leaned in, sniffed and shrugged. "Not really."

Not the hard *no* I was hoping for. Damn.

I handed him the ball, but before he could take it, I spun around and shot it myself, sending it swishing through the hoop. "Yeah, baby."

"Show-off." Bodhi laughed, racing for the ball.

We played for a while, shooting and dunking and goofing around, until Mabel called from the top of the staircase.

"Bodhi. Mav. Time to eat."

He tossed the ball one last time, then we jogged upstairs, finding everyone shuffling around the dining room table.

"Hey." I pulled Mabel into a hug before she could sit down. "Happy Thanksgiving."

"Hi." She held on for a long moment, arms tight around my waist.

"You okay?" I asked.

She nodded but didn't let me go.

My sister thrived on fuzzy socks, pumpkin spice lattes and autumnal-colored cardigans. Thanksgiving was her favorite holiday, and if she was hugging me like this, something was wrong.

Was it her ex? Bodhi's dad wasn't in the picture. That motherfucker—I refused to even think of him by his name— hadn't been since Bodhi was six months old and he'd left Mission, abandoning both his child and my sister.

The day that asshole had walked away from her and Bodhi was the day he'd become dead to me. For the most part, he was nonexistent. He lived in Washington or Idaho or Oregon. I'd stopped keeping track. But every once in a while, Mabel would hear something about him and it would put her in a funk.

"Hi, son." Dad came over, breaking up the hug to pull me in for one of his own, slapping my back a couple times.

"Hey, Dad."

When he leaned away, his gaze was watery. Wait, was he crying? Monty Houston didn't cry. Ever. What the fuck was going on?

"Thank you for cooking, Elle." Mom took her seat beside Dad's empty chair as the rest of us went to our usual places.

The same chairs we always sat in. Dad at the head of the table, Declan at the foot. Mom and Elle and Mabel on one side. Bodhi, Stevie and me on the other—Bodhi always between us as the buffer.

Mom had the mini pumpkin I'd made her beside her water glass. The sick blanket was still on her lap. She gave me a smile that didn't reach her eyes when I sat down across from her.

Okay, something was definitely going on.

Mabel dabbed at the corners of her eyes as she took her seat, and when Elle sat beside her, they held hands, so tight their knuckles turned white.

The table was piled with food, turkey and stuffing and potatoes and cranberries and rolls. No one moved to fill their plate.

Mom looked to Dad, and whatever passed between them made my stomach sink.

That sinking feeling only worsened as Dad struggled to say grace, pausing every few seconds to clear his throat. He was not a man who used many *ums* and *uhs*. He didn't stumble through a prayer.

"Let's eat," Declan said, scooping a heap of mashed potatoes onto his plate.

We all followed suit, loading up. But my side of the table seemed to be the only one with an appetite.

Mom picked at her food. Not unusual for someone not feeling the best. But so did Dad. So did Mabel. So did Elle and Declan.

Conversation was stilted, and rather than talk about

anything meaningful, we chatted about the weather. The fucking weather.

That sinking feeling was so deep by the end of the meal that I was regretting that second helping of turkey and stuffing.

"That was delicious," Dad said, looking to Elle and Declan. "Thank you, guys."

"Any time." Declan gave him a sure nod.

"Bodhi, you can go play or watch football," Mabel said. "We'll have pie in a little while. I'm too full for dessert right now."

That was a damn lie. Mabel hadn't eaten much of anything, even her mashed potatoes. She loved mashed potatoes.

"'Kay. Wanna watch a game, Uncle Mav?" Bodhi asked.

"Yeah, in a few. You get it going. I'll be down in a bit."

He seemed reluctant to leave the table, like he could feel the tension too. Like he knew the adults were about to discuss a topic clearly not suitable for children.

"Go on," I said, giving him a nod.

He pushed out his chair and went to the stairs.

"Close that door, Bodhi," Mabel said, knowing her son well enough to expect him to linger on the stairs and eavesdrop.

"Okay." He frowned but obeyed.

She waited a few moments, then stood and checked that he'd actually gone downstairs.

The only topic that we never, ever discussed around Bodhi was his father.

Did he want custody or something? Was he trying to get back into Bodhi's life? That asshole could rot. He'd given up his rights, and as far as I was concerned, he wasn't getting them back.

"What?" I asked at the same time Stevie said, "What's going on?"

Well, at least I wasn't the only person who was confused as fuck about this holiday gathering.

Mom and Dad shared another one of their looks, and my insides roiled.

"Thanks for coming," Mom said, her gaze sweeping around the table before it landed on me. There were tears in her eyes. Why was she crying?

"Mom." My voice cracked.

"I have cancer."

She might as well have kicked the chair out from beneath me.

Stevie gasped, slapping a hand over her mouth.

I shook my head, refusing to let that sentence be true. "No, you don't. You're just sick."

"Maverick." She gave me a sad smile. "It's cancer. And it's . . ."

She blinked too fast, swallowed too hard. Then she crumpled, leaning forward, chin ducked, to hide her tears. Right before my eyes, my mother, the best, strongest, kindest, most loving woman on this earth, crumpled.

"It's . . . what?" I whispered.

"Advanced." She sniffled, wiping away more tears when she finally looked up. "We'll try treatment. But the prognosis isn't good."

"What does that . . ." I couldn't finish my question. I couldn't fucking breathe.

"I'm sorry," Mom whispered.

I should have told her not to apologize. That she had nothing to be sorry for.

Instead, I rushed to the bathroom.

And puked up Thanksgiving dinner.

———

FUCK, it was cold.

I'd been sitting outside on the front stoop for, well . . . I wasn't sure how long I'd been outside. Long enough that I couldn't feel the tips of my ears or my fingers.

But the house had been too hot. Too sticky and stuffy. Too heavy.

So I'd come outside to breathe. To cool off.

And now I didn't want to go inside.

Acute myeloid leukemia.

Mom had explained the details of her cancer. Of her treatment. She'd be going to the hospital for chemotherapy. Something called induction. From there, she might need a stem cell transplant.

There were a lot of unknowns at this point. A lot of statistics. When Dad had started spouting numbers, percentages and survival rates, I'd tuned it all out. I'd stopped listening and stared at Mabel's uneaten mashed potatoes.

When they were finished explaining, I'd been close to getting sick again, so I'd come outside to breathe.

Wasn't leukemia for kids? Mom was in her late forties. She shouldn't have leukemia. She shouldn't have cancer.

Cancer. Cancer. Cancer. That word kept running through my mind on a loop.

I hung my head, forearms on my knees, and breathed

through my nose as the world spun and turned like I was riding a roller coaster.

I hated roller coasters.

My mom had cancer. And that cancer was likely going to kill her. She'd made it a point to tell me three times that the prognosis wasn't good. Like I hadn't heard her the first time.

Besides Stevie, everyone else at the table had already known. Wasn't that some bullshit? Why were we the last to find out?

I couldn't feel my toes. My shoes were still inside in the entryway. My socks were just plain, white socks. Mabel hadn't given me my fuzzy Thanksgiving socks.

We'd been too busy talking about cancer.

The door opened behind me. I didn't turn. It was probably Dad or Mabel. Maybe Declan. But the click of heels made me sit up straight as Stevie dropped to a seat beside me.

"Here." She handed me my shoes.

I pulled them on without a word, not bothering with the laces. Then she handed me the keys to my truck. Somehow, she'd guessed I wouldn't be going back inside.

"Thanks." I pushed to my feet and started down the sidewalk for the driveway.

"Maverick?"

I turned as Stevie stood, walking closer.

Her hazel eyes were swimming with tears.

Everyone inside had already dealt with this blow. They'd had the chance to let it sink in.

Not us. They'd told us at fucking Thanksgiving, with my mini pumpkin and smudged daisy on the table.

It felt like someone had shoved a hot poker down my

throat. My eyes watered, my nose was on fire. When was the last time I'd cried?

I wasn't sure who moved first. One moment, I was staring at the girl who'd hated me since we were ten. The next, she was in my arms. I clung to her the way she clung to me, in a hug so tight it was hard to breathe.

I closed my eyes before the tears could fall. I folded around her, my face buried in her neck as she burrowed into my chest.

When was the last time we'd hugged?

Probably twelve years ago, when we were kids. In the days when we used to be friends.

Best friends.

I needed my best friend today. So I hugged her, leaned on her. And breathed in the scent of her floral perfume. The orange blossoms in her hair.

I let myself lean on her for another heartbeat, then let her go.

Her hazel eyes were still full of tears. "I'm so sorry."

I didn't want her apologies either. What I wanted was for my mom not to be dying. I wanted to rewind time and go back to when we were ten. When Stevie didn't hate me. When we used to be friends. When Mom wasn't sick.

But we weren't friends. And my mother had leukemia.

Fuck cancer.

And fuck Thanksgiving too.

CHAPTER TWO

STEVIE

F*ive months later . . .*
Maverick's truck was in my parents' driveway. In *my* parking spot.

"Seriously?" I muttered, pulling my red Jeep to the curb.

What was he doing here? My question was answered when the devil himself came sprinting around the side of the garage, arms raised to catch a football that soared over the roof of the house.

Maverick caught it and let out a whoop. "Got it!"

Thirty seconds later, Dad came jogging around the garage, hand raised in the air to give Maverick a high five.

This wasn't the first time I'd come home to find Dad playing football with Maverick. It also wasn't the first time they'd challenged each other to toss the ball over the house and see if the other person could catch it in time.

The ladder was propped against the side of the house. Apparently, their earlier attempts hadn't gone as well as this one.

I shut off the engine and, on a sigh, climbed out of the Jeep.

"Hey, Steve," Dad called.

"Hi, Dad." My lip curled from the nickname I'd loathed since middle school—and from the sneer Maverick sent my way.

"Adair," Maverick drawled in his familiar baritone. It could have been a nice voice if it wasn't always laced with contempt.

"Houston."

Maverick tossed Dad the football. "One more time, Deck?"

"Let's do it. Ready?"

"Go." Maverick tore off around the house as Dad loaded up the ball and launched it over the roof. The second the ball was flying over our two-story house, he ran off toward the backyard to see if his throw had made it.

Given the cheers that came a moment later, I guess that was a yes.

With any luck, Maverick would leave now that they were done playing around. I needed a night sans Maverick's attitude.

Since Thanksgiving, he'd been nearly unavoidable. My parents and his parents had gone into hyperdrive, organizing impromptu family breakfasts and lunches and dinners. I'd spent the last five months suffering through Maverick's company over way too many meals simply because it made Meredith happy to have us all together.

We were all focused on Meredith, trying to soak up as much time with her as we could manage.

If it were just the family functions, I probably could have

tolerated Maverick. But the guy was freaking everywhere lately. In my four years at Treasure State University, I'd rarely crossed paths with him on campus.

This past semester? It was like our routes between lecture halls were always colliding. Even when I took the long way around, going out of my way to avoid the more crowded common areas, there he was. Walking with other guys on the football team. Flirting with some girl on a bench. I'd even bumped into him at Dolly's Diner the other night when I'd gone out to eat with my roommate Jennsyn.

At least the campus run-ins would be over soon enough. It was May, and in just a few more weeks, I'd be a college graduate. There'd be no more passing him in the hallways of the student union or seeing him in the fieldhouse gym.

And beyond that, well . . . I didn't want to think about how everything was going to change after Meredith died.

Our family, his and mine, would never be the same.

The idea of losing her made my throat burn, but I swallowed it down and went inside the house, where Mom and Meredith were in the living room on the couch.

Meredith was on the left side of the couch. Mom was on the right. My entire life, those were the seats they'd choose for the nights when Meredith would visit Mom and they'd gossip and drink a glass of wine. Even as the couch had changed, their places hadn't.

I couldn't imagine a world where Meredith's seat was empty. Where she wasn't just down the block if I ever needed advice or a warm hug.

When I'd run away from home at seven years old, it was to Meredith. I'd arrived at the Houstons' house with my backpack loaded with my favorite stuffie and a box of snacks. She'd come to nearly as many of my volleyball games as my parents. In a neighborhood brimming with boys, she always made sure to celebrate that I was a girl by painting my nails or braiding my hair.

We all needed Meredith, and she was withering away before our eyes.

I'd learned more about cancer treatment in the past five months than I'd ever cared to know. Chemotherapy. Consolidation. More chemotherapy. Growth factors. An autologous stem cell transplant. Bone marrow biopsies. Drug trials.

Through it all, the leukemia cells remained.

Despite the palliative treatment and supportive care, the cancer was killing her.

She kept getting thinner and thinner. After the induction chemo, she'd lost her hair. The green floral silk scarf she was wearing today was one I'd bought her when I'd gone to Hawaii with Mom and Dad for Christmas.

We'd all spent plenty of time researching her cancer. Researching options. None of us were giving up hope, but it was hard to feel much when the doctors tossed out statistics that seemed unbeatable. When the tests never came back in her favor.

So I took a moment to memorize her on that side of the couch before I walked into the living room.

"Hey." I plopped down on the middle cushion and gave them both a hug. "How's it going?"

"Oh, good. We were just chatting," Mom said. "And listening to your dad and Maverick throw that ball over the house."

"Or try." Meredith laughed. "It took them a while. Maverick drove me over so we could hang out, but then your mom said you were coming over tonight and we decided we might as well eat dinner together. Monty is on his way. He's getting pizza."

That Meredith wouldn't eat.

The current cocktail of drugs they had her on was ruining her appetite.

"You know I love pizza." I smiled on the outside, and on the inside, I stuck out my tongue and blew.

I loved pizza. If it was made the way I loved pizza. Extra sauce. Extra green peppers. I was okay with onions, olives and sausage, but I hated pepperoni and bacon and mushrooms.

Monty was a great man. He was Dad's best friend, a great dad and grandfather. He loved Meredith and treated her like a queen—this cancer was eating him alive too. I'd known him my entire life, and if I ever needed help, besides my parents, Monty was the next person I'd call.

But he still believed that if I just tried pizza or tacos or cheeseburgers "his way" enough times, my tastebuds would magically change.

He'd show up tonight with a meat lover's deep dish and a thin-crust supreme. Even if I picked off the mushrooms, I would still taste them.

I gagged even thinking about their texture.

It was fungus. Why was I the only person in this family who thought eating fungus was fraught with peril?

Whatever. I'd make chicken nuggets when I got home.

"I saw Mr. Wilson on his porch as I was driving over," I told Mom and Meredith. "I flipped him off."

"Good. What an asshole," Mom grumbled.

Meredith's nostrils flared. "I have never in my life wanted to throw eggs at a person's house the way I want to with his. Maybe I will."

"You just name the night," I said. "I'll start stocking up on eggs. Let them rot for a bit so they're nice and rancid. And I'll get us some ski masks too so he doesn't catch us on his doorbell camera."

"I love this plan," Meredith said, laughing with Mom.

Would we ever egg Mr. Wilson's house? No. But we could dream.

Wilson was a crochety old man and the neighborhood grump. My sophomore year in high school, he'd decided that me running around the neighborhood in a sports bra and shorts was indecent exposure. He'd called the cops.

Nothing had come of it, but it had been devastating for me at that age. I'd been fifteen, tall and strong. I'd never been a slender, willowy girl. I loved volleyball and soccer and running. I was fit and muscular.

I loved my body. Now. But at fifteen, I'd been coming to terms with the fact that I was different than the petite, popular girls at the Oaks. And having a police officer show up at my door, telling my parents that a neighbor was offended with me flashing too much skin, had been a major hit to my confidence.

But I'd clawed it back, one middle finger to Mr. Wilson at a time.

The incident had caused such a disturbance with the homeowners association, that most people in the neighborhood hated Mr. Wilson. My parents had even considered moving, but they loved being close to the Houstons.

They'd met at an HOA meeting twenty-something years ago, before Maverick and I were born. Meredith and Mom had been pregnant at the same time, bonding at that HOA meeting over heartburn and swollen ankles.

They'd decided that the debates over paint color

approvals and fence height limitations were too much drama, so they'd gone out for dinner instead.

They'd been best friends ever since.

Movement outside drew my attention. Maverick and Dad stood in the front yard, their tall, towering figures framed in the wide living room window.

Dad was talking, arms crossed over his chest. Maverick was nodding, the football tucked under his arm. Both had serious expressions. Then Dad held out his hand, taking Maverick's in a shake. They grinned, then Maverick tossed the ball into the back of his truck before he came inside.

He walked to the kitchen, probably for a glass of water, lifting a hand to wave as he passed the living room.

"I'm going to go say hi to Dad." I stood and slipped out the front door. Dad was still in the front yard, looking down the street. Waiting on Monty and the pizza. "Hey, Dad."

"Hi, buddy." He held out an arm, tucking me into his side for a hug. "How were classes today?"

"Fine." I shrugged. "I'm ready to be done."

"I'm ready for you to be done too. I think this is going to be our busiest year yet."

Dad owned Adair Landscape and Nursery. He'd started the business when he'd moved to Mission, moved into this house. His first office had been in our basement. For years, money had been tight as he'd built the business, living mostly on Mom's salary as a dental hygienist.

But with a lot of hard work, Adair had become the go-to landscaping company in Mission and the surrounding area. His reputation as a landscape architect was unparalleled.

I'd known since I was a little girl that someday I'd work for Dad. My major was environmental horticulture science, and as soon as I graduated, I'd go to work full-time for Dad.

After I got some on-the-job experience, I'd work toward getting my own architecture license.

"It's going to be a great season," I told Dad.

Every summer since I'd turned sixteen, I'd worked at Adair, usually in our small garden center. This year, I'd be on landscaping sites with Dad and, hopefully, pick up a few small clients of my own to start building a portfolio.

"Yes, it is going to be a great season." He hugged me tighter. "I just offered Maverick a job."

"What?" My jaw hit the lawn as I stepped away. "Come again?"

"I offered Maverick a job."

"No, you didn't." The color drained from my face.

Dad knew how I felt about Maverick. He knew we couldn't be in the same room without bickering. And he'd offered him a job?

"Why?"

"Steve." He stepped close, putting his hands on my shoulders. "Hear me out. It's been a rough year for Maverick. He's still got another season with the Wildcats, so it's not immediate. He doesn't want to work this summer, not with football and everything happening with Meredith. But after he graduates, it would be good to have someone to manage the business aspects of the nursery. Maybe look at expanding the garden center."

Manage. There was no way I was hearing this right. "You asked Maverick to be the manager?"

That was Dad's job. And eventually, it was supposed to be mine. Wasn't it? But now he was giving it to Maverick?

I shook my head, trying to make sense of this decision. "I don't understand. You're the manager. I thought I was going to be the manager."

Did that mean he wasn't going to let me run the business? Dad had always told me that Adair would be mine if I wanted it. And I *wanted* it. I'd always wanted it. Did he not think I was capable?

My heart started to fracture, tiny cracks that were growing and growing and growing, like roots spreading through soil. This wasn't happening. How was this happening?

"Adair is yours." He squeezed my shoulders, accentuating each word. "It's always been yours. But you'll need help. A business manager will free up your focus to be on landscaping and our customers. Let someone else deal with the staff and inventory and finances. You see how much I work."

Yes, I did.

Mom always joked that Dad's second wife was Adair Landscape. He worked tirelessly, year-round. And he'd been so successful that Mom had been able to retire early from Dr. Peterson's office.

They'd bought me the Jeep for high school graduation. Had I not gotten a scholarship to play volleyball at Treasure State, they would have paid for my education. And they'd bought a house for me and my roommates to live in this past year so we didn't have to rent—once I started full-time at Adair, I'd be purchasing it from them, getting a first-time homebuyer's loan from the bank to build up my credit.

His hard work meant I'd been lucky. Incredibly lucky and fortunate. But I'd always planned to work that hard too. Always.

"I want to work hard too." And if I decided someday I wanted to step back, couldn't I hire a business manager?

"I don't want this lifestyle for you," he said. "You're

young. You'll have plenty of years ahead to work your ass off. But I also want you to have help. To not feel like it's all riding on your shoulders. I need you to trust me. I'm doing this for you."

"And Maverick."

He gave me a sad smile. "Yes. And Maverick."

Because Maverick was the son Dad had never had. The son he'd always wanted.

If I was a boy, would we be having this conversation? Would he have decided to split his job in two, giving half to my archnemesis?

I wasn't sure I wanted the answer.

"Is this because of what's happening with Meredith?"

"Not really." He shook his head. "I've been thinking on this for a while. I don't know what's going to happen after Meredith . . ." *Dies.* None of us could say it. "But regardless, I would have offered this job to Maverick."

So he'd been planning this for months and months. And rather than tell me about it first, he'd gone straight to Maverick with an offer.

He hadn't even given me the chance to fight for Adair. To decide for myself how hard I was willing to work.

While my head was still spinning, Monty pulled into the empty space behind my Jeep.

"Hey, Monty." Dad crossed the front yard to help carry in the pizzas.

Monty was still dressed in his suit and tie. He was a financial advisor, helping people with their investments and retirement. He had a business of his own too.

Mabel worked for Monty. She was beginning to build her own portfolio as well as take over pieces of his. Why couldn't Maverick go to work for his own father?

"Hi, Stevie." Monty smiled as he walked up the driveway with Dad. He looked haggard, his suit not as well fitting as usual. He'd lost weight, and the dark circles beneath his eyes were becoming permanent.

I forced a smile. "Hi."

"Hope you're hungry." He lifted both boxes of pizza while Dad trailed behind with a six-pack of beer and a bowl of salad.

"Starved," I said.

"Coming in?" Dad asked.

"Yeah." My throat felt raw, like I was on the verge of screaming or crying. But I swallowed past the burn and followed them inside, taking the pizza boxes from Monty so he could go and kiss his wife.

"How are you feeling?" he asked Meredith.

"I'm good. Hungry."

We all heard the lie.

But at least she was here. At least she wasn't in the hospital like she'd been during and after her treatments. At least she'd felt well enough today to leave the house.

I carried the pizza into the kitchen, taking out a stack of plates and a handful of utensils. Everyone filtered in behind me, dishing themselves a plate.

I wasn't hungry. Not for pizza. Not after that announcement from Dad. But I took the smallest piece of the meat lover's pie and joined everyone at the table, tearing off the crust to nibble on it as I picked off the pepperoni and flicked away bacon bits.

"Dad, you forgot breadsticks for the food princess," Maverick said from his chair across the table.

My nostrils flared. Food princess? That was a new insult.

"Yes, I am a food princess. I'm picky. I know what I like." I leveled him with a glare. "And what I don't."

He scoffed.

God, we couldn't work together. What was Dad thinking? We'd kill each other.

My parents both shot me a warning glance.

Monty elbowed Maverick and gave him a slight headshake.

For years, our parents had tried to get us to make amends. They'd finally given up, choosing to simply accept our mutual hatred. They wouldn't sacrifice their friendships with each other just because Maverick and I didn't get along.

Part of me loved that they were so loyal to each other.

The other part wished my parents would have chosen me over the Houstons.

My only comfort was that for all of my suffering, Maverick had to suffer too.

For the most part, we did our best to ignore each other. Or we traded barbs when no one else was listening.

Maverick must have been feeling brave tonight to pick a fight with everyone at the table.

"Will you do something for me?" Meredith asked, placing her hand on her son's.

"Sure, Mom."

She gave him a sweet smile. "Go on a date with Stevie."

The crust I'd just bitten off lodged in my throat and I coughed, clearing it out before I could choke.

A date? With Maverick? I let out a hysterical laugh. "No, thanks."

"You must be feverish." Mav put his hand on Meredith's forehead.

"I'm serious," she said. "I want you two to go on a date. Figure out a way to be kind to each other again."

"That ship has sailed." Maverick plucked a mushroom off his slice, popping it into his mouth, smirking as he chewed.

I gagged.

"Please?" Meredith clasped her hands together. "Consider it my dying wish."

Maverick choked on his mushroom.

CHAPTER THREE

MAVERICK

"Whoa." Dad smacked me on the back. "You okay?"

I nodded and spat the mushroom that had just tried to kill me into a napkin. Once I could breathe again, I twisted in my seat to glare at my mother. "Do you mind?"

"What?" She feigned innocence. "If I'm going to die soon, I might as well guilt you kids into making up before I'm gone."

Why did she have to talk like that?

When her treatments had started, she'd held on to a glimmer of hope that the drugs would work. That the intense chemotherapy, that first induction, would be enough to kill the leukemia cells. But that glimmer of hope had faded when the biopsy results had come back with cancer cells. The hope had disappeared entirely after the reinduction and transplant and subsequent test after test.

Now Mom seemed determined to use that fucking word at every opportunity.

Die.

She was dying. But did we have to fucking talk about it?

"Can we not share dying wishes over dinner?"

She gave me a sad smile.

Mom was breaking my heart one sad smile at a time.

"Make the most of it." Her favorite saying.

Mom always told me to make the most of it.

"So? What do you say?" She looked between Stevie and me. "One date?"

Stevie's eyes were huge, and for a woman who absolutely hated meat lover's pizza, she shoved a huge bite into her mouth, gagging as she chewed, just so she wouldn't have to answer.

I glanced to Dad, hoping he'd come to my rescue.

He was focused on his meal. So were Elle and Declan.

"Uh . . ." I dragged a hand over my face.

The doorbell rang.

"I'll get it." I was out of my chair and jogging through the house before anyone else could move.

The door pushed open before I got there in time, Mabel's head poking inside. "Hello!"

"Hi." I took her arm, practically hauling her inside.

"Maverick, what—"

"Mom, Mabel's here," I called. "Without Bodhi. So now you can tell her what you told me in the truck earlier."

Mabel gave me a sideways glance. "Um, what's going on?"

"Mom is making dying wishes. Welcome to the worst dinner of all time."

She groaned, spinning for the door. "Maybe I'll skip the pizza and watch Bodhi's practice instead."

"Not a chance." I pushed her in front of me, both my hands on her shoulders, as I marched her into the dining room.

"Hey, everyone." Mabel held up a hand to wave.

"Hi, sweetie." Elle stood, rushing to the kitchen to get her a plate. "Hungry? What flavor?"

"Surprise me," my sister said.

"Bodhi is at baseball?" Declan asked as he pulled out the empty chair at his side.

"Yep. For another hour." Mabel didn't move, so I nudged her forward, earning a glare over her shoulder.

But she gave up the fight, sitting beside Stevie, who looked to still be chewing that same bite with a grimace.

"Mom just told us that her dying wish is for Stevie and me to date."

Mabel laughed. "That's funny, Mom."

"She wasn't joking." I stood behind Mom's chair, my arms crossed over my chest.

"I wasn't joking," Mom repeated.

Mabel scrunched up her nose. "They'll kill each other."

Stevie swallowed. "Exactly."

Mom simply shrugged and poked her slice of pizza with a tine on her fork. "Be that as it may, it's my wish. And like I told your brother as we were driving over, my wish for you" —the fork got aimed at Mabel's nose—"to go out with that doctor."

"Not this again." The moment that Elle handed my sister a plate with a slice of each pizza, Mabel stole a move from Stevie's playbook and shoved a huge bite in her mouth.

The doctor was a guy Mabel had met at the gym. Apparently, he was gorgeous. Divorced.

Mabel had slipped a month ago and mentioned to Mom that he was hot. And that he'd asked her out for dinner.

Mabel had her reasons for saying no. She was in no rush to date again, not after the shitshow that had happened with Bodhi's dad, even if it had been years and years ago.

Did that stop Mom from pushing? Hell no.

"Fine." Mom held up her hands. "You can all ignore me. But let it be known that my dying wishes are on record."

Could we stop talking about dying wishes?

Fuck, I hated this. I hated it so much I couldn't stand still, so I retreated to the kitchen, pacing beside the island as a wave of restless, angry energy rolled through my veins.

My fingers were jittery. My appetite had been smashed like a fly under a swatter. I wanted to scream and rage and that familiar burn in the back of my throat just wouldn't go away.

I'd never felt more helpless in my life.

Fuck cancer.

And fuck dying wishes.

I had no desire to date Stevie, and judging by the sour look on her face, she sure as hell didn't want to date me either.

We hated each other. Period.

Mom had been given over a decade to come to terms with that reality. Not even a date would change the facts.

Stevie considered me the enemy. It had been that way since we were ten.

One day, the two of us had been riding bikes around the neighborhood with some of the other kids. The next, she'd told me she never wanted to be my friend again. We'd started fighting before middle school and had simply never stopped.

All because I'd said something about her boobs.

Was it a stupid comment? Absolutely. I'd been a ten-year-old boy, stupid was on brand.

And when Stevie had started her own mudslinging, as a

stupid, ten-year-old boy, I hadn't let it go. Instead, when she'd told me I had an ugly, big nose and was chubby, I'd told her that she sounded like a donkey when she laughed. *Hee-haw. Hee-haw.*

She'd run away mad. And I'd cried when I got home. Maybe I'd known, deep down, even as a stupid, ten-year-old boy, that my friendship with Stevie was over.

Our parents had tried to force us to work it out and not let this animosity fester for twelve years. They'd pushed and we'd pushed back, against them and each other. Fight after fight had led us here.

I was the villain in Stevie Adair's story. And she was the adversary in mine.

Also my nose was fucking perfect. I might have been a little pudgy at ten, but I was ripped now.

There were plenty of women in Mission who liked my nose and abs just fine.

"Maverick, come and sit down," Dad said. "Before your pizza gets cold."

I sighed and returned to my chair.

"Please?" Mom put her hand on my leg. And with another sad smile, my resolve crumbled.

Say no. Just say no. "Fine."

Stevie's jaw dropped. When she spoke, her voice was a near shriek. "Fine?"

None of this was fine. But what the hell else was I supposed to say? "Would you go on a date with me?"

Maybe I was a bastard for putting her on the spot, but I'd let her be the asshole here and squash Mom's wish.

She must have realized what I was doing. Her nostrils flared.

There wasn't another soul on earth who could make a nostril flare look pretty. Stevie managed it every time.

Was that why I got such a thrill from provoking her?

In any mood, Stevie was beautiful. Pissed off? The gold flecks in her eyes danced like flames. They never got that way with anyone else. Just me.

Well, she could glare and snarl at me over one date. It would make my mother happy.

Or she could say no.

Break Mom's heart.

The ball was in her court.

Declan kicked her leg under the table.

"Ouch. Dad," she hissed.

He gave her pleading eyes. So did Elle.

When she faced me again, it was with a look that could flay meat from bone. "I'd love to, Maverick."

Mom exhaled. "I know you're doing this because you're being guilted into it. But I don't even care. Thank you."

Stevie gave her a tight smile, then stood, taking her plate to the kitchen. She put it in the dishwasher, slamming the door too hard, then headed for the front door.

"Be back." I stood too, and by the time I'd jogged to catch up, Stevie was nearly to her Jeep parked on the street. "Stevie."

She whirled, finger raised. "You. Are. The. Worst, Maverick Houston."

"This wasn't my fucking idea." I held out my arms.

"*You* should have told her no. Not left me to disappoint her."

"This is what she wants. It's one date. You can survive it."

She scoffed. "My reputation won't."

"What the hell does that mean?"

She waved a hand at my six-foot-four frame. "It means you're . . . you."

"Hot. Athletic. Sexy. Great nose and bone structure. Yes, your reputation will never recover."

She gritted her teeth, raised her fists and shook them in the air.

If only I had a dollar for every time that I'd pushed her to that gesture. God, it was fun pissing her off. Besides playing football, watching football or coaching football, it was my favorite hobby.

Well, except for sex.

"You are a manwhore," she said.

I huffed. "Can you even say 'manwhore' these days? It's not nice to judge people based on their sexual proclivities. And, for the record, I'm not a manwhore."

Stevie's expression flattened.

Okay, so I was kind of a manwhore.

In my defense, I'd had a hard time adjusting to Mom's diagnosis, and mindless sex had been my coping mechanism when football wasn't an option.

But this spring, those random hookups had started to feel shallow. I hadn't had sex in over a month. And I doubted I would anytime soon either, especially at my house.

Last week, my roommate and best friend, Rush Ramsey, had become a father. His girlfriend, Faye, had given birth to a healthy baby boy.

Rally Ramsey slept a lot, ate a lot, shit a lot and cried a lot.

He was fucking awesome.

That baby had been a blissful distraction. Faye had even let me babysit this morning so Rush could go to class and she could score a shower.

And not that a newborn would know if I was screwing a girl in the room downstairs, but that idea just didn't sit right with me.

But apparently, the fact that I was incredibly responsible with children and babies didn't win me any favors with Stevie Adair.

Nope, I was just a manwhore.

Hell, this date was going to suck.

"What if we just pretended to go?" Stevie asked.

"She'll ask questions." Meredith Houston was a trust-but-verify kind of mom. "By the time we get our story straight, we might as well have just gone to dinner."

She crossed her arms over her chest, her jaw working as she thought it over. As she came to the realization that this was happening unless she wanted to waltz back inside and break Mom's heart. "When and where?"

I knew she'd come around. "Saturday?"

We were in the slowest time of year for Treasure State Wildcats football players. We actually had weekends free at the moment.

"Fine." She kicked her toe into the grass.

"Six o'clock? Dolly's Diner?"

"No. Someplace obscure."

So she wouldn't have to be seen with me. *What-the-fuck-ever.* "Luna?"

It was the most expensive restaurant in Mission. Not a place overly crowded with college students.

"You're buying," she said.

"Obviously," I deadpanned. "It's a date."

Mom's dying wish. *Damn it.* I wanted to scream.

Stevie tipped her head to the sky.

And did it for me.

CHAPTER FOUR

STEVIE

Maverick was tapping his fingers on the table when I arrived at Luna. His pint glass was nearly drained, only an inch of beer remaining at the bottom. His lips were pursed, and given the disheveled state of his brown hair, he'd run his fingers through it no less than ten times.

I was thirty-six minutes late.

My phone had chimed the entire drive to the restaurant, but I'd left it in my purse, knowing it was Mav. There were probably a dozen texts waiting, and I doubted any of them were particularly nice.

Well, too bad. I wasn't feeling particularly nice either. He should have told Meredith no. Was it petty to punish him for being a coward? Yes. I'd even felt a little guilty on the drive over.

But the fact was, this was a waste of a Saturday night for us both.

I pulled out my chair, settling into the seat across from his. Then without a word or glance at Maverick, I pulled the book I'd brought along out of my purse, opening it to the page where I'd left off.

It was a spicy romance. The heroine had just overheard the hero jacking himself off in the shower and calling out her name. There was still fifty percent to go, but I already knew it was a five-star read.

"You're fucking kidding me."

My gaze flicked up from the page to find Maverick's light-blue eyes. If he didn't glare so much, he'd have beautiful eyes.

"Yes?" I asked.

He leaned his elbows on the table, checking over his shoulder before he lowered his voice. "You're late. And now you're reading on our date?"

I lifted a shoulder and dropped my eyes back to the book. "It's not a date."

As far as I was concerned, this was a family obligation. It wasn't the first time I'd ignored him by reading. I doubted it would be the last.

"Adair," he snapped.

"Houston," I drawled, not breaking from the page.

He huffed and leaned back in his chair, his knee knocking the underside of the table as he shifted. "Un-fuck-ing-believable."

"I haven't gotten to read for fun lately. I've been busy with school and volleyball. Besides, don't tell me you were actually looking forward to chatting tonight. We'll suffer through this meal in silence and move on."

He clenched his jaw so hard I heard his molars grind over the dull hum of restaurant conversation and clink of silverware on plates.

"What if I was looking forward to talking? What if I was taking this seriously?"

I arched my eyebrows, flipping a page. "You're not."

"Have you been playing volleyball?" he asked.

"Some."

"With the team?"

Was he actually trying to have a conversation? I glanced up. A smirk sat on his lips.

Asshole.

I wouldn't be able to read if he was talking to me. No matter how good this book was, it was hard to tune out his smooth voice. "A few times. Coach Quinn asked if I'd come in and practice with the incoming freshmen. Otherwise, I play every Sunday morning."

My roommates, Jennsyn and Liz, had both been on the Wildcats team with me this year. We were all graduating this spring, and though our volleyball careers were over, we all still loved to play, me especially. So I'd found a rec league team that needed a few other players.

"Any other questions?"

Maverick's smirk stretched wider. "You play center, right?"

"Setter." The center position was called middle blocker, something I'd told Maverick a hundred times. Just like I'd told him I was a setter.

But explaining volleyball to this man was a waste of my time. Maverick didn't give a shit about volleyball. Not because he didn't like the sport. Maverick Houston loved all sports.

You couldn't hardly tear him away from Monday Night Football. He talked ad nauseum with Dad about baseball teams. Maverick was in charge of the Adair-Houston March

Madness bracket pool, and he'd even convinced his parents to host a party for the FIFA World Cup.

But volleyball? It might as well not exist. He'd dismissed it simply because volleyball was *mine*.

Which was why I'd refused to learn anything about football.

I returned my attention to my book, not that I could concentrate. Reading was almost impossible with the weight of Maverick's stare on my face.

Another question was coming. I could feel it as clearly as I could feel the vibration from his knee bouncing beneath the table. But I refused to play into his antics. Maverick was a guy who was used to the spotlight. He loved attention.

Denying him mine was my favorite pastime. Yes, sometimes I couldn't resist a snarky reply or comeback. But it irked Mav the most when I pretended like he didn't exist.

Ignore him.

That had been my mom's advice all those years ago. The day Maverick had gone from my best friend to that fartface who lived down the street.

Maybe in time, I'd forget that day. Maybe not. I remembered it as clearly as if it were yesterday.

I'd ridden my bike to the neighborhood park to meet Maverick. He'd already been there with a bunch of boys from around the block. Other than holidays when Mom had forced me into a dress, I'd lived in shorts and T-shirts. For the most part, Maverick and I used to dress the same. But that summer day, I'd decided to wear a pink tank top and matching shorts.

A couple of the other boys had commented on the color, teasing me for dressing like a girl.

That, I could have waved off.

Except then Maverick had made fun of my boobs. He'd called me A Cup. All of the other boys had chimed in, cupping their hands over their chests, pretending like they had cleavage.

I'd ridden my bike home in tears.

When I'd told Mom about it, she'd told me to ignore him. That boys our age were usually awful, and the best punishment for Maverick was my cold shoulder.

A Cup. Thinking about it still grated on my nerves.

Our parents knew how this rift had started, but they hadn't counted on me holding a grudge for twelve years.

Maybe Meredith was right. Maybe it was time to let it go.

Maybe not.

I turned to the next page in my book.

Maverick let out a huff, then shifted in his chair, searching the restaurant for our waitress. He unrolled his silverware from his napkin, picking up his fork to twirl in his fingers. He scooted his chair in closer, bumping the table's edge.

My water glass was too full, probably because the ice had been melting for over thirty-six minutes, and Maverick's squirming sent a plop over the glass's rim.

"Do you mind?" I took a drink, setting it down with too much force.

"This chair is uncomfortable." He shifted it again.

"You're such a baby. Try sitting still."

"I have been sitting still." He leaned forward with a sneer. "I sat still for the first thirty-something minutes of this date."

"It's not a date." How many times was he going to say that word?

"Could they have given me a smaller table?" He crossed his legs, a knee knocking underneath again. And again, my water sloshed.

"Maverick," I hissed.

"Why is this table so fucking short?"

It was short. The tops of my thighs were just a few inches from the underside. If I wanted to cross my legs, I'd have to sit sideways.

Mav drained the last of his pint. "Where is our waiter?"

An excellent question. Not that I'd ever admit that out loud.

I'd been here for at least ten minutes. This was not the night for a dallying waiter. I wanted food, the check and a short goodbye.

A man in a long, black apron came walking down the aisle. The moment he made eye contact, I held up my hand.

"We're ready to order."

"You haven't even looked at the menu," Maverick said.

"Doesn't matter." I gave the waiter a bright smile when he stopped at the edge of this tiny table.

"Welcome." The waiter took out a small notepad and flipped to a fresh page. "Can I get you anything to drink, miss?"

"I'm fine with water." After this charade was over, I'd go home, treat myself to a glass of red wine and make a batch of my favorite chocolate chip cookies. "I'll have a side salad. No sunflower seeds. No feta. No mushrooms. Extra walnuts. House vinaigrette on the side."

He nodded, jotting it down. "Would you like that out before or after your meal?"

"That is my meal. The sooner you bring it out the better."

"Um . . . of course." He looked to Maverick. "And for you, sir?"

Maverick was staring at me. Scowling, actually. "Anything that resembles a burger. Medium. Fries."

"We have a gourmet bison burger with caramelized onions and a jalapeno relish."

Damn. That sounded good. That's what I wanted for dinner.

"Fantastic." Maverick handed over his menu.

The waiter hesitated before he collected my menu, like he could see the indecision on my face. But I handed it over so he could leave to, hopefully, expedite our order so we could get the hell out of this restaurant.

"Way to make an effort," Mav muttered.

"You could have made an effort to tell your mother this was pointless."

"It's one fucking dinner," he whisper-yelled. "Would it kill you to be nice?"

I was nice. Well, to everyone but Maverick. Maybe it was purely habit, but throwing sass his direction had become a favorite pastime. Snide retorts and sarcastic censure came so naturally when he was in the room it was like breathing. And thankfully, the snarkier, the better. It usually meant we spent as little time together as possible.

Avoidance was easier, for everyone.

But he was right, this was just one dinner. For Meredith.

"Fine." I closed my book with a slap, setting it aside. "How are you tonight, Maverick?"

"Annoyed as shit that you couldn't be here on time."

Fair. If I was in his chair, I'd be irked too. "I'm sorry for being late."

"Liar."

I lifted a shoulder. "Can you really blame me for not wanting to be here? It's not like we ever get along."

"And that's my fault?"

"Yes. Obviously."

He rolled his eyes. "All because I was a shithead when we were ten? When are you going to get over it?"

"Get over it?" My voice was too loud, and the people at the tiny, short table beside ours gave us a sideways glance. Maybe, if I was lucky, they'd complain to the restaurant manager and ask us to leave. Banishment from Luna seemed like the best outcome tonight. "You act like this is all my fault. *You* started this, Maverick."

"I. Was. Ten. And you said some shit when we were kids that was cruel too."

He wasn't wrong. I'd called him chubby once. Not my finest moment. And in middle school, my go-to insult was to call him Big Beak because of his nose—a nose he'd grown into over the years and was actually quite well-proportioned to the symmetry of his face.

We both had apologies to make.

If we truly started apologizing, we might never stop.

"Fine. I'll 'get over it' when you apologize and *mean* it." I crossed my arms over my chest. Not an A cup anymore. I was a C cup and had great boobs. So there.

Maverick had never given me a sincere apology for that day. He'd made excuses, saying it was the other boys who'd started it. Saying it was just a joke and I'd freaked out.

Meredith and Monty had forced him into a *sorry for teasing you.*

To which my parents had made me say sorry for calling him chubby and saying he had a big nose.

Neither of us had meant those apologies. Because

neither of us had let the insults go. Instead, we'd let them drive us apart.

"I'm not apologizing for something I said a million years ago," he said.

"Then we'll never get along. Congratulations." I tossed up a hand. "You've deprived your mother of her dying wish."

He scoffed. "This is such bullshit."

"Hence the reason I didn't want to come and showed up thirty-six minutes late." I picked up the book and returned to my page.

The hero in this story would never have teased the heroine for her boobs. In fact, he was obsessed with her breasts, as he should be.

"Fine, I apologize. I'm sorry I called you an A cup." Okay, that had actually sounded sincere. Maverick was rarely sincere.

I glanced up, romance novel forgotten, and met Maverick's gaze. "Apology accepted?"

It came out as a question. What was the catch?

"Good," he said. "Now it's your turn."

"I'm sorry for all the things I said to you in the last twelve years that wasn't the epitome of nice. For all the times I hurt your feelings, I apologize." It was sincere too.

"Thank you. But when I said it was your turn, I didn't mean for apologies."

"Oh. You didn't?" Why not? Weren't we trying to let bygones be bygones here? "Then what do you mean?"

"I want you to admit that you told Leah McAllister that I kissed Heather Olson."

There it was. That was the catch.

Damn it. Well played, Houston. Well played.

I'd been denying that for years, and I wasn't going to stop today. "I don't know what you're talking about."

"Of course you don't." He scoffed. "Who else could it have been?"

I set my book on the table. "Anyone on the football team? Or any of the cheerleaders? Because you did kiss Heather Olson. While Leah McAllister was your girlfriend. Don't make me out to be the bad guy here. You were the cheater."

"I was going to break up with her."

"Sure you were," I deadpanned.

His eyes narrowed. "So you admit you told Leah."

"That's not what I said." I tossed my hands in the air.

My gestures were always a bit too wild when Maverick was around. Like speaking—and yelling—wasn't quite enough to combat the absolute absurdity that came out of his mouth.

Was it me who'd told Leah? Yes. Because I had seen him kiss Heather, and Leah had been one of my closest friends in high school. My loyalty had been to her, not her cheating boyfriend.

Leah had dumped him, rightfully so. And as a bonus, Maverick had never been able to prove it was me who'd spotted him making out with Heather under the bleachers. It drove him nuts suspecting it was me but never having proof.

"You were friends with Leah," he said.

"I was friends with all the girls in our class. That doesn't mean I gave enough of a damn about who you were stringing along to get involved."

Other than the one incident with Leah and Heather, where Maverick was concerned, I'd usually remained neutral.

We hadn't gone to Mission High School like most kids in the area. Instead, Maverick and I had attended the Oaks.

It was a private school in Mission with a heavy focus on both academics and sports. We'd both been on traveling club teams, me for volleyball, him for soccer. And for a small school, their football program had been stellar. There was more than one player on the Wildcats football team who'd attended the Oaks.

Our graduating class had been a total of ninety-three. Half of that had been girls. I'd learned early on that there weren't enough people to escape girl drama, so I'd always done my best to stay neutral—Mom and Meredith's advice.

One of the most polarizing topics in our graduating class had been Maverick. At one point or another, every single girl at the Oaks had harbored a crush on him. Well, except me.

When girls found out our parents were friends, and I was forced to spend my weekends in his company, there were always questions. Expectations. *Is he dating anyone? Does he like me? Can you give me his number?*

The first and last time I'd given a friend his number, Leah, had ended in disaster.

"Can we move on to a different topic?" I asked.

He studied me for a long moment, and I fought the urge to squirm. Maybe someday I'd tell him the truth about Leah and Heather. Or maybe I'd take that truth to the grave.

"Your dad offered me a job." He stared at me like he wasn't sure if I knew that already.

"I'm aware." The edge to my voice was sharper than a steak knife.

"And you hate that, don't you?"

"More than mushrooms."

Maverick smirked.

Where the hell was my salad? I was searching the restaurant for our waiter when a man appeared at the edge of our table.

"Maverick Houston?"

"Yes." Maverick stood, taking the man's proffered hand.

"Nice to meet you. I'm a big Wildcat football fan. Just wanted to say hello. Wish you luck on your season next year."

"Thank you." Maverick gave him a kind smile. "I appreciate that. I think we'll have a hell of a team."

"I agree. It'll be sad to see you seniors go. Any plans to pursue a professional career?"

Maverick chuckled. "No. I'll leave that dream to Rush. He's the best there is. I'm excited to cheer him on when he makes it big."

Rush Ramsey was the star quarterback and Maverick's roommate. For most of my life, Maverick had been the star athlete. The guy who thrived in the limelight. It was actually kind of strange to see him so comfortable giving the glory to someone else.

Though I guess I hadn't really spent much time with Maverick in public since high school. Other than the random crossing of paths on campus, I only saw him at family functions. And that was, well . . . different.

Maverick wasn't a Wildcat football player when we were sitting at my parents' dining room table. He wasn't the most eligible Treasure State University bachelor when he was dressed in ratty sweats, watching a movie with his sick mother.

He was just Maverick.

The boy who used to help me build tents in the basement. The kid who learned how to tie his shoes before me and would help if my laces came undone. The ten-year-old who'd made me feel self-conscious about my growing chest. The teenager who'd made out with almost every girl at the Oaks.

This Maverick was almost . . . gracious. Humble.

My head started to hurt, like my brain was physically protesting that it needed to process this vision.

"Well, I'll let you get back to your date." The man shook Maverick's hand again, then he gave me a small nod before escorting his companion to the door.

"What?" Mav's glower was back as he took his chair.

"Nothing." I picked up my book and tried my best to read.

How did he feel about his sports career ending?

I know I'd had a lot of feelings going into my last season at Treasure State. There'd been times when I'd been so ready to be done with grueling practice and travel schedules. Then there'd been times when I'd cried myself to sleep because volleyball had been a part of my entire life.

Sure, there were rec leagues and fun tournaments for adults. But in my heart, I'd played my last real volleyball game.

After we'd lost in the first round of the NCAA tournament to Oregon, and I'd locked myself in a bathroom stall to cry for ten minutes.

Was Maverick anxious for his last season? I closed my book, about to ask, when I looked up to see his phone pressed against his ear.

"Hey, baby."

Hey, baby?

No. No, he did not. He was not calling another woman while he was supposed to be on a not-real date with me.

I ripped open my book so hard I heard the spine crack.

He was still a fartface. That was never going to change, was it?

Maverick had deserved to get dumped by Leah McAllister. And later by Heather Olson.

"What are you doing tonight?" he asked, his voice quiet.

Was that his bedroom voice? Did women actually fall for that low, gravelly purr? I rolled my eyes so hard it hurt.

He laughed at something she said. It wasn't his condescending chuckle or the booming laugh he reserved for playtime with Bodhi. This was sultry and dark, and damn it, I hated that I kind of liked it.

"Want to meet up later?" He paused. "Yeah, I could be there in twenty."

Twenty? We hadn't gotten our food yet.

He ended the call and tucked the phone in his jeans pocket. "Is this date over?"

"Most definitely."

He stood, digging out his wallet. He tossed a hundred-dollar bill on the table, then without a word, strolled to the door.

The moment it closed behind him, the waiter appeared with my salad and Maverick's burger.

I ate them both and finished reading my book.

It wasn't a good date.

But I'd had worse.

CHAPTER FIVE

MAVERICK

Mom opened her front door before I had a chance to knock. "So? How was the date?"

The sparkle in her eyes was gut-wrenching.

There hadn't been much to sparkle about lately, and it was a welcome change from the dreary, tired fog that usually clouded her blue eyes.

If I told her the truth about the date last night, that sparkle would vanish in a blink.

"It was good." I kissed her cheek and stepped inside, kicking off my slides in the entryway.

"Good." Mom pressed a hand to her heart. "How good?"

Stevie and I hadn't killed each other. We hadn't started a fistfight or screaming match in the restaurant. Hell, that was a goddamn success in my book. "Pretty good."

"Pretty good as in there will be a second date?"

I fucking hated disappointing my mother. Especially now.

"Mom." I put my hands on her shoulders, giving her a sad smile. "Stevie doesn't like me."

She frowned. "Oh. Does that mean you like her?"

"She's great."

If great meant she was a menace.

I still couldn't believe she'd shown up with a fucking book. Like my company was really so dull and boring that she needed fiction to entertain her through a meal. A meal I hadn't even eaten. Instead, I'd hit the drive-through at McDonald's for a cheeseburger and fries before I'd gone home to explain to my best friend and roommate, Rush, why I'd called him and pretended he was a hookup.

Rush hadn't been all that happy to pretend to be a woman when I'd called, faking a date.

What-the-fuck-ever. He'd played along long enough to torment Stevie for a few minutes before I'd walked out of Luna.

She thought I was a playboy? Fine. I'd be the playboy.

Not that she was exactly wrong. I had a reputation for a reason. But that was in the past, and even if I told her I was taking a break from the hookups and casual sex, she wouldn't buy it. Stevie Adair had made up her mind about me a long, long time ago.

Mom's shoulders slumped. "So that's it?"

"Hey, we tried." I slung my arm around her too-thin shoulders and pulled her into my side. "How are you feeling today?"

"Meh."

"Can I do anything to help?"

"Go on a second date with Stevie."

I groaned. "Mom."

"Just . . . try. Harder. What if you become friends again? What if you realize there's something special between you both?"

"I don't think that's going to happen."

"Why not? This is Stevie we're talking about. You two have so much in common. She's smart. Beautiful. Sweet. Loves sports. She keeps your ego in check."

And she had a stubborn streak that ran bone-deep.

To Stevie, I was enemy number one. And yeah, maybe I'd antagonized her over the years. The problem here was history. There was simply too much between us.

Mom pulled away and clasped her hands in front of her heart. The skin over her knuckles seemed too thin, like tissue paper. Translucent, so I could see the blue of her veins.

Every visit I seemed to find something else different about my mother.

Fuck, this was hard.

"Please, Maverick. Try again. One more time. One more date. And then I promise, I'll leave this alone."

No, she wouldn't.

Just like she wouldn't stop nagging Mabel to go out with that doctor who'd asked her on a date.

I had a feeling that if I cracked into Mom's phone, I'd find a list of things she wanted to do before she . . .

Nope. Not going there. I wasn't even going to think about what happened beyond the here and now. Not when this morning had been a decent morning.

I'd woken up early and gone to the fieldhouse with Rush to hit the weight room. After a shower, I'd stopped by my favorite coffee shop for a muffin and latte. Then I'd come here to relax and hang with Mom.

"Want to watch football?" I asked, walking down the hall for the living room.

"Maverick."

I sighed, tipping my head to the ceiling. "Mom, Stevie and I aren't going on another date."

"Because you haven't asked her yet."

I dragged a hand over my face. "Mother."

"Maverick. Please?"

A snarl tugged at my lips. *Damn it.* How did Dad say no to this woman? Oh, wait. He didn't.

None of us told her no. And that really had nothing to do with the cancer. Mom had always been impossible to argue with. We loved her too much. Because she loved us even more.

The scales were always tipped in her direction, because without a doubt, my mother would move heaven and earth to make us happy. She was the best mom in this entire world, and I'd fight anyone who believed otherwise.

So when she asked for something for herself, which was as rare as a double rainbow in a snowstorm, none of us refused.

"Fine." I marched for my slides, stepping into my shoes.

"You're leaving?" she asked. "I thought we were watching football."

"Either I go to Stevie's now, or I'm not going at all."

"Oh. Good." She opened the door for me, smiling as I kissed her cheek. "Tell her I said hi."

"Yeah," I grumbled, then headed outside into the fresh Sunday morning.

May was my favorite month in Mission. The mountains were still capped in snow, but spring was blooming in the valley, the fields shifting from brown to green. The sky was a brilliant blue streaked with rays of white sunshine.

I rolled the window down as I drove across town to Stevie's place, but I couldn't even enjoy the clean, cool air and fresh wind on my face. Not when I was about to have a door slammed in it.

The only reason I knew where Stevie lived was because I'd had to help move her shit into her house last summer.

Elle and Declan had bought a house in town as a rental property investment, then leased it to Stevie and a couple other girls from the volleyball team. While Stevie had been off in Europe, her parents had agreed to help move everything out of her old rental.

Which meant my parents had offered to help. Then they'd volunteered me and my truck too.

I hadn't been back in nearly a year. There was no reason for me to visit Stevie's place. But I drove there like I came every day, pulling into the driveway and hopping out without delay.

She'd better be home. I wasn't coming back.

I pounded a fist on the door, then crossed my arms over my chest, waiting for an answer.

Please be gone. Please be gone.

The door swung open.

Shit.

Stevie's smile morphed into a sneer when she spotted me on her porch. She was wearing a pair of lavender leggings, the fabric molding to her long legs. Her sports bra was the same color with thin straps at her shoulders, leaving her midriff exposed. Her silky, chocolate hair was in loose waves that hung nearly to her waist.

She had the body of an athlete, tall and strong, but the feminine curves made her a damn knockout. Add in that hair, and she'd been the inspiration behind many of my teenage fantasies.

Not that she'd ever know.

She was beautiful. Too beautiful for her own damn good. Certainly for mine.

There was a strange pinch in my chest as I took in the toned lines of her body, from her strong arms all the way to her bare toes.

Huh. Weird. What was that? I rubbed at my sternum. Was this anxiety? A heart murmur? How did I make sure it never happened again?

"Yes?" She took a bite of the cookie in her hand. The scent of sugar and vanilla wafted from inside the house.

Stevie made the best chocolate chip cookies in all of Mission. Whenever she brought them to my parents' house, I'd sneak a handful when no one was looking.

My stomach growled. "Can I have a cookie?"

She arched her eyebrows and shoved the rest of the cookie into her mouth. Her foot started tapping on the hardwood floor.

"My mom asked that I try again. The dating thing."

Stevie choked, coughing up a crumb before she smacked her hand over her mouth, holding up her other hand as she finished chewing and swallowed. "What?"

"She wants us to go on another date."

Horror. That was the only way to describe the emotion on her face.

"Fucking hell, Adair. You look at me like I'm a monster."

"Well, Houston, you're the guy who called a hookup while you were on a date with me."

"It wasn't a real date."

She huffed. "Does that matter? Why would I want to subject myself to that again?"

I exhaled and let out a frustrated growl. "Look, I just

want Mom to be happy. She asked me to try, so here I am, trying, okay? Can we just . . . talk? Please?"

The dismay on her face vanished as she shifted to the side and waved me in. Her feelings toward me aside, Stevie wanted Mom to be happy too.

I stepped out of my slides and followed her past the open living room and into the adjoining kitchen. There was a plate of cookies on the counter covered in plastic wrap.

She moved to the cupboards, taking out two glasses. When they were each full of milk, she slid one to me and waved to the cookies. "Go ahead."

"Thanks." I took one, dunking it in milk as she did the same.

The butter and sugar and chocolate melted on my tongue, and I held back a moan. No person as infuriating as Stevie should be able to make such good cookies.

"Are your roommates home?" I asked as I grabbed my second cookie.

"No."

Good. I didn't need an audience for what I was going to suggest. "I have an idea."

"I'm already terrified."

"So am I," I muttered, giving myself a moment to inhale the second cookie.

She didn't even blink when I went for number three.

When it was gone, I wiped a hand over my mouth and gulped my milk until the glass was empty. Then I braced my hands on the counter. "What if we came to a mutually beneficial arrangement that would also please my mother?"

"I'm listening," she drawled.

"We start fake dating."

"I'm not lying to my family, Maverick. Or yours."

"It's not a lie. We actually date. No one needs to know it's hopeless. A dead-end street. It's not *if* we break it off, but *when*."

She didn't immediately say no. That was something. "For how long?"

I shrugged. "For as long as it takes to convince Mom we've made up. That we gave it our best shot. We just weren't meant to be."

"We've been fighting for over a decade." She picked up another cookie. "That could take another ten years."

"Yeah." It was definitely going to take a while.

Maybe, down the road, Stevie and I would naturally bury the hatchet. We both would move on with our lives, find jobs and relationships. Except my mother wouldn't be there down that road to see us move past our juvenile disagreements.

Hence, this proposal.

"I told you that your dad made me that job offer."

"Yes." Her lip curled.

"I won't take it."

Her eyes blew wide for a moment before they narrowed. It was something I'd seen her do countless times. That was the thing about Stevie. I could read her expressions like an open book.

And this meant she was intrigued. Good. I could work with intrigued.

She took a bite of her cookie, staring at me as she chewed. If I had to guess, she'd had cookies for breakfast. And if anyone ever criticized her for it, she'd wave them off with a flick of her wrist.

Stevie wasn't a woman who skimped on food. If she was hungry, if she wanted cookies, then she ate cookies. She'd probably devoured my entire cheeseburger after I'd left Luna last night.

She put her all into everything she loved. Food. Friends. Family.

I was counting on it.

I was counting on her love of my mother.

"How would this work? I need specifics."

"We go on dates. Real dates. That's it. I give Mom her dying wish. You avoid having me as a coworker."

She set her cookie down. Picked it up. Set it down again. "This could work. But I have stipulations."

Of course she did. "And they are?"

"No other women. I don't need to be made a fool. If people believe we're actually dating, then you can't be going off for hookups like you did last night."

I hadn't hooked up with anyone. But if I told her that the person I'd been talking to was Rush, that it had all been a ruse to piss her off, well . . . she'd just get pissed. "Fine. Same goes for you. No other guys."

"Fine. When would we be going on these dates?"

"Saturdays." That gave us a week in between them. A week to recover. "Starting the weekend after graduation."

She worried her bottom lip between her teeth.

I knew that look like all the others. She was going to say yes. I did a mental fist pump.

"All right." She nodded. "We'll fake date for a while. Saturdays only. Do our best to convince your mom we're mending broken bridges. And when it comes time, you'll tell my dad you've had a change of heart and turn down the job at Adair."

"Deal." I held out my hand.

She slipped hers into mine, our palms molding, and a jolt shot up my arm.

I let her go at the same moment she tugged free.

Static. That's all it was. Static electricity. A shock.

She smoothed her hand over her side, down that pale purple fabric and the perfect line of her hips. Then she cleared her throat and took a gulp of her milk.

When her hazel eyes flicked to mine, there was something in them I hadn't seen before. It almost looked like she was shy.

Stevie wasn't shy.

Maybe I had a few things still to learn about this woman. Good thing we were stuck together for the foreseeable future.

Before she could change her mind, before she realized this was doomed for failure, I took three more cookies off the plate. Then walked out the door, not letting myself look back.

CHAPTER SIX

STEVIE

My cap was pinned to my hair, and my black graduation gown hit above my knees, hiding the skirt of the floral dress I'd worn today. The lawn outside the fieldhouse where the ceremony had taken place was packed with graduates and families, including mine.

Mom dabbed at the corner of her eye. She'd spent most of today wiping away tears and taking pictures.

Dad's proud smile beamed brighter than the afternoon sun.

It was mostly because of this achievement. Dad was ecstatic that his one and only child had a degree and would now be stepping into her role within his business. He'd been smiling all morning.

I was trying not to let it bother me that his smile had grown impossibly wide when Maverick—thorn in my side and pretend boyfriend—had opened his big, fat mouth an hour ago.

The jerk had told everyone we were going on another date.

Not that I wanted to ever come to Maverick's defense, but he'd gotten cornered during the ceremony. Every person in our group had pestered us to share details of our date at Luna.

I'd waved it off and left to join the other graduates in my class for the ceremony. While I'd been in a sea of students, Maverick had been stuck in the stands with our parents.

They'd worn him down.

So he'd told them we were going on another date. Next Saturday.

Everyone seemed a little too excited about the prospect of me and Maverick sharing another meal. Well, everyone except Mabel.

She'd been giving me skeptical glances ever since I'd joined them once the ceremony had finished.

"One more picture," Mom said for the seventy-ninth time. She wasn't going to stop until she had at least two hundred on her phone. "Mabel and Stevie. I don't have one of you together."

We came to stand beside each other, our arms locked and smiles wide as Mom lined up her camera.

"So what's really going on with you and my brother?" Mabel asked, still smiling through the photo.

"Nothing." It wasn't a lie but it wasn't the truth. The word tasted sour. "We're just . . . hanging out. We both realized your mom was right. We can't fight forever. So we're making amends."

Mabel looked at me like I'd grown two heads. "One dinner at Luna and now you're buddy-buddy? No way."

"He's not so bad."

"You're a horrible liar."

Yes. Yes, I was.

Maverick and I were never going to pull this off. Not in a million years.

"Maverick, your turn." Mom came to my rescue, waving him over from where he'd been tossing a mini Wildcats football with Bodhi. "Stand beside Stevie."

"Oh, let me get my phone too." Meredith opened the flap on her purse, taking out her own phone. She stood beside Mom, and while Mom's smile was showing, Meredith's was covered in the white mask she'd worn today.

Her immune system was weak and her body vulnerable. We'd all tried to convince her to stay home, to avoid the crowd today, but she'd refused, not wanting to miss my big day.

Dad shuffled beside Mom, taking out his own phone. Then Monty came to Meredith's side, doing the same.

All four parents, lined up and ready to capture me and my fake . . .

Boyfriend?

Absolutely not. I was not calling Maverick my boyfriend.

He was just . . . Maverick.

The object of my frustration jogged over, raking his fingers through his soft brown hair to brush it off his forehead.

He was wearing a pair of jeans that draped to a pair of white Nikes. His Treasure State quarter zip was pushed up his forearms and molded to his broad shoulders. The corners of his jaw looked sharper than normal today, probably because he'd actually shaved. He was missing the stubble he usually had on the weekends.

Well, if I was going to fake date someone, Maverick Houston was the hottest guy I could have picked.

His arm was warm as he threw it around my shoulders, tugging me into his side so hard I nearly lost my balance.

"Sorry," he murmured.

"It's fine." I righted my feet and did my best to ignore the heat from his body that seeped through this flimsy gown. The scent of his clean, woodsy cologne filled my nose, and *wow*, he smelled good. Really good.

"Relax," Mav whispered, his hand sliding to my bicep, giving it a squeeze as our parents tapped their screens in rapid succession.

"Don't tell me what to do." I plastered on a smile that I hoped was convincing.

"Yay!" Mom tucked her phone away and clapped her hands together. "Should we head to the house?"

"Finally." Bodhi raced over, mini football in hand, and clutched his stomach. "I'm starving."

"Me too." Monty took Meredith's arm, keeping her close as we started for the parking lot.

She'd been a trooper today, enduring the ceremony that had dragged on and on. But her energy was waning. Her eyes seemed heavy, and though I couldn't see her mouth, I'd caught more than a few yawns.

"Mom's getting tired," Maverick said as we walked behind the group along the sidewalk.

"I would have understood if she wanted to stay home." Something I'd told her at least five times.

"She wasn't going to miss this," he said.

Meredith had come to my graduation.

Because there was a very real chance she'd be gone for Maverick's. He still had another year of eligibility for football, so even though we'd started our freshman year at the same time, he was just now going into his senior year. If she didn't make it to next spring, I doubted he'd even attend his own ceremony.

"I think everyone's a little surprised we're going out again next weekend," he said. "And a little too excited about it."

"I noticed."

Everyone—besides Mabel—seemed beyond thrilled at the prospect of me and Maverick spending time together. Maybe they simply wanted us to be friends again. Maybe the joyful exuberance today was solely due to my graduation.

But the wistful smiles, the over-the-top enthusiasm, the questions about where we were going to eat and what I was going to wear, said there was more here than just hope for simple reconciliation.

"You told them it was just a dinner, right?" I asked.

"I said it was a date."

"Do they think it's a romantic date?"

He shrugged. "What other kind of date is there?"

I frowned.

"This is what you agreed to. We're dating."

"Dating-ish. It's dating adjacent."

"It's dating," he said. "If you need to clarify the technicalities in your own head, fine. But we made a deal."

"I know," I murmured.

Saturdays. We were stuck with each other on Saturdays.

Maybe it wouldn't be so bad. If he showed up dressed like this, wearing that cologne, I could almost fool myself into thinking it might be fun.

If we could keep from bickering.

I slowed a few steps, Maverick doing the same so there was more space in between us and our parents. "I think we need some rules."

"Rules for what? We're going out on Saturdays. We'll date—"

"Exclusively."

He rolled his eyes. "Yes, we already agreed to that. I remember. What other rules do you need? Stop overthinking this."

Overthinking was my specialty. He'd always been the spontaneous person between the two of us.

"I can't," I admitted. "Doesn't it feel like we're not prepared for this? They're going to ask questions." I flung out a hand to our families.

"And we'll answer them with the truth."

I stopped walking, crossing my arms over my chest. "Like how you called another woman to arrange a hookup before the waiter at Luna ever delivered our meals."

"Like how you showed up thirty minutes late and brought a book." He faced me, hands on his hips.

We glared at each other for a moment, and it was like all of the uncertainty vanished. It was as welcome as a cool breeze on a hot day.

This, I could deal with. This was familiar.

Our first argument of the day. The knot in my stomach loosened.

We'd been thrown together, on and off, since we'd arrived this morning before the ceremony, and so far, we'd gotten along. Granted, he'd mostly hung in the periphery while I did what was needed for graduation, but on a normal day, he would have teased me for the gown. Maybe flicked the tassel on my cap.

Was that why we argued so much? Because it was our normal? Because it was easier?

Not something I was going to overthink at the moment.

"Are you guys coming?" Dad asked, glancing back.

"Right behind you, Declan." Maverick's grin was menacing as he inched closer, his hand lifting to my face.

"What are you doing?"

Before I could swat him away, he tucked a lock of hair behind my ear, his fingertips skimming the shell.

My breath hitched, lodged in my throat as he leaned closer.

Oh God. Was he going to kiss me?

This was why we needed rules. Did he expect me to kiss him through this? Fake dating did not require kissing and public displays of affection. Or did it?

Were we telling people we were friends? Or more than friends? Why hadn't I asked more questions before agreeing to this?

"Don't look so horrified," Maverick said, his voice low. "It's not like I'm going to kiss you."

He made a face. A face that said the last thing in the world he would do was kiss me.

It stung. More than it should have. I took a step away, moving to follow our parents, my gaze locked on the concrete sidewalk.

Maverick fell into step at my side, his hand coming to my elbow. "Rules. All right. You can't recoil when I touch you."

"I didn't recoil."

"Sure." He scoffed. "Work on that for me, yeah?"

"Fine." I flicked my wrist. "No recoiling."

"Stop fucking scowling at me."

I looked up to him and scowled. "No promises."

His nostrils flared as his hand latched around my elbow, drawing me to a stop. "Look, the only way we don't bury ourselves in lies is if this isn't a lie. I'm going to act like your boyfriend, because for all intents and purposes, you're my girlfriend. That was our deal."

He was right. The best way through this was to have as many truths as possible. Our parents simply talked too much. They were too close, and they, without doubt, were watching.

We'd be under a microscope.

Maverick was my boyfriend. Temporarily. Rather than think of this as a fake relationship, maybe the right way to treat this was with an expiration date.

And a reward. Adair Landscape. I was doing this for my future. So I could someday take over Dad's business as the owner and manager.

"Okay." My voice sounded defeated.

"Good." The back of Maverick's hand brushed my knuckles, and I did everything in my power not to shy away.

"Relax, Nadine. I'm not going to hold your hand."

Nadine.

My middle name. My grandmother's name.

"You haven't called me Nadine in a long time," I said.

He shrugged. "Guess I forgot."

No, he hadn't forgotten.

Nadine was the name he'd called me when we'd been friends. Maybe this was him trying to get us back to that point.

He'd come up with the nickname when we were eight or nine. I couldn't remember exactly when. A teacher had seen my name on the class roll and expected a boy. I'd been sad about it at recess, so he'd called me Stevie Nadine for weeks. Eventually, he had shortened it to Nadine.

Maverick was the only person in the world who knew

that I didn't love my name. It was one of those insecurities, those secrets, I'd buried deep.

My parents had had two stillborn boys before I was born. They'd planned to use the name Stephen to honor Dad's dad, my grandfather. A man who'd been Dad's hero. My grandpa had died from a heart attack while Dad was in college.

So when I was born, they'd named me Stevie.

Dad called me Steve, and it made me feel like less, every single time.

"We can do this," Maverick said.

"You really think that?" I asked.

"No."

But we'd both try anyway. For the woman ahead wearing a silk scarf over her head. The woman leaning against her husband, drawing from his strength those last few steps to the parking lot.

Yes, a part of me was doing it for Adair Landscape and Nursery. But part of me was doing this for Meredith too.

"Stevie?" Mav took my wrist, pulling me to slow down and face him again. "Thanks."

"Welcome." The truth was, even if he hadn't offered to walk away from Dad's job offer, I would have done this for his mom.

His blue eyes roamed over my face, lifting to my tassel. "Congratulations."

It was sincere. Sweet. Too much niceness from Maverick. I started to feel icky again.

He flicked the tassel, sending the strings into my nose. "I didn't get you a graduation present."

There he was.

I batted his hand away before he could flick the tassel a second time. "God, you're a child."

"Can't help it." He chuckled. "You're my favorite person to annoy."

I elbowed him in the ribs.

It only made him laugh louder.

"Stevie!" A shout from behind made us both turn. A guy dressed in a cap and gown jogged to catch up. His polished loafers clicked on the concrete, his tan slacks swishing with every step.

"Oh no." I grimaced, covering it up with a smile and finger wave. "Hey, James."

"Hey." He stopped in front of us, breathing heavily. How far had he been running? "Just wanted to say congrats."

"Thanks. You too."

He eyed Maverick for a moment, then dismissed him with a slight tilt upward of his nose.

What a snob. Seriously, what had I been thinking, going out with this guy.

We'd gone out on exactly two dates. He'd kissed me after the first. Invited me to his place after the second. When we'd been on his couch, making out, he'd pushed my head toward his lap.

I'd righted the bra he'd pulled over a breast and left less than a minute later.

That was three weeks ago. And James had yet to take the hint that I was no longer interested. No matter how many calls I sent to voicemail or texts I ignored, every time I bumped into him on campus, he asked if I wanted to go out again.

Hard pass.

"Are you celebrating tonight?" he asked. "I'm having a

few people over later. You should come by for a drink. I make a killer spicy margarita."

I opened my mouth to tell him I had plans, but before I could speak, Maverick draped his arm around my shoulders.

"She hates limes. But nice try, man."

James studied us together, taking in Maverick's arm. How he'd tucked me into his side and, oddly enough, how I fit.

"We've got plans with family," I told James, tugging on Maverick's shirt as I took a backward step. "Have fun at your party. And congrats."

"Is that my competition?" Mav asked when we were out of earshot.

"No." I glanced over my shoulder. Thankfully, James was retreating toward the fieldhouse. "But we went out a couple times."

"If that's the type of guy you're dating, no wonder you're so uptight."

I smacked him in the arm. "Has anyone ever told you that you're ridiculously good-looking until you open your mouth and ruin your face?"

Maverick laughed. "Yes. You."

"Well, it's still true."

He flashed me a megawatt smile. "*Ridiculously* good-looking?"

"Better write it down. I won't repeat it again in your life-time." I wish I hadn't said it in the first place. Damn it.

"Better looking than James?" he teased.

"Hmm." I tapped my finger to my chin, turning to take another look at James as I pretended to think it over.

James was attractive. Fit. His style was a bit pretentious but something I'd been willing to overlook. Yet if I was being honest with myself, I'd known ten minutes into the first date he wasn't for me. My own desperation was the reason I'd even agreed to date number two.

Because I was getting desperate.

What if Maverick—

Absolutely not. I shut that thought down before my brain could even see it to completion.

No. I was desperate but not that desperate.

The last person on earth I'd ask to take my virginity was Maverick Houston.

CHAPTER SEVEN

MAVERICK

S tevie's cheeks were flushed from the cold, her eyes glued to the firepit in her parents' backyard. There was an empty bottle of wine on the ground beside her chair, and she swirled the last of the cabernet in her glass as she stared at the flames.

I hadn't seen her drunk since high school when I'd shown up at a kegger in the mountains and she'd already been there, three sheets to the wind.

She'd been happy that night, dancing and laughing with her friends as she'd ignored me completely. Not that I'd paid her much attention either. I'd been too busy getting drunk with my friends, then passing out in the back seat of my truck.

Tonight's drunk Stevie was not a happy, laughing Stevie.

In the hours since graduation, her smile had gotten smaller and smaller until it had disappeared completely. She looked like she was about to cry.

"There's room to expand for the garden center," Declan said. He'd angled his chair toward mine over the last hour, almost turning his back on Stevie so he could face me at his side. "That little place, Hollis's Greenhouse, closed down after last season. They only did potted annuals and perennials. Quick season too, open a few months. But a lot of locals shopped their center. It's too late to add much this season but definitely something to consider in the future."

"Yeah," I muttered, finishing the last swallow of my water.

Declan had been talking to me about Adair Landscape for what felt like eons. He talked like I'd not only accepted his job offer, but worked there already. Every minute was excruciating with Stevie listening in. And that sunken, sad look on Stevie's face told me that this was the first she was hearing about a garden center expansion.

Why wasn't he facing her instead?

The night air was cold, even with the fire. Stevie had taken off her cap and gown once we'd gotten here for the party. Her dress was pretty but her arms were mostly bare and so were her legs. Every few minutes she shivered.

Was she afraid that if she went inside where it was warm, I'd go back on our deal? That I'd take Declan's offer?

"I'm getting a little chilly," I said, pushing up out of my chair. "Think I'll head inside."

"Me too." Stevie grabbed the empty bottle and stood. Then she turned for the lawn, tossing out the rest of her wine as I fell in step behind her for the door.

"I'll take care of the fire," Declan said. "Meet you guys inside."

Stevie kept marching to the sliding door, stepping inside where Elle and Mabel were visiting.

Mom had fallen asleep on the couch after dinner, so Dad had taken her home. Elle was exactly where she'd been for hours, sitting on a stool at the kitchen island, sipping her own glass of cabernet as she talked to my sister. From the sounds of the TV in the living room, Bodhi was watching ESPN.

The kitchen was decorated with crepe paper and shiny streamers. There was a bouquet of clear balloons, each filled with confetti, on the dining room table. The arched opening to the dining room was strung with a banner that read *CONGRATULATIONS GRADUATE!*

The barbeque leftovers were all stowed in the fridge. The cupcakes had been inhaled. Now that the wine was gone, it was time to go home.

"Hey." Elle greeted us with a wide smile. "Is it getting cold out there?"

"Yeah." Stevie nodded. "I'm going to head home."

"What?" Elle frowned and slid off her stool. "I thought you'd spend the night."

"I think I want to sleep in my own bed."

"Oh, all right." Elle pouted and pulled her daughter into her arms. "I'm so proud of you."

"Thanks for everything, Mom." Stevie hugged her back, then collected her purse from the kitchen counter. "Tell Dad I said good night."

Yep, she was mad. Stevie hugged everyone goodbye. Always. Well, everyone except me.

"I'd better get Bodhi home too," Mabel said, sliding off her own stool. "Want a ride, Stevie?"

"That's okay. I'll call an Uber."

"I'll drive you home," I said.

Stevie scrunched up her nose.

It was a reaction I'd seen a hundred, a thousand, times. And a reaction that was perfectly fine when we were enemies.

Except she was, technically, my girlfriend. We were going to need to work on that.

"Thanks, Elle." I gave her a quick hug, then put my hand on Stevie's lower back. "Ready?"

She stiffened, then realized her mother and my sister were watching, so she nodded and let me escort her to the door.

Bodhi came running out after us, jogging to the driveway. "See ya."

"Good night, kids." Elle waved from the doorway, then slipped inside as we started for my truck.

"You two are doing a horrible job of faking this," Mabel said.

"Who said it was fake?" I asked.

Stevie dropped her gaze to the concrete beneath her shoes.

"I get why you're 'dating.' " Mabel added the air quotes. "Just don't do anything that will hurt each other, okay? Or anyone else. I think everyone is going to pretend right along with you for Mom's sake. And I think everyone likes the novelty of you two getting along, so they're willing to go along with this for a while. But be careful that it doesn't become a lie so big it breaks hearts. Especially Mom's."

"I'm not going to do anything to hurt Mom, Mabel." I crossed my arms over my chest. "Mom asked us to make up. That's what we're doing. It's a handful of dates on Saturday nights. That's not a lie."

Stevie only gave my sister a shrug.

"Whatever." Mabel held up her hands. "I'm sure the first time Bodhi dares you to kiss each other it will all fizzle anyway."

Stevie scrunched up her nose again.

"Would you stop fucking doing that?"

"Doing what?" she snapped.

I flicked the tip of her nose. "That."

She jabbed a finger into my ribs. "Don't tell me what to do."

I bared my teeth.

Stevie sneered.

"I don't know why I'm even worried," Mabel said. "I give this one more date, maybe two, before it implodes."

I wanted to argue. But she was probably right.

"Okay, I'm leaving." Mabel pulled Stevie into a hug.

Stevie hugged my sister back with the first genuine smile I'd seen in over an hour. "Thanks for coming."

"Of course. I wouldn't have missed it. Congrats." Mabel let her go, then turned to me. "See ya, loser."

"Later, nerd." I gave her a sideways hug, then as she went to her car, I went to the truck.

Stevie and I climbed inside without a word, and that silence continued as I drove across town. She leaned against the door and stared out her window like she wanted to be as far away as possible.

"I never told your dad I'd take that job," I said. "I realize how it sounded when he was talking about the garden center and—"

"I know that wasn't you. It's fine, Maverick."

"Is it?"

She shrugged and curled closer to the door.

The drive through town was quiet, the streets lonely, even for a Saturday. Downtown was probably a ruckus with graduates celebrating at the bars. Or maybe people had found house parties to attend, like douchebag James.

The night was cloudless, the stars glittering above like

their own version of celebration sparkles. Like the town of Mission itself was out to celebrate Stevie Adair.

"Congratulations," I said.

"You told me that earlier."

"I still mean it."

She pushed off the door and heaved a sigh that seemed to deflate her entire body. "Do you think Bodhi will dare us to kiss?"

That's what she was worried about? "Probably."

It was definitely something I would have done at that age.

"Is it really that appalling? Or are you afraid you'll like it?" I waggled my eyebrows.

"Eww."

I huffed a laugh, gaze shifting back to the darkened road. "You're hell on my ego."

"Someone has to keep it in check."

And she'd been that someone since we were kids. Before and after our falling out, Stevie was always the person who'd tell me to be nice or share or shut up. She was the voice in the back of my head, the conscience impossible to tune out, no matter how hard I tried.

"Did you have fun today?" I asked.

"Sure."

If "sure" meant "no."

Maybe she should have taken James up on his offer for that margarita. *Nah.* That guy was a fucking moron, and though poor James hadn't quite taken the hint, Stevie wasn't interested.

He was too smarmy. Too much of a snob. Not her type.

What was her type? Maybe another athlete? Maybe a

guy who loved the outdoors too? Or was she out there dating assholes like James?

She hadn't dated in high school. And in college, she'd never brought a boyfriend to a family function. Maybe that was because they were all like James.

Because we'd all hate a James.

Unless she'd had plenty of boyfriends and I just hadn't met them. Mom would ask her about dates. Maybe Stevie had brought a guy to her house, to meet her parents, and I'd simply missed it.

Who? I squirmed in my seat as a strange feeling crept beneath my skin. A feeling I couldn't quite name, but I sure as fuck didn't like. My grip tightened on the wheel, and my hands only loosened when I pulled into her driveway.

The lights were all off inside.

"Where are your roommates?" I asked.

"Probably out celebrating."

"Downtown? Want me to take you somewhere?"

"No." She unbuckled her seat belt and hopped out, slamming the door closed without a goodbye.

We didn't need a goodbye. I'd brought her home and was free to leave.

Instead, I put the truck in park and killed the engine.

"Damn it." I jumped out and hurried after her, jogging to the stoop. "Stevie, wait."

Her shoulders sagged as she slowed and turned. "What do you want, Maverick?"

Not a clue. I guess . . . I didn't want her night to end like this. I didn't want her sad on what was supposed to be a special night.

"I'm sorry," I said.

"For what?"

Everything. For being a shithead when we were ten. For never relenting on the quippy comments and comebacks. For needling her for over ten years.

"For this fake dating thing."

"Does that mean you want to call it off?"

"No." I shook my head.

She sighed. "Then I guess I'll see you Saturday."

"Yeah. Guess so."

Stevie turned, moving to the door. But she was still sad.

"We've kissed before," I blurted.

She hesitated, and for a moment, I thought she'd continue on inside. But then she spun around and met me at the edge of the stoop.

It was a single concrete stair that meant when she stared at me, we were eye level.

"We kissed when we were toddlers," she said. "That hardly counts."

"I'm just saying, would it really be so shocking?"

She scrunched up her nose, again, and damn if it didn't make me want to scream and laugh, both at the same time.

"Maybe you're afraid you'll like it."

She scoffed. "Trust me, I won't."

"I bet you would."

"I won't."

I inched closer, the toes of my shoes hitting the stair as I held her stunning hazel eyes. "Will too."

"Will not." She jutted out her chin.

"Will too."

"Will. Not." She poked a finger into my chest with each word.

We sounded like kids. Like squabbling teenagers? My pulse spiked. A thrill shot through my veins. What did it mean that I loved to argue with this woman so fucking much?

"Are you scared to kiss me?" It was a dare.

And Stevie rarely backed down from a challenge.

"No." She jutted out her chin. "Just irked at the prospect."

Nervous. Not irked. Nervous. That's what she really meant. She was nervous about if—when—it would happen.

She'd stress it. Overanalyze my movements. She'd start to wonder if I'd go back on the deal if she refused to kiss me. That, or she'd make me pick a date and she'd put a count-down in her phone, and until that day arrived, she'd fret over this entire arrangement.

"It's just a kiss," I said. "Not like it means anything."

Stevie hummed, worrying her bottom lip between her teeth.

Let the fretting commence.

Damn it, she'd drive me up a fucking wall if she was already spiraling around this. So rather than let her work herself into a mess, I took her face in my hands.

And crushed my mouth to hers.

Stevie's eyes blew wide as she froze, staring at me as I pressed in deeper, holding my lips to hers.

What the fuck was I doing? For a split second, I almost let her go. I almost called this entire façade off and vowed to avoid her for the next six to twelve months. Except her lips were warm and soft. And damn it, she had a great mouth. I couldn't pull myself away, not yet. Instead, I had the over-whelming urge to lick the seam of her mouth.

Her breath hitched, her mouth parting, and before I could stop it, my tongue moved without my permission, sliding past her full lower lip.

The moment the tip of my tongue touched the tip of hers, a current zinged through my bones. A lightning bolt that shot through every vein at that first taste of her mouth.

Fuck. Delicious. Sweet. The hint of wine lingered on her lips.

I groaned, and before I could tear myself away, I sank into the kiss, my eyelids heavy as they drifted closed. I delved into her mouth, tangling my tongue with hers and earning another gasp.

But she didn't push me away. A mewl came from her throat and then she melted. Stevie, my former childhood friend turned archnemesis, fucking melted.

She didn't reach for me. She didn't shift closer. She just let me hold her face, meeting every flicker of my tongue with one of her own until our mouths were fused together.

Oh fuck, it was good. I slanted my mouth over hers, needing more and more and more. My arms itched to haul her into my chest, to trap her against my body, except I was afraid the moment I let go of that delicate line of her jaw, this would end.

So I kissed her, exploring the different corners of her mouth, my lips moving over hers.

A sound echoed from down the street, and it barely registered past the blood rushing in my ears. But it was enough to startle Stevie.

She jerked, our eyes opening in tandem. We stared at each other, our mouths still touching, until she leaned back an inch, ending what might have been the best kiss I'd had in, well . . . ever?

I didn't let her face go. We just stared at each other. Breaths ragged. Hearts pounding. Minds visibly whirling.

What. The. Fuck.

Stevie had the same three words written all over her beautiful face.

The sound I'd heard a moment ago came again. A car door slamming from one of the neighbors. Laughter echoed through the night.

This time, when Stevie backed away, it was enough that I had to let go.

"I told Leah McAllister that you kissed Heather Olson," she blurted, then slapped a hand over her mouth, eyes wide.

Huh. All I'd had to do to get Stevie to finally, fucking finally, admit the truth was kiss her too. I'd suspected as much for years. Strange how I'd thought it would make me mad. Instead, I didn't really care.

"Okay."

She dropped her hand, eyebrows coming together. "That's it?"

I shrugged. "Guess so."

It bothered me more that she'd use it to reinforce the invisible brick wall between us. That my mouth was still wet from hers and she was already pushing me away.

She backed away, one step, then two. Then the next door slamming was hers.

I stared at it for a long moment, trying to clear the fog. I ran a hand over my mouth, my lips tingling.

It was just a kiss. A kiss didn't mean a damn thing. I'd kissed hundreds of girls before. It was just a silly kiss.

Right?

"Huh." Maybe we'd both have something to fret over for the next week.

CHAPTER EIGHT

STEVIE

K issing didn't count.

After a week of stressing over that kiss with Maverick, I'd come to the conclusion that kissing didn't count.

It didn't mean anything. It was nothing. It was merely a test to see if we could pull off a convincing relationship.

There'd been those first few moments when I'd frozen, too stunned to hide my initial shock. But after that had faded, after I'd turned off my brain and relaxed into Maverick's lips, it had been . . . good. Incredible, actually. I'd never been kissed like that before. Lazily, like he was savoring every moment. Thoroughly, like he was making sure it wasn't something I'd soon forget. Deliciously, like he wanted the taste of his cinnamon gum to linger for days.

Well, it sure had.

No wonder so many women on campus were infatuated with the man.

Fucking Maverick and his fucking cinnamon gum.

Well, I refused to let one kiss scramble my brain. Kissing

didn't count. And sooner rather than later, I'd stop thinking about it, right?

Right.

"Ugh," I groaned, dropping my face into my hands as I sat at the dining room table.

Not only had I kissed Mav, but then I'd admitted to snitching on his kiss with Heather Olson in high school. The confession had come out so quickly, it had shocked me too.

Maverick hadn't gotten angry. Why? He should have been furious. But he'd just shrugged, unfazed by the truth.

I wished he had gotten angry. I think I'd said it hoping for a fight.

It was easier when we argued.

Well, maybe I'd get that argument tonight.

I'd been dressed and ready for my date with Maverick for hours, but it wasn't time to leave yet. So I'd been sitting here long enough that the chair was getting uncomfortable, reminding myself the whole time that kissing didn't count.

This dinner tonight didn't need to be any different than the last. My book was already packed in my purse.

"Hey."

"Ah!" I jumped, the legs of my chair scraping across the floor as Jennsyn walked into the room. "Shit. You scared me."

"Sorry. I thought you heard me come downstairs."

There was an overnight bag on her shoulder. The duffel was stuffed so full the zipper couldn't close in the middle.

Jennsyn's *overnight* visits at her boyfriend's house next door lasted days. When she eventually came back, that bag would be empty. She was moving into Toren's place one bag at a time.

"You look pretty," she said, setting her stuff on the floor.

"Thanks." I smoothed down the front of my black dress.

A dress I wore not because I wanted to impress Maverick, but because it was my favorite.

The skirt was a little short for family functions and the straps that crisscrossed in the back left a lot of skin on display.

It was my favorite, even though this was the first time I'd worn it out. Favorite-ish. Favorite adjacent.

"Going to Toren's?" I asked her.

"Yep." She beamed, tucking a lock of her shoulder-length blond hair behind an ear.

I was going to miss her when she eventually stopped pretending like she still lived here. Our other roommate, Liz, spent most nights at her boyfriend's place too. This house was becoming much too quiet. Too lonely.

But at least Jennsyn was only moving next door.

She'd transferred to Treasure State for our senior year, and since she'd been new to Montana, our coach had asked if I would mind another roommate. It had taken us a while to get to know each other, to become friends. But over the past year, she'd become my best friend.

Jennsyn and I were both adjusting to life without volleyball. Without school. And now that we'd graduated, she and Toren could finally stop hiding their relationship.

They'd met at a summer party before the school year had started last year. They'd hit it off, except they hadn't realized at the time that she was a student athlete and he was one of the football coaches.

They'd kept their relationship a secret for months, but eventually, I'd started to suspect something was happening. She was good at sneaking out at night, but not that good.

It was nice that the secrecy was over. That she didn't have to pretend she wasn't head over heels for Toren Greely.

As far as I knew, they weren't broadcasting their relationship widely, but they weren't denying it either. They simply weren't telling anyone when they'd started dating. No one needed to know it had been months, not weeks.

"Are you guys doing anything tonight?" I asked.

"We talked about going out to dinner, but I doubt we'll go." She laughed. "We're in that stage where we're perfectly content to spend every waking hour in bed. You know how that feels. I want to soak it in."

No, I didn't know how that felt.

Not even close.

Jennsyn didn't know I was a virgin. Neither did Liz. In the year we'd all lived together, my sex life—or lack thereof— hadn't come up in conversation. If they ever asked, I'd be honest, but I certainly wasn't going to offer it up freely.

In my heart of hearts, I knew it was nothing to be embarrassed about. I was picky. I had high standards. That wasn't a bad thing. For so long, I'd been hung up on giving my virginity to the *right* guy.

Now I wasn't even sure a right guy existed.

None of the boys in high school had ever measured up, and those I'd dated in college hadn't either. Not that I'd dated much. With a full-time class schedule and volleyball, there hadn't been much free time for parties. Most of the guys in my classes had been threatened by a woman who was taller and, if our grades were anything to go by, smarter too.

I'd spent the time between volleyball seasons working for Dad at Adair. There'd been a few landscaping guys over the years who'd been hot. But I was the boss's daughter. Beyond flirting, none had been brave enough to ask me out.

Virginity had been a redeeming virtue at fourteen. At sixteen, the few girls at the Oaks who'd *done it* were snickered about. By eighteen, I'd been in the minority of girls who hadn't.

As time had gone on, it had become this *thing*. This hurdle. But I'd told myself that if I'd waited until I was twenty, then I might as well wait for that *right* guy. A good guy. Apparently, all of the good guys had vanished or were taken.

Another year had passed with my virginity intact. Then another. Now I was twenty-two and I just wanted to get this over with.

I wanted to know what it felt like to have sex. I wanted to not fake conversations with my roommates about being in bed with a man.

"What are you doing tonight?" Jennsyn asked, her eyes sweeping over the curls in my hair and the dress. "Hot date?"

Yes, actually. Maverick was a hot date.

I cringed. How the hell had I gotten myself into this position?

This was Meredith's fault. Her dying wish. I loved her too much to be angry.

"Yeah, I have a date."

"Really." She shimmied her shoulders. "Tell me everything. Is it that James guy you went out with a few times?"

"No." I scrunched up my nose. "He's too much of a snob. I'm actually going out with, um . . . Maverick."

Jennsyn's jaw hit the floor. "Maverick Houston? As in the kicker on Toren's football team? As in your archnemesis from high school and the bane of your existence?"

Good to know that she'd been listening the few times I'd bitched about Mav.

"Yep. That's the one."

"I thought you hated him."

I lifted a shoulder. Hate was exactly the word I'd used before, but today, it felt too powerful. Too extreme. I'd never really hated Maverick. "He's . . . Maverick."

"Am I supposed to know what that means?"

Considering I didn't know what it meant? "No. It's complicated."

"But you like him now?"

"Yes?" That answer shouldn't have come out as a question.

Did I like Maverick?

We certainly weren't friends. And I didn't have a crush on him. But he had his moments. Mostly, I liked *me* around Maverick.

I could just be myself. I didn't have to laugh at his jokes if they weren't funny. I didn't have to stroke his ego—I worked tirelessly to temper it instead. I didn't have to try to impress him or pretend to be anyone but myself.

He knew me, good and bad. Just like I knew him.

I liked that we could be real with each other.

Even if this was fake.

And though I wouldn't admit it to a soul on this earth, I liked that kiss.

"I don't know what's happening," I told Jennsyn. It was the truth. "We're just going out to dinner. We'll see what happens."

"All right. Just be careful, okay?" His reputation with women was the unspoken reason behind that warning.

Maverick was nothing if not notorious.

One of the younger players on our volleyball team, Megan, had been crushing on Maverick last year. I'd told her to be careful. Maverick was the type to chew her up and spit her out. Had Megan heeded my warning? No. She'd been determined to climb into his bed.

But we'd all listened to her fawn over him in the locker room for weeks. Then one day, nothing. She'd never mentioned Maverick again. Probably because he'd chewed her up and spit her out.

Judging from the look on her face, Jennsyn was worried that would happen to me too.

"Don't worry." I waved it off. "I know what I'm doing."

Did I?

"Okay." She didn't believe me. Not even a little bit. "Well, I'd better head over. Have fun tonight."

"Thanks. You too." There were butterflies in my stomach as I headed for the garage. They kept flapping their insufferable wings as I drove downtown to the sports bar where Maverick and I were meeting for dinner.

He'd texted me this morning asking if I was up for somewhere other than Luna. Of course he'd pick a place where there were TVs mounted on every wall. Fine by me. He could watch whatever game was on while I read my book.

I'd had a busy week working at Adair. Mostly, I trailed Dad around, acting as his shadow. But he worked long hours, and as his shadow, that meant I worked long hours too.

The bar where we were meeting was on Main Street. As I walked inside, I gave my eyes a moment to adjust to the dim light. It was one of the more popular hangouts in Mission, and as I spotted a few tables full of college students, those butterflies in my stomach transformed into hornets.

People were going to think I was another random woman on Maverick's arm. Another notch in his bedpost. Another girl in a short skirt.

I cared what people thought. No matter how much I pretended outside opinions didn't matter, they did.

What was I doing here? Why had I picked this dress? What was happening to me? This past week, I'd questioned everything. I'd worried and fretted and turned myself inside out.

"Stevie." Maverick's voice cut through the sounds of glasses clinking and people talking and TV announcers blaring.

I scanned the bar and spotted him at a high table toward the back. His seat was perfectly positioned in front of the largest television in the room.

Weaving through tables, I made my way to his side, staring at the three empty chairs. One beside his. Two across.

If I sat beside him, I'd be able to watch TV too. If I sat across from him, the screen would be above my head and I'd have every excuse to read.

Before I could second-guess myself, I pulled out the chair beside his.

"Hi." My voice was flimsy and pathetic. That single word sounded more like a swoon. I cleared my throat and tried again. "Hey."

Maverick gave me a sideways glance. "You okay?"

"Super-duper." What the . . . super-duper?

Maybe I should feign illness. Go home and think about my word choices for the next five to seven business days.

No. This was a date. I'd agreed to Saturday. So I took a deep breath and looked anywhere but at Maverick.

A few years ago, the owners had remodeled this place. The rectangular bar sat in the center of the space, giving people four sides in which to place their orders. There were mirrors behind the shelves of liquor, and the exposed posts and beams were stained a dark brown, adding to the moody atmosphere. Against the red brick walls, tall, leather booths gave people more intimate seating.

And the massive garage door with black-paned windows at the front of the building was open, letting in the sound of traffic from Main Street. A breath of wind carried through the bar, raising goose bumps on my arms.

I hated this dress.

"Nice dress," Maverick said, his gaze dropping down the bare skin on my back.

There was appreciation in his gaze. Was that why I'd plucked it from an abandoned corner of my closet? Because I'd wanted that sort of reaction?

Yes.

This was all Maverick's fault. He'd kissed me and then I'd spent a week overthinking a kiss that didn't count but maybe it did count and I was using this dress as my own personal revenge for him twisting me into a knot.

My head was starting to hurt.

The waitress swung by, a tray tucked under her arm. "What can I get you?"

"Water, please."

"And a shot of Fireball," Maverick said.

She left two menus on the table, then hurried to the bar. I was still squirming in my seat, trying to nonchalantly tug down the too-short hem of my skirt when she returned with my water and his shot.

The scent of cinnamon hit my nose, and it was like a portal to the past. I wasn't in a bar. I was on my porch, Maverick's lips sealed to mine, our tongues tangled.

I breathed through my mouth.

"Here." He slid the shot in front of me.

"I don't want that." I gave it a sideways glance, then slid it away.

There would be nothing cinnamon in my mouth tonight. Not that shot. Not his gum. Definitely not his tongue.

"Why not?" he asked. "You're nicer to me when you're a little tipsy."

The tone of his voice was flirty and sultry. Sexy and low. The voice he'd used on that phone call at Luna. The voice he used to seduce women.

My belly did a strange flip. I didn't like that voice. But I kind of did.

Seriously, no wonder he was a playboy. It was almost hard to blame him. I doubted he had to work for attention at all.

"Don't use your sex voice on me."

"My what?" He barked a laugh. "Sex voice?"

"You know what I mean." I flicked my wrist. "That voice you use when you're talking to a hookup. Like that girl you called at Luna. Save that voice for your harem, not me."

"I don't have a harem or a sex voice. And for the record, I didn't call a girl at Luna. I called Rush and pretended he was a girl because I knew it would piss you off."

So I'd punished him by being late. And he'd thrown it right back in my face. Maybe I should have suspected it that night. Maverick had always been the best opponent. I bit the inside of my cheek to hide a smile. "Jerk."

He chuckled. "Couldn't help myself. If you want this shot, you can have it. But you don't have to."

"I'm not drinking tonight." I lifted my chin, eyes glued to the TV. "I'm driving."

"I'll take you home."

So he could ambush me with another kiss on my front stoop? "Absolutely not."

Maverick heaved a sigh, leaning back in his chair as he raked a hand through his hair. "There's the brick wall," he muttered.

I crossed my arms over my chest. "What's that supposed to mean?"

"Nothing." He snatched my glass of water and took a long drink. "Do you want something to eat?"

"Sure." Food seemed like a great way to avoid conversation. And oddly enough, this was the same feeling I normally had on dates. On edge. Jittery. Not exactly hungry, but eating meant I didn't have to make small talk.

Wait. When the hell had this become an actual date?

"Hey, Mav." A petite blond appeared at the end of our table. She leaned her forearms against the edge, pressing her breasts together as she flashed him her cleavage.

"Hey," he muttered, barely sparing her a glance.

The woman looked at me, then back to Maverick, her smile widening when he tore his eyes from the TV. "How's it going?"

He stared at her for a long moment, almost like he was trying to place her. Then he threw an arm across the back of my chair, his hand wrapping around my bicep. His thumb started tracing patterns on my bare skin. "We're good."

We're good?

It took everything in my power not to let my mouth flap open.

We're good. Like we were a couple. Like I enjoyed the tingles on my arm from his thumb.

I did like them. But she didn't need to know that.

"Want to split a burger, babe?" he asked, leaning into my side and holding up a menu for us both to read.

Babe?

He squeezed my arm, a silent plea for us to sell this date to the blond. Did he even know who she was?

Another night, I might have let him suffer. But this woman was bold enough to interrupt and she wasn't getting the hint.

"Sure, sweetie." I leaned into his side.

We should have auditioned for the senior play at the Oaks. Instead, we'd both been on stage crew.

"Well, I just wanted to say hi," the blond said, clicking her nails on the table.

"Hi." I gave her my sweetest, saccharine smile, then tapped the menu with my free hand. "Oh, let's get nachos instead. No cilantro or—"

"Olives. I know."

He did know. He knew what foods I liked and those I didn't.

His icy blue eyes met mine, and the knot in my stomach loosened. The hornets buzzed off.

So did the blond.

"One of your girlfriends?" I asked.

"I don't have girlfriends." He took another drink of my water. "What about you? Am I going to run into another boyfriend tonight?"

"No." The closest thing I'd had to a boyfriend lately was, well . . . Maverick.

"You know, I was thinking last week. You've never brought a guy home."

"So? You've never brought a girlfriend home either."

"Because I don't have girlfriends."

"Until now."

"Until now." His eyes stayed locked on mine, and they transformed from serious to playful in a blink. I knew that mischievous glint. He'd been torturing me with it since birth.

"What?" I inched away.

"When was the last time you had a decent fuck?"

My gasp was instant. Then I gave him my best scowl as I dipped my fingers into the water and flicked the drops into his face. "You're such a pig."

"Truth." He chuckled, wiping his nose dry. "I'm just joking."

"Liar," I muttered, elbowing him in the ribs.

"Okay, fine. I'm curious. I was thinking about it all week."

"About what?"

He shrugged. "Why you've never brought anyone around."

"So that you could ridicule him?"

It wasn't a reason. There simply hadn't been a guy to bring home, not one I'd wanted to introduce to my parents. Or maybe there hadn't been a guy I'd met who could handle Maverick.

Whether I wanted to admit it or not, Maverick was always a part of my thought processes. At least where our families were concerned. Maybe the reason I hadn't brought anyone home was because I'd known it would end in a dumpster fire.

Shit. I'd ponder that one later.

"Next topic, please," I said.

"This one making you uncomfortable?" He bumped his shoulder into mine. "How long has it been since you've dated anyone seriously?"

"I haven't," I admitted. "I've been busy. I haven't had a lot of time for a boyfriend with school and volleyball. And no one has come along that's made me want to make space."

Maverick studied me for a moment, then hummed. "Fair enough."

I waited, expecting him to pester me for more. But he dropped the subject, taking a drink of water even though my fingers had been in it just a minute ago.

The waitress returned with another glass, this one for me, and took our order. Then we sat together, both staring at the TV.

He seemed entertained by the baseball game, but I couldn't seem to concentrate on the game. Every few moments, I'd steal a glance at Maverick's profile.

How long were we going to have to keep this up? Weeks? Months? How many Saturdays would we meet in this very bar, where he could watch a game and we could pretend to be enjoying a date?

Wouldn't it be easier, and cheaper, to just meet at a house?

Except I wasn't sure I was ready for him to invade my house. My roommates would have questions. If we went to his place, his roommates would have questions.

What if I used this situation to my advantage? What if I stopped waiting for someone special? What if I got this over with?

It wasn't the first time I'd had this idea in the past week. No, I'd considered it as often as I'd replayed that kiss. On. Loop.

I didn't want to be a virgin. I was dating a man who had no qualms about casual sex. And as a bonus, Maverick was a known quantity. We might fight, he might drive me up the wall, but deep down, he was a good guy.

Not that I'd ever admit that to his face.

"What?" Maverick pivoted to the side, eyebrows raised. "You keep staring at me. And I can tell by the look on your face that you're thinking something. Do I want to know what it is?"

"Probably not."

It was a horrible idea. It was fraught with peril and there wasn't a doubt in my mind I'd regret it.

But what if . . .

Kissing didn't count. What if sex didn't count either? What if it didn't have to mean anything? What if I could just check the box on this *thing* and move on?

"Spill," he ordered.

Don't do it. Do not.

I snatched that shot of Fireball, tipping it to my lips. The alcohol burned as it slid down my throat, warming my belly. I grimaced and chased it with a gulp of water.

Then, before I lost my nerve, I spilled.

"I think I want you to have sex with me."

CHAPTER NINE

MAVERICK

M y ass went from the stool to the floor in less than a second. It should have hurt except I was too shocked to feel pain.

What did she say?

Stevie gasped and leapt off her own seat to crouch beside me, gaze sweeping me for injuries. "Oh my God. Are you okay?"

No, I wasn't okay. Because either my brain had conjured up the wildest goddamn dream of my life. Or Stevie had just said those words herself.

"Fuck." I dragged a hand over my face as the pain began to register. It spread, hot and sharp, through my hip and elbow.

The waitress rushed over, eyes wide.

"I'm fine." I waved her off and pushed up off the floor, giving my stool a wary glance before returning to the seat.

Every eye in the bar was aimed my way. Another day, I might have felt embarrassed. But I wasn't a stranger to attention, and right now, I had more pressing shit to worry about.

"Did you just ask me to have *sex* with you?" I whispered.

Stevie stood, her mouth opening and closing, but before she could answer my question, she buried her face in her hands.

"Look at me," I ordered, tugging at her wrist.

When she dropped her arms, her cheeks were bright red. For a moment, I thought she'd take a seat and we could talk this out. But before I could stop her, she swept her purse off the table and rushed for the door, the short-as-hell skirt of her dress swishing around her hips.

"Stevie," I hissed.

She kept walking.

"Damn it." I slid off the stool, keeping my feet this time, and fished my wallet from my jeans. I smacked a hundred on the table, and like our first date, I paid for a meal I wouldn't get to eat.

I flew out the door, scanning up and down the sidewalk. Stevie rushed for her Jeep parked toward the corner of the block. "Stevie!"

She did what she did best. Ignored me.

A growl came from my throat as I raced to catch her, but she was fast. As kids, she'd been the fastest in the neighborhood. Even faster than me.

By the time I made it to the Jeep, she was behind the wheel, engine roaring to a start.

I pulled on the passenger door's handle, trying to open it, but it was locked. "Don't you fucking dare drive away."

She drove away, leaving a nice hole in the line of cars along Main Street.

"You've got to be kidding." I tipped my face to the cloudless blue sky, feeling like I'd just been punched in the nuts.

This was why I didn't have girlfriends. This was why

casual hookups were so much easier. Women didn't typically run out on me, but the couple of times a girl had snuck out of bed before I'd woken up, I hadn't cared. I definitely hadn't wanted to chase her down.

I think I want you to have sex with me.

She'd said that, right? Stevie had asked me to have sex with her. I was almost certain I hadn't made that up in my head.

Not a chance I was leaving that unsettled. So I changed directions, marching for my truck parked on the next block over. Then I tore off for the other side of town, my truck practically steering its way to her house.

For a week, I'd pondered that kiss. I'd let myself replay it so many times that I'd nearly convinced myself it was a dream. It should be a dream.

The best kiss of my life couldn't belong to Stevie Adair.

Except it did.

Was this my punishment for frivolously kissing girls in the past? Was this my penance?

Or was it the reason she wanted to have sex?

Maybe she was going through a dry spell. Maybe she just wanted an orgasm. Maybe she was fucking with me to see what I'd say. But this was not something I was going to guess about. I needed a damn explanation. Now.

My foot pressed the gas pedal deeper. There wasn't a speed limit I didn't break on my way to Stevie's.

The garage door was closing as I pulled into her driveway. I parked behind her stall, blocking her in so she couldn't drive away again. Then I shut off my truck and stalked for the house.

Standing on the stoop felt like returning to the scene of a crime.

I dragged a hand over my face, taking a deep breath as I tried to calm my racing heart. Then I pounded a fist on the door, straining my ears for footsteps, waiting for her to open up.

Nothing. Not a single sound came from inside.

I pounded on the door again, then rang the doorbell.

Silence.

"You don't get to ignore me," I said, pushing the doorbell in rapid succession.

Ring. Ring. Ring. Ring. Ring. Ring.

I dug my phone from my pocket and pulled up her contact, hitting her name so it would ring too.

It took another minute until finally I heard the stomp of feet on hardwood. Then the door whipped open, the chime of the doorbell drifting outside.

"Maverick, I don't—"

"Shut up." I stepped inside, forcing her backward on bare feet. Then I slammed the door closed, blocking out that cursed stoop and all thoughts of that kiss. "You don't get to drop that bomb on me, then walk away. We're going to talk."

Stevie gulped as her gaze dropped to the floor. "It was a mistake. Forget I ever said anything."

Yeah, because that was something I could forget. "What is happening?"

"I don't know," she whispered, wrapping her arms around her middle.

"Liar."

Her gaze flicked up, narrowing to a glare.

I arched my eyebrows. "The truth. What the fuck is going on?"

She groaned, her face contorting as she turned and trudged into the house. Instead of leading me to the kitchen, she changed paths for the living room, skirting the end of the couch. Then, without any hesitation, she face-planted into the cushions.

The skirt of her dress flopped up, revealing a sliver of her black panties. I forced my gaze away, inspecting the living room.

It was comfortable and clean with neutral colors and a vanilla candle on the coffee table beside a book that looked like it was for decoration, not reading. The TV was too small, but otherwise, it was a nice house. It was exactly what I'd expect for Stevie, classy and inviting.

Though she'd never invited me here before.

Nope. She'd just asked me for sex.

"Stevie," I barked. "Explain. Now."

"Uh-rar-rar-rar-rar."

Did she expect me to understand that? "In English, please."

She punched the couch beside her hip, then turned her face, not climbing off the couch, just freeing her mouth. Her hair fell over her eyes. "I'm a virgin."

I rocked on my heels, those three words hitting me square in the chest. "You're a what?"

"Don't make me say it again," she groaned, turning her face back into the cushion, doing her best to hide.

Or suffocate.

I was supposed to be the dramatic one. That role had been mine for years. How dare she try to switch places?

With a scowl, I stomped around the couch and shoved her legs to the side, making room for myself on the end of the couch. "Would you look at me?"

She kicked my thigh.

I pinched the skin on her ankle, earning a yelp.

"Hey." She twisted, kicking at me again, but it forced her out of the cushion and up to a seat. She leaned her elbows to her knees, letting the curtain of her hair fall forward and shield her face.

My fingers itched to push it aside, to tuck it behind her ear, but if she needed that wall of soft brown waves between us, so be it.

"You asked me about my boyfriends and why I'd never brought anyone home. It's because there wasn't anyone to bring home. You know I never dated anyone from the Oaks."

Not a single one had been good enough for her. Stevie and I might not have been tight, but we'd hung out in the same circle of kids in sports. She'd gone to prom with a group of girls from the volleyball team. A few of her teammates had dated guys on the football, basketball or baseball teams. But Stevie had always stayed single.

And now, looking back, I wasn't sure how I would have reacted to my buddies hitting on Stevie. We'd all been pigs—to steal her word from earlier. We'd been teenagers. We'd been hyperfocused on sex.

I hadn't warned any of them away from her, but I might have reminded a few of them on occasion that our families were close. That the only guy who could give Stevie shit was me.

Not that she needed to know that.

"But what about college?" I asked.

She shrugged. "I told you. I've been busy. And every guy I've dated has been . . . meh."

"Meh?"

"Yeah. Meh."

"What does that mean?" I had an idea—James's face popped into mind—but I wanted specifics.

"Freshman year, I went out with a guy three times. He'd come to my dorm room and asked me to change shoes so I wouldn't be too tall."

"Dick. Who else?"

She sighed. "A guy my sophomore year took me to a house party and slipped something into my drink."

"What the fuck?" I yelled, shooting off the couch. My pulse spiked as a burning rage spread from my chest through my veins. "Who?"

"It doesn't matter. A couple of friends showed up and knew I wasn't the type to get that drunk, so they took me home before anything happened."

"Motherfucker. I'm going to kill him."

"He doesn't go to school here anymore. I reported him to the campus police. And that was my last house party."

My hands fisted at my sides as I stared down at her. "Who was it?"

"No one you know, Maverick. He was in one of my classes." Her shoulders curled forward. "I haven't told many people about that. It's not exactly something I like to relive or admit. But even though nothing happened, it made me not want to date much for a while. So I didn't."

"No shit." I crossed my arms over my chest. "That's more than *meh*."

She shrugged again. "It's in the past."

"That doesn't make it okay."

"I stuck close to the team after that."

We all stuck close to our teams. Most athletes didn't do much with other students. We stuck to those we trusted. Those who understood the demands of being a student athlete. The people who wouldn't take pictures of us and post online.

Sure, I'd hook up with jersey chasers, those women more interested in scoring with a guy on the team than much else, but it wasn't like we'd hang out after.

"What about James?" I asked.

"Not my type."

"Who else?"

"Guys I've met at school, mostly. I've gone on a handful of dates but usually it ends after dinner and a movie."

Did she kiss these losers? Did she let them inside her mouth?

The idea of another man on her stoop, claiming that mouth, made something twist in my gut.

"I haven't met anyone I wanted to invite into my bed," she said, her voice dropping quiet. "You know I'm picky."

She said it like it was a bad thing.

Okay, so the guys she'd met had all been fucking idiots. That still didn't explain this proposition of hers. "Why would you want me?"

"It's humiliating, Maverick." Finally, she looked up at me, hazel eyes swimming with tears. "It's become this thing, and I just want it over with. I'm tired of feeling like I'm different. Like I can't talk to my friends about sex because I don't actually know about sex. I don't want to have to explain it to future boyfriends like it's some sort of secret. I don't want someone who wants to take my virginity for bragging rights, and I also don't want a guy who makes a big deal over it."

Well, it was a big deal. "That still doesn't answer my question. Why me?"

"Because you're you." She flung out a hand, gesturing to my body. "It's not exactly like you have qualms against meaningless sex. You know what you're doing. At least, I hope."

I gave her a flat look. Of course I knew what I was doing.

"This is embarrassing for me, but you've already seen me at my most embarrassing moments, so why not just add this to the list."

Like the time she'd gotten carsick on a camping trip and puked all over the front of her shirt.

I hated that this was an embarrassment for her. But I understood it too. There weren't many women our age who'd kept their virginity unless it was for a specific reason. Maybe they were saving it for marriage. Maybe it was a religious belief.

Stevie didn't want to be different. She was special, talented and unique. But she'd always been content to be a part of the crowd, not to stand apart.

But this?

I couldn't do this. I couldn't take this from her, even if she was asking. It should be with someone who'd make it count. Who she'd look back on with fond memories, not contempt or regret.

Except before I could open my mouth to let her down gently, a tear dripped down her cheek. "You're safe."

The room seemed to tip upside down, then right side up. A complete spin, end over end. Except, when it settled back to normal, nothing was normal.

I was safe.

That was why she'd asked. Despite all the other reasons, it was the only one that mattered.

What the hell did I do now?

"Maverick?"

"Yeah," I choked out.

"Can you leave now?" Her voice sounded hollow. Ashamed. Shaky, like she was having a hard time keeping the rest of those tears from falling.

Leaving was the last thing I wanted to do. There was too much to discuss, too much to consider. But the crack in her voice, the way her shoulders curled in on themselves, sent me from the house.

Date over.

CHAPTER TEN

STEVIE

Dad rapped his knuckles on my office door. "Hi, buddy."

"Hey, Dad." I smiled as he settled into the empty chair across from my desk. "What's up?"

He crossed an ankle over his knee. There were still a few streaks of mud left on the soles of his boots, just like on mine.

The spring rain from this past week meant the entire valley was soggy, and we'd both gone on field visits this afternoon.

"How'd your meeting go?" he asked.

"Good." I picked up my notebook, scanning the page of scribbles I'd made. "I've got some questions, but I'll rough out the plan, then run it by you."

"Sounds good."

This was my second week as a full-time employee at Adair, and today's visit was my first solo client visit. Last week, Dad had kept me close, taking me on his own client meetings so I could shadow him for a while. But the last inquiry that had come through our website, he'd assigned it to me.

It was a small and simple job, and the client had requested a weekend or evening consultation. The other landscape designers at Adair worked weekdays, seven to four, and at the end of May, everyone was fairly booked for this season. The only person with bandwidth at the moment was me. So Dad had bypassed the typical onboarding process and sent me on my own.

It meant working on a Saturday, but since I had no desire to stay home where I'd undoubtedly dwell on last Saturday with Maverick, here I was.

I'd been so nervous that my hands had shaken the entire visit, hence the awful handwriting of my notes, but I'd been smiling ever since I'd left the jobsite.

"How is everything else going?" Dad asked. "Any . . . issues?"

"No." But I really didn't like that tone in his voice. It was almost as if he had the answer and was trying to see if mine matched. Like the time he'd busted me in high school after I'd told him I was spending the night with my friend Maggie —she'd told her parents she was staying the night at my house—and we'd gone to a camping party in the mountains instead. "Why?"

"No reason." He waved it off.

"Okay. Are you sure?"

His smile didn't reach his eyes. "I'm sure. It's usually an adjustment, adding another person to the team."

Ah. So I might not have any issues, but someone else in the office did. "What happened?"

"Nothing worth stressing over."

If that was true, he wouldn't have asked if there'd been issues. "Did someone complain about me?"

"I wouldn't call it a complaint. Samantha just overheard some grumbling in the break room that you were already getting clients."

Dad's assistant, Samantha, was new to Adair this season. His former assistant had retired last year, and he'd hired Samantha this spring. She was my age, also a recent graduate from Treasure State, and had gotten a degree in teaching. Except she didn't want to be a teacher. She'd just finished her courses to earn her bachelor's because she didn't want to start over in a different major.

I could understand not wanting to go back to the beginning and drag out college. She fully admitted to taking this job for the paycheck until she could figure out what she really wanted to do.

Maybe Dad had brought her on because we were the same age. Because he thought we'd become friends.

Well, so far, I couldn't stand Samantha. She was a gossip and spent the majority of her seven-to-four shift kissing Dad's ass. Her smiles were fake and her laughter forced. In just two weeks, it had become so awkward that I'd started using the back door to avoid seeing her at the reception desk.

"Did Samantha say who was grumbling?" I asked. Not that I didn't believe her, but I also didn't believe her.

I'd known the other designers for years. They'd known me for years. Yes, only as a part-time employee and Dad's daughter. But it shouldn't have come as a surprise to anyone that I'd eventually have clients of my own. And I couldn't see any of them squabbling over tiny projects.

"She didn't want to throw anyone under the bus, being new to Adair and all."

"Sure." That, or she'd made the whole thing up.

"Don't worry about it. I guess I'm just overly sensitive. I don't want anyone giving you a hard time since you're my daughter, and I'm making exceptions to the rules."

"I've worked here for years," I said, like he didn't already know that. "Maybe not as a designer, but I know this business."

Dad nodded. "Yes, you do. I'm sure it's nothing major, but if something does happen, I want you to talk to me about it."

"Of course," I lied. Not in a million years would I tattle to my boss, even if my boss was my dad.

"Are you busy tonight? Want to come over for dinner with Mom and me?"

"Actually, I have a date," I said too brightly, hoping to hide the dread in my voice.

"With Maverick?"

"Yep."

At least, I think I had a date with Mav. I hadn't heard from him since last weekend when I'd made a huge fool of myself.

I'd spent a week in agony from a humiliation the level of which I'd never experienced before. It physically hurt every time I replayed last Saturday, from the bar to my living room. Work had been a lovely distraction, but it wasn't enough to erase the memory of my verbal diarrhea.

Not only had I asked Maverick to have sex with me, but I'd told him about my virginity.

No one knew about that. No one.

What demon spirit had possessed me to share with that man, of all people, my secret truths?

Maverick's silence for a week probably meant that this

charade was over. I was praying for it at this point. I wouldn't blame him in the slightest for running far, far away from the drama of a twenty-two-year-old virgin and her sexual dilemma.

"So you guys are really dating?" Dad asked.

"Yep." It wasn't a lie. I kept telling myself it wasn't a lie. We were going on dates. They just weren't romantic dates.

It still felt like a lie. Not giving my parents the whole story felt like a betrayal.

"Huh." Dad rubbed a hand over his jaw. He hadn't shaved today and his whiskers, more gray than brown these days, scratched against his palm. "I know it was Meredith's idea. That she pushed you kids into this. Part of me is proud that you'd do this for her. But the other part, your dad, worries about you. I'm well aware that Maverick isn't your favorite person."

And yet he'd still decided to offer Mav a job. He'd talked at length about a garden center expansion the night of graduation. How could he be worried about these dates but not see a problem with bringing my not-favorite person on at Adair?

I kept my mouth shut, not wanting to get into that discussion today. It wouldn't matter anyway. Maverick wasn't taking the job.

"He's growing on me," I admitted. "And it was time to let go of the past. Meredith was right about that."

A whole truth. It was time to bury our hatchets.

"I'm glad. When he comes to work here, it will be better if you two are on speaking terms."

When. Not *if.* When. In Dad's mind, that job was already Maverick's, even if Mav hadn't accepted his offer.

"He's still got a year left of school, Dad. Maybe he won't want to work at Adair after he graduates."

"Maybe." Dad shrugged. "Maybe not. I guess a guy can hope."

Was this his version of shoving us together? It wasn't the same as Meredith's dying wish, but the pressure of his *hope* settled on my shoulders like a forty-pound bag of potting soil.

Before I could say anything else, the chime from the office's front door dinged.

Dad twisted in his chair, peering out my open door to the hallway. We were the only two in the office today, but through my window, I'd kept an eye on the garden center since I'd arrived after my client visit.

The parking lot outside our greenhouses had been full for hours. The staff had spent the day hauling wagons of petunias and irises and geraniums for those customers who were too impatient to wait until after Memorial Day to do their planting, despite our warning that there was still a risk that the flowers would freeze. From what I could tell, we'd sold quite a few larger shrubs and trees from the nursery too.

But customers didn't wander into the office, so as footsteps thrummed on the floor, I expected a staff member to emerge from the hall.

Instead, my date filled the doorway with his broad frame.

Maverick was wearing a pair of jeans that hung low on his hips and a quarter zip with the sleeves pushed up his sinewed forearms. His hair was combed. His jaw clean-shaven. He looked ready for a date.

Well, he hadn't stood me up. That was something, right? Or maybe he was here to call it off.

"Hi, Maverick." Dad practically leapt from his chair as a beaming smile lit up his face. He shook Mav's hand like it had been a year, not two weeks, since they'd seen each other. "How's it going?"

"Not bad." Mav returned Dad's smile, then his blue gaze settled on me. "Hey."

"Hello." A flush crept into my face, and I couldn't seem to hold his eye contact.

My fingers found the end of my braid, toying with the ends as I focused on my monitor, as if I could actually focus on the spreadsheet on the screen.

"How's spring practice going?" Dad asked Mav.

"Not bad." He crossed his ankles, relaxing against that door like he'd spent countless days visiting me at work.

The space wasn't large, just enough room for my desk, a bookshelf in the corner and a couple of chairs for clients or coworkers. But with Maverick here, the room might as well have collapsed in on itself.

He and Dad chatted about football, about the Wildcats training regimen and the coaches and the season schedule, all while I closed out of my tasks and tried to ignore the heady scent of Maverick's cologne tinging the air.

Another day, it would have irked me that he and Dad were talking about football. They usually talked football—though lately, this job offer was also on the topic rotation. They'd bonded over football years ago, and I'd always wondered if the reason Maverick talked about it so often was because it forced me out of the conversation.

Today, they could talk about it ad nauseum for all I cared. Anything to buy me time to stop the trembling in my hands.

Last Saturday had been a giant clusterfuck. But there was no going back in time. We'd figure it out. We'd stick to the plan.

Once we were alone, I'd beg him to forget it had ever happened. Then I'd fulfill my end of the bargain, date him long enough to convince Meredith we'd tried. And after a string of Saturdays, we'd have our inevitable breakup. He'd tell Dad he couldn't take the manager job. And it would be over.

"I'm excited to watch you play this year," Dad told him. "Should be a great year."

"I think so too."

Dad turned, giving me a smile. "It'll be strange not to spend our weekends at volleyball tournaments. We've been doing that for so long, I don't know what Elle and I are going to do with ourselves on Friday and Saturday nights."

My parents were loyal supporters of the Wildcats volleyball program. If there was a tournament within three hundred miles, they'd come and watch me play. They'd been regulars at Upshaw Gymnasium, so familiar that most of my teammates and players had known them by name. And before I'd started college, they'd been just as supportive during my years in high school. They'd driven me to countless club tournaments, sacrificing their own nights and weekends to make sure I never missed a practice.

I wasn't the only person mourning the loss of volleyball.

Was that why I'd asked Maverick to take my virginity? Was that my grief over a finished volleyball career manifesting in a moment of crisis?

"Well, I should let you kids get out of here." Dad clapped Maverick on the shoulder. "Good to see you, son."

"You too." Mav shifted out of the way, letting Dad through the door.

"Bye, Steve." Dad held up a hand. "See you Monday."

"Bye, Dad." The moment he was gone, Maverick closed the door, and the office shrank again.

Maverick rounded my desk, taking a seat on its edge. "Hi."

"Hey." I rolled my chair backward, putting an extra foot of space between us. That cologne was stronger now that he was closer. Rich and masculine and clean, like soap and citrus and fresh cedar.

Why couldn't he smell like he did when we were thirteen? Like stinky feet and onions. And why couldn't he have grown up to be gangly and ugly? It wasn't fair that Maverick was this handsome.

Was that why I'd pitched this sex thing? Because at least I could say I'd lost my virginity to a smoking-hot guy?

At this point, I had no idea why I'd made this suggestion. All I could do was regret it. Over and over and over again.

"You good?"

"Not really," I confessed.

I couldn't look at his face and not hear myself.

I think I want you to have sex with me.

Mortification spread through my veins like poison, and I covered my face with my hands, not wanting him to see as I fought the urge to scream.

Why couldn't I have just kept that to myself? Why, of all people, had I told Maverick? Was I really that desperate?

I didn't want to be a virgin anymore, and I was so fucking tired of caring. Except I did care. Even though I knew it shouldn't matter, I cared.

"You don't have to be embarrassed." His voice was low and gentle. It was not a voice I'd heard from Maverick often, but it was my favorite. It was the way he talked to his mom or Bodhi.

It was the Maverick he hid behind layers of arrogance and flippancy.

"Are you going to look at me?"

"No," I murmured into my palms as I shook my head.

"What if I was a normal guy? A boyfriend you wanted to date. Would you have told me?"

I gulped and forced my hands down to my lap, keeping my eyes glued to my fingers. "Probably not."

"Want me to pretend you never told me?"

"Yes," I whispered, even though I knew it was something neither of us would forget.

"Nadine."

The nickname made me glance up.

His ice-blue eyes were waiting. "Talk to me."

"I don't know what to say." Hadn't I already said too much?

"It's not a big deal. You know that, right?"

"Isn't it? It makes me feel like less. I just . . . want it over with. The longer it's gone on, the longer it bothers me. If you were a twenty-two-year-old virgin, wouldn't you feel . . . different?"

"I suppose. I don't think you're less, but I get it."

I exhaled, trying to let go of the tension in my chest. "I wish I'd never said anything. I don't know how to do this. I don't know where we go from here."

"It's a Saturday." He stood and held out a hand. "We go on our date."

It wasn't that simple, but I didn't let myself overthink it. This was the plan. Stick to the plan.

So I put my hand in his and let him pull me to my feet. Then, with his hand clasped around mine, I let him lead me outside and to his truck.

"What are we doing?" I asked as we both fastened our seat belts.

"It's a surprise."

"I don't like surprises." I glanced to the back. To the red cooler behind us. "What's that?"

"Dinner."

"What kind of dinner?"

"Mushrooms. Lots and lots of mushrooms."

I scrunched up my nose. "You'd better be joking, Houston."

Maverick chuckled. "There she is."

CHAPTER ELEVEN

MAVERICK

"Where are we going?" Stevie asked as we headed out of Mission.

"Fourteen minutes."

"Huh?"

I tapped the clock on the dash. "It took you fourteen minutes to ask. I'm impressed. I didn't think you'd make it out of the parking lot at Adair."

She rolled her eyes but there was a ghost of a smile on her lips.

Maybe what we both needed to get back to our normal was the teasing and ridicule.

I'd spent a lot of time thinking about Stevie over the past week. Up until about an hour ago, I'd planned to forget this entire thing. To drive to my parents' house and disappoint my mother.

Except then I'd found myself packing a cooler of food. And when I'd climbed in my truck, I hadn't once considered turning off the route to Adair. I'd had a hunch she'd be at work today, and when I'd parked beside her Jeep, all of the doubts from the past seven days had disappeared.

I couldn't explain it. I couldn't put this feeling into words.

I just wanted to spend time with her.

Like how it used to be when we were little kids. During the summers, when I wasn't at football or basketball or soccer camp, I'd wake up and, before breakfast, ask Mom when I could go play with Stevie.

That's why I'd chosen the mountains for this date. We needed space. Some fresh air. A spot we could go and not get interrupted by fans or ex-hookups or waiters.

Just Stevie and me.

"So are you going to tell me where we're going?" she asked.

"Guess."

That won me another eye roll. Did she realize I liked them?

"The mountains." She pointed down the narrow two-lane road ahead toward the foothills and forest in the distance.

"That's not a guess. That's stating the obvious."

"You're kind of a smartass. Has anyone ever told you that?"

"Yes. You. On multiple occasions."

"Maybe you should write it down so you don't forget."

"I haven't forgotten." I shifted, draping an arm over the steering wheel. "I just refuse to change."

She turned, meeting my gaze. Her eyes were serious, all of the humor gone.

"No snarky comment?"

"No." She swallowed hard, then faced forward.

The playful mood from moments ago might as well be roadkill in my rearview mirror.

All right. Guess I shouldn't have said I refused to change. Is that what she wanted? A different Maverick?

I didn't know how to be anyone else. This was me, for better or worse. If there was a soul on this earth who knew me, good and bad, it was Stevie.

"What did I say?"

"Nothing." It was a blatant lie.

"Stevie."

She sighed. "If you refuse to change, and I refuse to change, will we ever really be friends again? Part of me wonders if we're doomed and this is a waste of our Saturdays."

Was this her way of ending this arrangement? Was this her way of calling it quits before we had to have the hard conversation about last Saturday?

This virginity issue wasn't only hanging over her head now. It was looming over mine too. And it wasn't something I could forget.

What had she expected me to say? Yes, and sweep her away to bed? To fuck her senseless and then walk out?

Yeah, I'd done that with other women. But this was Stevie. She was different. Special.

She deserved more than a meaningless night.

We drove in silence for a few more miles, neither of us sure what to say. Until she broke the quiet.

"We're going to that place where we used to go camping, aren't we?"

The corner of my mouth turned up. We hadn't even turned off the highway yet. "Yeah."

"Why?"

"It's a Top Five."

I held back a grin as she stared at my profile. She wouldn't ask what I meant by Top Five. She'd already figured out Top Five meant my favorite places. But she was undoubtedly trying to figure out what the other four were.

"I can hear the gears turning in your head."

"The family campsite." She held up one finger, then two. "And the Wildcats stadium. Those are two of the five."

"Yep." The obvious choices. If she got the next three, then I'd really be impressed. I hadn't meant for this to be a test, but maybe it was.

If Stevie knew me well enough to name the Top Five, then I could know her well enough to take her virginity, right?

She hummed, thinking it over, her eyebrows knitted together.

I slowed, taking the turn off the highway to a gravel road that would lead us into the mountains. It took until the first bend before she guessed again.

"McDonald's."

"Fast food?" I gave her a sideways glance. "You really think I'd pick a cheap burger place as a Top Five?"

"I'm right." She spoke with sheer confidence.

I chuckled. "You're right."

A smile, beautiful and brilliant, lit up her face. God, she was gorgeous. It wasn't a matter of attraction. Not a damn bit. If she were any other woman, sex wouldn't have even been a question. I would have fucked her on that couch last week, then whisked her to bed for another round.

Then she would have pulled away. Then she would have spent the next decade ignoring me.

And now that I'd sort of gotten Stevie back, I wasn't ready to lose her again.

"I almost took us to McDonald's tonight," I told her. "It's been a while. You could have gotten a chicken nugget Happy Meal."

"I do love a Happy Meal." She laughed. "I thought you and your mom went there every couple weeks."

"We used to." Every other week, Mom and I would meet for lunch at the local McDonald's. She'd ask me about school and football and girls and whatever else she wanted to know. It was basically an inquisition, but I'd answer all of her questions with limited grumbling as I inhaled a couple burgers and fries.

"After she started treatments, her taste buds changed. All she could taste was the salt."

"Oh. Sorry," Stevie said.

"Me too." I missed those lunches with Mom, so much that it was actually a shock that McDonald's was still a Top Five. I doubted I'd ever go there again after she . . .

Maybe it was time for me to redo the Top Five.

"Okay, two more." Stevie drummed her fingers on her knee, chewing on her bottom lip as I kept driving.

She was the only person I knew who'd spend the time to guess. Who'd give it all her brainpower simply to see if she could get it right. Most would have given up by now and asked for the answer. But Stevie wasn't the give-up type.

It was as endearing as it was infuriating.

"Give up?"

She shot me a scowl. "No. Don't rush me."

I'd learned a long time ago not to rush her. She did things when she was ready.

Maybe that was part of the virginity thing too. She

hadn't been ready before. And now she was, which meant it would be foot on the gas, no brakes until it was done.

If it wasn't with me, she'd find someone else. That idea made my entire body tense and my hands tighten on the steering wheel.

Sex would mean lighting the fragile remains of our relationship on fire. But I didn't want her screwing some random guy either. I didn't want her with a James. I didn't want her hitting the bars and picking up a one-night stand.

That wasn't Stevie. She'd regret it.

And she'd regret sleeping with me too. If it didn't mean anything.

What if it meant something?

What if it didn't happen soon, but someday? Someday when we didn't hate each other. When we could survive meals together. When we were friends again.

When she actually wanted *me*.

Shit, was I actually considering this?

"This truck," she said, tearing me from my thoughts. "It's a Top Five."

"It's not a place."

"Yes, it is. Behind the wheel, it's one of your favorite places. Am I right?"

"You're right." I'd been sure she wouldn't guess that one. "Pretty good, Adair. Still got one to go."

"It's your bed. Number five is your bed."

A place she'd never seen, at least not since we'd become adults, but she'd guessed it anyway.

And damn if she wasn't right again.

"How'd you know?"

She giggled, pride lighting up her hazel eyes. "Lucky guess. It was that or the gym."

126

"Definitely not the gym. I like working out but not that much." I slowed as the road narrowed into a two-lane track that was the final stretch to the campsite.

"I haven't been up here in years," she said, gaze wandering beyond the windows as she took in the soft evening light.

The sun was on its way toward the horizon, casting the treetops in rays of gold and yellow. By the time we made it home, it would be dark, but it was worth the drive to watch the sunset.

The campsite was nothing more than a small, oval-shaped meadow in the trees. There was a fire ring of stones, and once upon a time, there'd been a picnic table too. After it had broken from too many years in the elements, someone had cut it up for firewood.

The grass in the meadow was lush and green, growing tall from the spring rains and afternoon sun. In the summer, there'd be flowers of every color in this spot. Our families used to come up here and camp for a few weekends every year.

Dad would load up our fifth wheel and Mom would stock it with enough food for a month. I'd always spend the night in a tent. So would Stevie.

The moment I parked, she opened her door, letting in a blast of cool mountain air. It smelled like pine and wind and rain.

She shivered as she took in the view, the chill sinking past her green Adair Landscape and Nursery T-shirt and jeans.

I reached for the Wildcats hoodie I'd left in the back seat, taking it along as I joined her outside. "Here."

"Thanks." She pulled it on, fishing her braid free. The

hem hit her thighs, the sleeves so long they covered her fingertips.

It was just a hoodie. Given the stain on the sleeve, I couldn't tell her the last time I'd put it in the washing machine, but hell if I didn't like seeing her in my clothes.

I tore my eyes away, forcing them to the view of the jagged, snowcapped peaks in the distance. To the evergreens swaying in the breeze.

Stevie meandered past my side, stopping where the gravel around the firepit met the edge of the grass.

"Mom wants her ashes scattered up here. She told Mabel and me over dinner on Wednesday."

Stevie's spine went rigid. She turned over her shoulder, eyes instantly filling with tears. But she swallowed hard and didn't let them fall. Instead, she gave me a sad smile and held out her hand.

I was stuck beside the truck. Maybe she knew I was having a hard time putting one foot in front of the other. So I took her hand, her fingers holding tight to mine, and let her tug me into the meadow.

This was another Top Five that would change soon, wasn't it? If we all came up here and scattered Mom's ashes, I doubted I'd ever visit again.

Stevie stopped in the grass, tilting her head to the sky as she filled her lungs.

I did the same, letting the fresh air and mountain scents chase away the sadness in my heart. If my time up here was limited, then I wanted to enjoy it.

The link between our hands changed. She'd been holding me up until this point, but I laced our fingers together, this time holding her.

She looked up at my profile, the tip of her nose as rosy as her cheeks. Her lips.

Stunning. Absolutely fucking stunning.

There wasn't a moment in my life when I hadn't thought she was the prettiest girl around. Sweet. Caring. Feisty. Competitive. She could be absolutely vicious when she wanted to win.

So could I.

What happened when we both lost? Complete and total annihilation? Would we ever speak to each other again? Would this fake relationship of ours eventually destroy us both and cause a rift in our families?

It was possible. Probable, even.

Maybe it was the reason we'd started fighting in the first place. Or kept fighting. It was easier than admitting there might be more beneath the surface. That if Stevie and I truly imploded, if we broke each other's hearts, it would screw with the vibe of our families.

The smart thing to do right now would be to let go of her hand. Walk away. Ignore the pull to Stevie Adair like I'd been doing for a decade.

Instead, I tugged her closer until the tips of her shoes were touching mine.

Her eyes searched my face as I memorized the swirl of colors in her irises. Brown and gold and green and gray. They were a forest of their own, as breathtaking as the one around us.

"What?" she whispered.

You're beautiful. "Nothing."

Her eyes narrowed, reading the lie.

I didn't want to get into an argument. Not here. So I did

the only thing that was guaranteed to keep her mouth shut. I captured it with my own.

Stevie gasped as I sealed my lips over hers. With my free hand, I cupped the back of her head, my fingers sliding into those chocolate strands of her braid. I used the hold to angle her face, to keep her exactly where I wanted, neck stretched and chin lifted, so that I could slide into the furthest corners of her mouth, tasting them all.

Taking them all.

A moan vibrated in my chest as our tongues tangled.

Stevie whimpered, rising on her toes for more. Her free hand came to my arm, fisting the fabric of my shirt.

Fuck, she tasted good. Like sunshine and honey. I licked her bottom lip, then nipped the top with my teeth. And when she whimpered again, I unleashed, giving everything I had to that kiss, getting back even more.

That was Stevie. She wasn't going to be upstaged. For every flick of my tongue, she did the same. She sucked on my lower lip as she balled my shirt in both hands, pulling on it so hard it strained across my shoulders.

We clung to each other and let the world around us fade into a blur.

It should have been awkward. It should have been detached or messy. But it was fucking phenomenal. The best kiss of my life, surpassing even that one on her stoop.

God, this woman. How was this possible? How was this happening with Stevie?

When I finally broke away, my chest was heaving, my body flaming, my cock aching. I forced my eyes open just to make sure this wasn't a dream.

Stevie's breaths came in heavy pants. Her mouth was wet as she stared up at me with hooded eyes. Bedroom eyes.

Yeah, I wanted to see her in a bedroom. Stripped bare. Her cheeks and chest flushed. Her lips just as wet as they were now.

She wasn't mine. But she kind of was.

"Okay," I said, more to myself than to her. I was doing this.

She blinked. "Okay, what?"

"Nothing," I murmured.

Selfish as it was, I didn't want her with another man. Her first time was going to be with me. I'd make sure it was good. Comfortable. Safe.

As long as she wanted me. As long as she chose me on merit.

Not just some guy. *Me.*

That meant I needed to make her my girlfriend. For real. How the fuck did I do that?

CHAPTER TWELVE

STEVIE

Maverick cleared his throat, opened his mouth and closed it. He put his hands in his pockets. Took them out. Put them in again. Took one out. He was walking so fast along the sidewalk downtown that I had to skip every other step to keep pace.

We'd met a few minutes ago, both parking on the same block for our weekly date. He'd made reservations for us at a local brick-oven-pizza place, and if he didn't slow down, we'd be ten minutes early.

"What's the rush?" I asked.

"Huh?" He looked at me, like he'd forgotten I was beside him. "Oh. Shit. Sorry." He altered his stride to the point where it was basically a crawl.

"You're acting weird."

"No, I'm not." He scowled, dark eyebrows knitting together.

"Yes, you are."

It was the kiss in the meadow. When we finally broke apart, he'd looked at me with fear in his eyes. And I'd known on the drive back to town, he was going to be weird.

We'd left the mountains as the sun had begun to drop below the jagged horizon. By the time we'd made it to Adair and my Jeep, night had fallen. I'd been grateful for the dark. And that cooler of food. We'd had chips with peanut butter and jelly sandwiches to occupy our mouths on the trip to town so that we wouldn't have to talk.

We should talk. Probably. Not that I had any clue what to say.

I'd told him I was a virgin. And he'd kissed me. Was that his way of agreeing? Or testing the waters?

God, I wish I understood men.

"Maverick?" I slowed to a stop, waiting for him to do the same. Then, when he turned to face me, it was my turn to open my mouth and close it, completely at a loss for what to say. "This is hard."

"Yeah." He raked a hand through his hair, the strands sticking on end before he smoothed them out. "When did this get so complicated?"

"About the same time I asked you to have sex with me."

He chuckled. "So it's your fault."

"Yes," I grumbled. Being wrong was worse than losing. "Can we please, *please* forget it ever happened?"

"Sure." That was a lie.

I couldn't even get mad at him for it. This entire awkward situation was my doing. Why hadn't he run away screaming? Was he really that desperate to prove to Meredith we could do this? But if that was the case, why take me to the mountains? "Why do you keep kissing me?"

He shrugged. "Why not?"

"Is this like you testing the waters or something?"

"What?"

"I don't know." My face was starting to get hot. "Are you considering . . . it?"

He was, wasn't he? That's why this was getting weird? Because he was actually considering sex. With me. Were we actually having this conversation? Or was this a nightmare? It felt very much like a bad dream.

Maverick frowned, then reached out and snatched my hand, clasping it tight as he pulled me down the sidewalk. "I realize this is something you're chomping at the bit to do, but can we just go on this date?"

"Oh my God." My stomach pitched so violently I came to a fast halt, my head spinning as I thought about this from his standpoint.

What the actual fuck was wrong with me?

All this time, I'd been so concerned with my virginity. With having sex so I could be done with it. I'd asked Maverick for his help like he was some sort of tool at my disposal. Meaningless sex was his specialty, right? So why wouldn't he want to help?

I hadn't once thought about how he might feel used. Feel cheap.

"Maverick, I'm so sorry. I can't believe I did this. It was wrong and insensitive and I'll understand if you want to go home and never speak to me again."

He stopped and turned, giving me a sideways glance. "What are you talking about?"

"I propositioned you. For sex." My skin crawled. I was actually the worst.

A throat cleared behind Maverick. And then a couple emerged past his broad shoulders. A couple I'd seen at the fieldhouse on campus and in the weight room countless times.

Ford Ellis, the head coach of the Wildcats football team. And Millie Cunningham, an assistant athletics director.

They were arguably the most beautiful couple in Mission.

Please, *please* say they hadn't heard me.

Maverick gave Ford a tight smile. "Hey, Coach."

"Maverick." Ford's eyes softened with pity.

Without question, they'd just heard me.

Never in my life had I wanted to walk into traffic before, but as cars zoomed down Main Street, it was tempting.

I tugged on my hand, still in Maverick's grip, but his fingers clamped tight. There was a warning in the pressure of his hold not to make this worse.

"We were just walking by and thought we'd say hello." Millie pulled in her lips like she was trying to hide a smile. "Hi, Stevie."

"Hi." My face had to be as red as the fire hydrant on the next block.

Shit. This was a disaster. This was karma for how I'd treated Maverick.

"I don't believe we've met." Coach Ellis held up a hand in a wave since my right hand was clearly not free to shake. "I'm Ford Ellis."

"Nice to meet you, Coach Ellis." I gave him a wobbly smile.

"Stevie was a setter on the volleyball team," Maverick told them, giving me a glance. "She set the school record for assists last year."

Wait. He'd actually gotten my position correct—setter,

not center. And he knew I'd set that record? My parents prob-ably bragged about it, but those were normally the types of details that went in one of Maverick's ears and out the other.

"Really? That's awesome." Coach Ellis nodded. "Congratulations."

"Thank you?" The unnecessary question mark at the end of what should have been a statement floated around my head. *Kill. Me. Now.*

Coach Ellis was being nice, but I still wanted to run far, far away. Anything to escape the cloud of embarrassment and its torrential downpour of humiliation.

"We'd better get going." Millie came to my rescue, pulling on Ford's hand. "Bye, Stevie. Maverick."

"See ya," he said. "Later, Coach."

Ford clapped Mav on the shoulder, then they were gone.

"That didn't just happen." I slipped my hand free of Maverick's and buried my face in my hands.

"Oh, it happened." He sighed, then two, strong arms wrapped around my shoulders, pulling me into a hug.

Even with my hands still on my face, his scent surrounded me. Laundry soap and citrus and woodsy cologne.

"I'm sorry, Houston."

"It's fine, Adair."

Maybe reverting to last names would make this less awkward. Probably not, but at this point, I'd try anything.

He let me go, pulling at my wrists until I had no choice but to meet his gaze. "I don't think you're using me for sex, especially considering we haven't had sex. So stop stressing it, okay? I don't feel propositioned."

I cringed at his use of my own damn word. "I wish I could take it all back."

"I don't."

"Really?"

He shook his head. "Do you think you're the first woman who asked me to fuck her?"

"No," I muttered. But I really didn't want to think about him and other women.

Mav glanced over his shoulder, making sure we were alone. "If I don't want to have sex, then I don't. Simple as that. You want me to forget it. I'm forgetting it. But you have to do the same. You're not forcing me into anything, babe."

I scrunched up my nose. "Babe? Eww. No."

"Of course that's what she hears," he muttered. "Can we go to dinner now? I'm hungry."

"Fine." I fell into step beside him, stealing a look at his profile. "Promise?"

"Promise." He hooked his pinky finger to mine.

Just like I'd made him do when we were little kids and he made me a promise.

A pinky promise.

"Think we'll actually make it through a dinner date together?" Maverick asked as we neared the restaurant.

I laughed, about to answer, when the door to the pizza place opened and a stream of people, none looking particularly happy, walked outside.

"What's going on?" Maverick asked a guy as he passed.

"Their oven died."

Maverick's shoulders sagged. "So much for pizza."

"Want to try somewhere else?"

He rubbed a hand over his jaw, then gave me a smirk. "I've got a better idea. Come on."

We retreated to the lot where we'd parked, and when we got to his truck, Maverick opened the door to the back.

"Um, is there something wrong with the passenger seat?"

"Get in, smartass." He jerked his chin to the cab, so I climbed inside, sliding down along the bench as he followed me inside.

"Mav, what are—"

My question was cut short by his mouth crushing mine.

There was a glint in his eyes as he stared at me, his tongue dragging along my bottom lip before he pulled away. "You know what I was thinking about the other day? That party in the mountains in high school. You were drunk and happy and I wish we had been fake dating back then so I could have made out with you in the back of my truck."

Instead, he'd been chasing after one of the other girls, a junior. What was her name? I was pretty sure they'd had sex in his truck.

Wait. That's not what this was about, was it? I gulped. "I thought you were hungry."

He shook his head, bending to kiss the corner of my mouth. "Not anymore."

My eyes fluttered closed as my belly flipped. Kissing didn't count. I had to remember that kissing didn't count. Otherwise, I was going to get myself in a lot of trouble.

Maverick's mouth trailed along my cheek toward my ear. "You look hot tonight."

I was in jeans and a black tank top. I wouldn't go straight to hot. But maybe that's what he told women in his back seat before he stripped them out of their clothes.

"People will see us." My voice was breathy, damn it. Making out in his truck was not something that should be appealing, but there was a pulse blooming in my core.

"Who cares?" he asked.

I held back a moan as he took my earlobe between his teeth. "I don't think I can do it back here."

"We're not having sex. We're just kissing."

"Oh. Good." I didn't want my first time to be in a truck. So why did I sound disappointed?

"Stevie," Maverick whispered my name, his breath on the shell of my ear sending tingles down my spine. "You're overthinking this."

"I am not," I lied.

I was so stuck in my head I could visualize the tension creeping into my muscles, like they were slowly changing colors, from relaxed pink to angry red.

It was the same thing that happened whenever I was alone with a guy. He'd be touching me, whispering in my ear, feeling me up and my mind would start to wander. I'd lock up, until all I wanted to do was escape.

So I'd make up an excuse and hustle my way out the door.

Maverick growled, leaning away with an exhale. "I meant what I said on the street. If I didn't want this, I wouldn't be doing it. Understood?"

That's not what I'd been thinking, but it was now. "Are you sure? You can say no, and I'll still fake date you for your mom's sake."

"I'm sure."

"How sure?"

He pinched the bridge of his nose. "Very sure."

"How do I know you're not just saying that?"

"Woman." He looked to the cab's roof, his jaw flexing as it worked. When he faced me, there was a new intensity in his blue eyes. "Do I say stuff I don't mean?"

"No." Not to me, at least. Maverick might be an asshole, but he was honest. Brutally so. We both were to each other.

"Can we make out now?"

"Why do you want to if it's not going any further?"

He blinked. "The guys you've dated are truly dickheads, aren't they?"

Well, yeah.

"I just want to kiss you. That's all that's going to happen. It's not anything more than that. I like kissing you. Do you like kissing me?"

"Yes."

"Then fucking kiss me."

"But—"

Before I could argue, his mouth was on mine again, silencing both my voice and my brain. It was like Maverick knew how to find the off switch. Maybe he'd tell me where it was hidden. Or maybe he'd just keep kissing me.

One stroke of his tongue against mine and all of the noise went quiet.

This kiss was different than the others. In the meadow, there'd been desperation and hunger, like he'd needed a good memory before they all paled against the inevitable sad. The one on the porch had been laced with shock and surprise.

This kiss was lazy. Patient. Liquifying. The languid strokes of his tongue were an exploration. A slow discovery.

God, he tasted good. I melted against the seat, letting him plunder my mouth as my hands roamed his broad chest. My palms pressed against every hard muscle. My fingers found every dip and cut of his pecs and arms.

The heat in my core spread to my limbs. It chased away any of that lingering tension until I was pliant. At Maverick's mercy.

He kissed me for what felt like hours, until my lips were swollen and the windows were fogged. When he finally broke away, the ache in my center was almost unbearable.

"Fuck, you can kiss." He dragged a hand over his mouth, collapsing against the seat at my side.

It should have been strange, kissing Maverick. Except each time, I only wanted more. Did he feel the same? Or was this how he was with all of the women he'd been with?

Kissing didn't count, right?

The doubts, the noise, came crashing in like a hailstorm.

"You don't have to do this," I said. "You don't have to kiss me. I know we're faking this for other people, but we don't have to fake it to each other."

"Thirty seconds." He loosed a dry laugh. "That's all it took for you to start overthinking this again."

"I'm being serious."

He frowned and grabbed my hand, lifting it in the air. Then, with his gaze locked on mine, he brought it to the zipper on his jeans. The denim strained over a bulge. A very large bulge.

Maverick was rock-hard. Oh. My. God.

"Does that feel like I'm faking anything?"

Definitely not.

"That's what I thought." He bent and nipped at the corner of my mouth. Then he opened the door, letting in the cool, outside air as he hopped out, adjusted himself, and climbed in the driver's seat. "Are you going to ride back there?"

"Where are we going?"

"I'm hungry."

I pulled in my lips to hide a smile as I crawled through the gap to the front seat.

When we got to McDonald's, he didn't ask what I wanted. He just ordered me a chicken nugget Happy Meal.

CHAPTER THIRTEEN

MAVERICK

Bodhi was drooling on his sleeping bag as I zipped the tent's door flap closed, trying my best to sneak away quietly so I didn't wake him up.

Once the tent was shut, I stood, stretching my arms above my head, wincing at the ache in my back. Fuck, I was tired.

It had been a long week with spring practice and a few extra workouts, plus running some errands to help out Dad. Mabel had needed someone to take Bodhi to baseball practice Tuesday, so I'd volunteered. Rush and Faye had wanted to go on a date Thursday, so I'd spent an evening babysitting Rally, letting him spit up on my shirt after a bottle. It was the first time they'd left the house together, and Faye had only called six times in the hour they'd been gone.

I'd planned to relax last night, to catch up on laundry at home, but then my parents had asked Mabel and me over for dinner.

While we'd had burgers and hot dogs, Bodhi had begged to do a campout, and since I couldn't say no to him, I'd hauled out the tent from the garage and set it up in my parents' backyard. Normally, I didn't mind camping out. I'd burrow into a sleeping bag and be dead to the world as soon as my head hit the pillow.

But I'd tossed and turned instead, struggling to shut my brain off. I'd had a hard time sleeping anywhere lately, tent or bed.

I couldn't stop worrying about Mom. In the late hours, with nothing to act as a distraction, my mind would wander toward the future. Toward life without Meredith Houston.

We needed a miracle.

And we probably weren't going to get one.

The cancer was slowly taking over her body, despite the drugs the doctors had her on to prolong her life. So she was making her time count. Spending as much time with us as she could.

Fucking cancer.

It had changed this house. It had changed our lives. And it wasn't done wreaking havoc on my family yet.

The lights were on in the kitchen as I padded, barefoot, across the dewy lawn. When I slipped through the back door, I was greeted with the scents of coffee and eggs.

Dad was at the stove, pushing a spatula across a frying pan. "Morning," he said, his voice low.

"Hey, Dad."

"How was the campout?"

I shrugged, shuffling to the coffeepot and taking a mug out from the cupboard. "Not bad. A little chilly."

"Thanks for staying out there with him."

"Any time."

Dad had done his fair share of campouts, each of us filling the role of father for Bodhi. But Dad stayed close to

Mom these days, always at the ready to help if she needed something. Since she'd been diagnosed, he'd taken over laundry, cooking and cleaning.

He made sure that any meal she wanted was fresh, taking daily trips to the grocery store. Any leftovers from last night's dinner would be going home with Mabel or me. Leftovers had too big of a risk for foodborne illness.

Their friends from around town would send flowers over with their well wishes. Dad would snap a picture, then take the bouquets to Elle and Declan's house. Elle had also adopted every one of Mom's houseplants. Flowers and soil and plants meant mold. We couldn't have mold in this house.

Hands were washed often. If Bodhi had even a hint of a stuffy nose, Mabel would stay away. And the Adairs were really the only people Dad would let through the front door.

We were all doing what we could to keep Mom from germs, but Dad had taken his role as protector to a whole new level. Not that I'd ever doubted his love for her, but I sure as hell wouldn't question it now. His entire world revolved around her.

He was desperate for a miracle too.

While we prayed and hoped and waited for one, he made sure she stayed as strong as possible.

"Hungry?" Dad asked, nodding to the scrambled eggs.

"Not quite."

He opened the spice cabinet, fishing out three different jars, shaking them into his eggs. "Oregano, some sea salt and garlic. It's my new favorite seasoning mix."

"I'll have to try it."

"I've found that since your mom wants no seasonings, I'm doubling up to compensate." He chuckled, shutting off the burner and taking out a plate and fork. He dished his eggs and took them to the table.

I sat in the chair across from his, watching as steam floated off his meal. "I'm sorry you're having to do all of this, Dad."

"I'm not." He steepled his fingers in front of his chin as his eggs cooled. "Your mom did everything for a long time. I took it for granted. But the truth is, I like cooking for her, even if she doesn't eat much. We're both trying to find the good things through all this. Turns out, I'm a decent cook. And there's something special about making a meal for the people you love. Besides, she told me it was time to learn."

Not just so he could help while she was sick. But so that he could cook for himself, after she . . .

"This is hard, Dad."

"Yeah, son. It is." He kept his eyes on his plate as he nodded, blinking too fast while he vanished tears. "But we will be okay."

Would we?

"How's it going with Stevie?" he asked, taking a bite.

"Good."

"That's great." His relief was palpable.

Every person in this family, including the Adairs, seemed to have hung all of their hopes on my relationship with Stevie.

Dad had to know we were doing this for Mom, but he hadn't said anything about it. I doubted he would. Neither had Declan or Elle. Mabel had delivered that one warning, but otherwise, she hadn't brought it up again.

If me dating Stevie meant there was something other than cancer to discuss over meals, so be it.

"We've got a date tonight," I told him. "Every Saturday."

"What are you guys going to do?"

I shrugged. "Not sure yet. Probably go out to dinner or something."

Though every time I'd attempted that, it had turned into a mess. The picnic had been good, even if we'd just scarfed peanut butter and jelly sandwiches in the truck. Last weekend, after the make-out session, I'd bought her a Happy Meal at McDonald's. But that was another meal eaten in my vehicle. And the moment we'd returned to her Jeep, she'd hopped out and gone home.

Maybe it was time to try something else again.

"Hey, Dad?"

"Yeah," he said, his mouth full.

"Got any recipes I could try?"

———

STANDING in the spice section of the grocery store, I searched for paprika. The recipe called for paprika. Stevie would probably have that at her house, right? I snagged a bottle anyway, adding it to my cart.

There wasn't an aisle at the grocery store I hadn't gone up or down. I was on my second pass, getting the last of the ingredients on the list Dad had made me this morning.

The list Mom had reviewed and approved.

She thought the idea of me cooking dinner for Stevie was absolutely adorable. She'd smiled more this morning than I'd seen her smile in weeks.

If there was a reason not to screw this up with Stevie, it was Mom's smile. So I was going to do everything in my power not to screw this up, one paprika bottle at a time.

"Maverick?" My name came from behind, from where

I'd passed the boxed cake mixes, and when I turned, a familiar brunette sauntered my way, a finger twirling the end of her shoulder-length hair.

Megan. *Oh, hell.*

I'd made a lot of stupid decisions in my life with women. But Megan? She ranked close to the top of the list.

She was on the volleyball team, a year younger than Stevie. Over the better part of last fall and winter, she'd flirted with me mercilessly.

And I'd flirted back. Had I strung her along for months? Yeah. I wasn't proud of it. But I hadn't let it go any further than flirting. I'd always made a point to hook up with girls who weren't in the athletics program. It got too complicated otherwise.

It wasn't like the volleyball and football teams had joint practices or training sessions, but we all shared a weight room at the fieldhouse. And though there were times when it was reserved for each individual team, it was mostly free for any student athlete to use. Coaches too.

Megan had been working out one day when I'd gone in to lift. It had been quiet, most everyone gone on winter break. We'd picked up that flirting we'd been doing for months, and when she'd asked if I wanted to hang out at her place, I'd broken my own damn rule and spent the night in her bed.

The next morning, when she'd asked if I wanted to go out again, I'd known I was fucked. I'd told her I had some family stuff going on that I needed to focus on. That I wasn't great at relationships. But what I hadn't done was give her a firm no.

Any other woman, I would have made it crystal clear.

But any other woman, I didn't have to worry about crossing paths in the fieldhouse hallways.

I was trying to keep it from getting awkward.

But it was getting awkward.

"Hey, Megan."

"What are you doing here?" She batted her eyelashes.

"Shopping." Obviously.

"Right. Dumb question." She giggled. "I haven't seen you lately."

"Been busy."

"How's everything going with your family?" she asked.

"Not great." I shuffled backward, trying to position the cart so it was between us, but she just sidestepped it and came into my personal bubble.

"Oh, I'm sorry. It's your mom, right? I overheard someone talking."

Of course people were talking. Was it too much to ask that people minded their own goddamn business? "Yeah, it's my mom. She's got cancer."

"Maverick." Instant pity filled her eyes. It was genuine, I'd give her that. "I'm so sorry."

"Thanks."

She reached for my arm, placing her hand on my elbow. "Is there anything I can do?"

Not unless she had a miracle in her pocket. "Nope."

"Are you sure?" Her hand slid up my arm, fingers trailing under the sleeve of my T-shirt.

"Yeah." I forced a smile and jerked my chin over my shoulder. "I'd better get through checkout."

"Sure." She dropped her hand, giving me a warm smile. Then her gaze flicked past me, down the aisle. Her smile changed. It widened and sharpened. "Hey. Apparently the store is the place to be today."

"Apparently." That was a voice I'd know anywhere.

Shit. I twisted, following Megan's gaze, to find Stevie ten feet away.

Her face was pale, her smile tight. She was dressed in a pair of biker shorts and a baggy sweater that draped off a shoulder. Her hair was loose, hanging to her waist in sleek panels like she'd spent time straightening it today.

Probably for our date.

"How's it going, Megan?" she asked.

"Good." Megan shrugged. "Just ran into Mav. How's life postgraduation?"

"Can't complain," Stevie said, her gaze locked on her former teammate.

I might as well have been invisible for the way she stared through me. "Hi."

"Hi." Her voice sounded small. I hurt. "Well, I'd better get my shopping done. See ya."

"Later," Megan said.

With a basket looped over her arm, Stevie spun and headed in the opposite direction.

"Me too." I turned and followed, not sparing Megan another glance.

By the time I reached the end of the aisle, Stevie was gone. But she didn't seem to be in line at the checkout registers, so I took a chance, turning right and starting down the rows, scanning each until I found the swish of her chocolate hair.

"Stevie," I called.

She kept walking, three steps, then four. I was sure she'd keep going, that she'd make me chase her through this entire store. But she must have realized I'd do exactly that so she stopped and faced me.

The wheels on my cart rattled as I closed the distance between us. Then I pushed it to the side so it wasn't between us.

Given the angry look on her face, I didn't trust Stevie not to shove it at me. A cart handle slamming into my dick was not something I needed today.

"What?" she snapped.

"You're pissed at me."

"Yep."

"Because of Megan? Did you really not know?"

I wasn't sure what happened in the women's locker room, but if it was anything like the men's, then the entire volleyball team would know Megan and I had hooked up.

"I did. I just . . ." She cringed, and I felt it sting through every fiber of my being. "I guess I forgot these past few weeks that you're a manwhore."

I took the hat I'd worn today off my head to rake a hand through my hair. "Nice, Steve."

Her nostrils flared. "Am I wrong?"

It was a petty insult, using the nickname she hated, but I was kind of feeling petty. "No, you're not. I can't change the past. What do you want from me? Other than my cock?"

When she flinched, I felt that too.

Too far. I usually took it too far.

"Fuck. I didn't mean that." I was being an asshole, my specialty. I scrubbed both hands over my face. When was I going to learn to not say every mean comment that came to mind? "I'm sorry."

My apology came too late.

When I dropped my hands, Stevie was already gone.

CHAPTER FOURTEEN

STEVIE

There was an abandoned basket at the grocery store with chocolate chips, vanilla and brown sugar. Some poor clerk would have to put it away.

I should have done it myself, but I'd been in such a rush to leave, I'd set everything down and bolted for the sliding doors.

So much for making Maverick cookies before our date.

The drive home had been a haze of rage and humiliation and that other, green emotion I refused to name. Freaking Megan. I'd never liked her much before today. But seeing her feel up Maverick's arm like she had every right to touch him, watching as he hadn't made a move to shy away, meant I hated her now.

I wasn't his biggest fan either.

After parking the Jeep in the garage, I slammed the door and stomped inside the house, immediately walking to my room where I flopped, face-first, onto my bed and screamed into a pillow.

What was I doing? Why did I care? This wasn't real.

Kissing didn't count. So why did I feel like screaming again? Or maybe crying for a solid six hours?

This was Maverick. I'd known the score when I started this. I'd thought I could handle it, tolerate him for a while. And now I was terrified that I'd gotten in over my head.

As much as I wanted to blame him for this mess, it was all on me. If I could rewind time, I'd go back to that dinner weeks ago, the dying wish dinner, and tell Meredith there was no way I'd date her son. I'd take it all back just so I wouldn't have to feel this.

Whatever *this* was.

There were so many emotions shouting inside of me that I couldn't pick the loudest.

Humiliation. Regret. Jealousy.

I'd spent years ridiculing Maverick for his sex life. I'd chided him relentlessly about being a playboy. I'd known he'd slept with Megan—she'd made sure the entire volleyball team knew she'd been with *the* Maverick Houston.

She'd also told us all in the locker room that they were getting together, that they'd had a real connection.

The Diet Coke I'd been drinking had spewed from my nose when she'd made that announcement.

Everyone knew he wasn't serious about her. That he'd gotten all he'd wanted. Poor girl had been utterly delusional.

Part of me had actually felt sorry for her. Felt pity that she hadn't figured him out.

And here I was, in the exact same position. Well, sort of.

Okay, my situation was entirely different than Megan's, other than the fact that Maverick had put his tongue in both our mouths.

"Ugh," I groaned into the mattress, fighting another scream.

A scream named envy.

It was beating out all of the other emotions.

I couldn't stand the idea of him with Megan. It was hard enough not to think of him with other women, more experienced women, when they were just nameless, faceless girls from school. But Megan? She'd been my teammate for years. She played libero, and besides her penchant for gossip, she was good. Pretty. Confident.

Fucking Megan.

I hated that I was jealous. I hated that she'd had Maverick first.

Not that I even had him. This was nothing but a mutually beneficial arrangement.

I flopped over, not wanting to suffocate myself in the mattress, and blew a sigh toward the ceiling.

Why did sex and relationships have to be so complicated? When it came to school or work or sports, I wasn't this person. I didn't second-guess every decision. Maverick teased me for overthinking, but it wasn't about everything. I didn't doubt my every move. But when it came to men, I was a timid, blundering mess.

All of my insecurities were wrapped up in a single word.

Virgin.

I didn't know how to date. I didn't know how to relax and be myself around a guy. I wasn't sure how to initiate an intimate moment. I questioned every touch, every shift in body language.

But I knew Maverick's movements. I knew his expressions and his habits. He was safe.

Except I wasn't sure how to get over the idea of him with the Megans.

A month ago, it hadn't bothered me. A month ago, he hadn't kissed me since we were toddlers.

How did I stop this from bothering me?

Running out of the grocery store probably wasn't the answer.

The sound of a door slamming outside made me jack-knife to a seat. Then I leapt off my bed, racing through the house.

Jennsyn breezed down the hall, heading for the door as the bell rang.

"Don't answer it," I whisper-yelled.

She slowed, giving me a sideways glance. "Um, okay. Why not?"

"Because it's Maverick."

"Oh." She looked to the door, then back to me. "I thought you were dating."

"We are." Though if he was here to call this whole thing off, honestly, I couldn't blame him. No guy should have to suffer through dating Stevie Adair. Who would have thought? Between the two of us in this relationship, *I* was the bigger disaster.

The doorbell rang again, followed by a knock so loud it had to be Maverick's fist pounding against the wood. "Stevie, I know you're in there. Open up."

I took a backward step, shaking my head.

"I'm not leaving." He pounded on the door again. "Not until you talk to me."

"Did something happen?" Jennsyn asked, lowering her voice. "Did you break up?"

"No. I just don't want to talk to him."

"Okay," she drawled.

"I don't give a fuck if you don't want to talk to me,

Stevie," Maverick called. "It's a Saturday. You promised me Saturdays. And if you're going to go back on your end of this bargain, then I'll go back on mine."

I scrunched up my nose.

"What bargain?" Jennsyn asked.

"Nothing," I said.

"Let me in, Adair," Maverick called.

I crossed my arms over my chest, a silent go away.

"Nadine." His voice was lower, gentler.

"Nadine?" Jennsyn mouthed. "Who?"

"Me." I pointed to my chest. "Nickname."

"Okay. So are we answering the door?"

"No," I said at the same time Maverick yelled, "Yes."

We really needed a thicker door.

"Ugh. Fine." Maverick was a stubborn ass who'd sit outside all night to prove his point, so I stomped past Jennsyn for the entryway.

I flung the door open, ready to berate him for being that stubborn ass, but when I found him with a bag of groceries looped over his arm, my beratement died a quick death.

My chocolate chips and brown sugar were peeking out from that plastic sack.

"Here." He shoved the bag into my chest. "There's more in the truck."

More? He turned and stalked to the open back door.

"Did he just bring you groceries? I kind of like him." Jennsyn took the groceries from my hand. "I'll take these to the kitchen. You can help him with the rest."

"Gee. Thanks," I deadpanned.

She only smiled. "You're welcome."

With an eye roll, I trudged to Maverick's truck, holding out a hand for a couple of bags. "What's all this?"

"Dinner."

How many dinners? This was enough to feed a family of six for a week. Before I could give him a snarky comment, Jennsyn appeared at my side, hand lifted for a wave.

"Hey, I'm Jennsyn Bell. We've seen each other around but never officially met."

"Nice to meet you," Mav said, dipping his chin.

"You too. Bye." She spun around, and in her bare feet, crossed the lawn that separated our house from Toren's next door.

Why she was still coming home was a mystery. All her stuff was at his place now.

Maverick watched as she walked to Toren's driveway, toward the open garage. And as Toren stepped outside, hauling Jennsyn in for a kiss, his jaw dropped. "Is that Coach Greely?"

"Yeah."

"Huh." He jerked up his chin to Toren. "Hey, Coach."

"Hi, Maverick," Toren called, giving him a wave. Then he tugged Jennsyn into the garage, closing it as they disappeared inside.

"How long has that been going on?" Mav asked, taking out the last of the sacks.

I shrugged a nonanswer. If Jennsyn wanted to tell him the truth someday, that was her decision. So I carried the groceries inside, taking them to the kitchen counter as Maverick followed. "I'm sorry about the store."

"So am I. What I said was a dick move. Sorry."

I sighed, taking ingredients from the bags and putting them on the counter. He'd bought spices I already had, but I kept that to myself. "I don't know how to do this."

"I can't change my past, Stevie."

157

"I know."

"Are you going to get upset every time we bump into a girl I know?"

"Maybe? I don't know," I admitted.

His jaw clenched.

"This is something I've never had to deal with before. I'm out of my element." And I was jealous. Ninety percent jealous with ten percent being reserved for crushing insecurities.

I hated that he'd have to teach me things. I didn't like Megan, and I hated knowing that she was better at something. "I feel like I'm late to a game that I don't know how to play."

"It's not a game. It's not a competition," he said.

"Says the man who turns everything into a competition."

He'd once made a contest out of who could drink hot chocolate at the highest temperature. He'd used a candy thermometer and a meat thermometer from his mom's kitchen so that he could judge the winner.

I'd had a scalded tongue for a week but I'd beat him by five degrees.

"Fair," he said. "But not this. There's no winner or loser."

I desperately wanted to believe him. "Well, I feel like a loser."

"You're not." He nudged his elbow to mine. "Ceasefire?"

"Ceasefire." I motioned to the food. "What are we making?"

"Chicken and wild rice. A recipe of Dad's. He's been cooking a lot and told me this was a new favorite."

"What can I do?"

He stepped away from the counter, surveying the kitchen. "Point me toward a pan."

Other than some direction on where to find utensils and cookware, Maverick didn't let me help, so I sat on the island, watching as he cooked. Admiring the way that man moved around a kitchen.

"Moment of truth," he said when the chicken was plated and we sat across from each other at the dining room table.

I took a bite and moaned. "Okay, this is really good. Better than I could have made myself."

"How hard was that to admit?"

"Very." I smiled. "I didn't know you could cook. Or that your dad could either, actually."

Monty had brought pizza for the last family dinner. But otherwise, whenever we went to the Houstons' house, Mom would cook for us all. I guess he'd been learning for all the meals in between.

"He's taken over in the kitchen since Mom's been sick."

"And he taught you?"

"No, she did." He gave me a sad smile. "It started years ago. Little lessons, here and there. Mostly how to read a recipe. But Dad never made a meal when I was growing up other than grilling burgers and steaks in the summers. She told me she wanted me to be able to make a decent meal for my future kids on the nights that my future wife needed a break."

Meredith wouldn't meet those future kids or that future wife, would she? Not without a miracle. The burn in my throat was instant, as was the ache in my heart.

"How are you doing with all of this?" I hadn't asked him how he was holding up enough lately. Everyone was so focused on Meredith, but we needed to start thinking about Maverick and Mabel and Monty.

"I'm good." A lie. He was far from good. But if he didn't

want to delve into the emotional turmoil of his mother's terminal illness, I couldn't blame him.

"Anything I can do?"

"Don't get upset with me for shit I can't change."

"Okay." I gave him a small smile, and when he went back to eating, I did the same, both of us taking a moment for the sadness to pass.

When we were finished, we did the dishes in silence, and then, standing side by side at the sink, Maverick dropped a kiss to the top of my hair.

"I'm going to take off."

"Oh, all right." I barely managed to mask the disappointment in my voice. "Thanks for dinner."

"Welcome."

I followed him to the front door, standing on the stoop as he walked to his truck.

He paused beside the door, fingers on the handle. "When this agreement of ours is over, can you do something for me? Can you be my friend again? I've missed you."

My entire chest cracked down the middle.

How hard was it for him to admit that? To be the person who put years and years of feuding to an end?

God, I'd been hard on him. We'd been hard on each other. "No matter what, we'll always be friends."

"Promise?"

I held up my pinky finger. "Promise."

"Make the most of it, right?" He nodded, staring at his truck door for a moment like he was debating opening it or coming back inside.

Don't go.

I almost said it. I almost asked him to stay. To kiss me again.

But before I could work up the courage, he was behind the wheel and reversing out of my driveway, giving me a quick wave over the dash before he was gone.

Maybe friendship was where we needed to draw the line. Maybe that was better for us both.

There was a reason we'd been fighting for ten years. It was easier, safer, to keep each other at arm's length. It was easier to bicker than admit there might be something more beneath the surface. Because if we truly imploded, if we broke each other's hearts, it would change the dynamic of our families forever.

So I retreated into the house. And made chocolate chip cookies alone.

CHAPTER FIFTEEN

MAVERICK

The moment I pulled up in front of Mission Mini Golf, Stevie groaned. "You can't be serious."

"Oh, come on." I shut off the truck. "It'll be fun."

"I don't like mini golf, Houston. You know this."

Only because when we'd come here on a family outing years ago, not long after the owners had opened the place, she'd scored dead last. Even behind Bodhi, who'd been three or four.

Not one of us had let her live it down.

"Give it another try," I said. "Go into this with a bit more finesse, and I bet you'll love it."

Her eyes narrowed. "I have finesse."

"Sure you do. Let's go."

"Nope." She crossed her arms over her chest.

"Tough shit, Adair. As your fake boyfriend, I'm obligated to take you on at least one cutesy date. And what is cutesier than mini golf?"

She scowled. "I'm not cutesy. And neither are you."

"We are tonight, baby." I winked, then opened my door, waiting by the hood for her to finally join me outside.

"Don't call me baby." She stormed past me for the arched gateway that opened to the course.

Cutesy was the only way to describe Mission Mini Golf. It was more of a garden showcase than an amusement area. There were flower beds and pots everywhere, adding color to green space. The windmill was sided in cedar shakes. The trickling stream and fountains meant that at every hole there was the babble of water.

That Stevie didn't like it here, when the woman loved flowers and the outdoors, was a testament to just how much she hated to lose. That single loss had tainted the whole sport for her.

"How many?" the clerk asked from the hut just inside the course's gates.

"Two." I fished out my wallet from my shorts pocket, handing over my credit card.

With my receipt, she handed over two golf balls, one blue, one pink.

Stevie snatched the blue from my hand and picked out a putter from the rack beside the hut. Then she collected a scorecard and tiny pencil, smacking both against my chest. "I'm going first."

"Go for it."

She set the ball down, lined up her putter and hit the ball so hard it bounced outside the concrete borders of the turf onto the lawn.

I rubbed a hand on the back of my neck, ducking my chin to hide a smile.

"Not. One. Word." She pointed the end of her putter at my face.

"Wouldn't dream of it, honey."

Her nostrils flared, but she didn't tell me not to use the endearment.

"That one didn't count." She picked up her ball and brought it back to the starting point. Then she hit it again, this time sending it around the curve.

I tucked the scorecard in my pocket, then twisted my hat backward as I took her place. With a quick sweep, my pink ball rolled across the turf and dropped with a plunk into the hole.

"See? Finesse." I couldn't help a smirk.

She rolled her eyes. "Good job."

I laughed, giving her a playful push toward her ball. "Just have fun. No one cares if you're good or bad at mini golf."

"Fine." She stuck out her tongue and blew, exactly like we used to do to each other as kids.

Despite what Stevie believed, I hadn't brought her here for torture. If she relaxed, if she didn't take this too seriously and didn't have so many people heckling her bad shots, I knew she'd like it, both the sport of it and the scenery.

She lined up and finished the hole in two. When she bent to retrieve both balls, I had the perfect view of her perfect ass.

Mini golf was fucking great.

I'd told her we were going casual tonight, so when I'd picked her up, she'd walked out of the house in a pair of cutoff denim shorts, a black-and-white-striped crop top and all that hair piled in a messy knot. I'd been fighting a boner ever since.

She didn't even realize she was sexy, did she?

It was getting harder and harder to hide my physical reaction. Ever since that first kiss, it was like the years I'd had smothering this attraction to Stevie, practicing my indifference, had been erased.

I was a teenager again, seeing her as a beautiful woman, and there was no way to ignore her beauty.

"You go first this time," she said, walking to the next hole, a curved bridge over a trickling creek.

My ball sailed to the other side, not a hole in one, but close.

Hers flew off the side and into the water.

I didn't even bother updating the scorecard after that hole. We both knew exactly what was happening tonight.

She'd get her ass kicked. And while she probably expected me to rub it in her face, I was going to keep my mouth shut and just enjoy the night.

Fuck, but I loved Saturdays.

These dates of ours had become the highlight of my week.

"What if we went out a different night?" I asked as we moved to the third hole.

"Are you busy next Saturday or something?"

"No. Just thought it could be fun to mix it up."

"Oh." She nibbled on her lower lip, and I tightened my grip on my putter so I wouldn't reach to tug that pout free. "When?"

"Whenever." Monday. Tuesday. Wednesday. I'd take any day. Time with Stevie meant everything else faded away.

There was no cancer. There were no explanations. She already knew everything that was happening with Mom. I didn't have to answer questions because Stevie was in the thick of it too.

"How about Wednesday?" She took her shot, missing the tunnel where the ball would shoot into the hole, but only by about six inches.

"Wednesday it is." Maybe I'd go to her place, cook her dinner again.

It had taken all of my willpower to leave last week. To keep my mouth off hers. To keep from laying her over the kitchen counter and having her for dessert.

But I'd needed time to think. To figure out where to go next.

Stevie had been jealous of Megan, hadn't she? She wouldn't admit it, but if it was jealousy, then it was a game changer.

Maybe I was getting under her skin. She'd sure as hell crawled under mine.

Maybe I could figure out this girlfriend thing after all. And maybe there was a chance she wanted me on my own merit. Not so I'd turn down Declan's job offer. Not to make Mom's dying wish come true.

If Stevie was jealous, then she might just want me for *me*.

I'd never worked this hard for a woman's attention before. I kind of liked it.

"How's work going?" I asked as we moved through the course, taking our time as the people ahead of us laughed and meandered hole to hole.

"Good. I've only got a few clients of my own. It's been a lot of learning so far, shadowing Dad. But I'm enjoying it. The other designers are great. If I could just keep Dad from hovering, it would be perfect."

"Did you expect Declan Adair to do anything but hover?" I chuckled. "You're his baby girl."

Her father had been the helicopter over her shoulder since the day she'd started wearing training bras. Declan would move every mountain around Mission if it meant she was happy.

"It feels different than him being protective. It feels like he doesn't have confidence in me."

"Oh." *Damn.* "Really?"

"I think some of it is his new assistant. Samantha." Her lip curled as she set down her ball. "She offered to proofread my proposals, which he thought was a great idea. Except she's nitpicking everything I'm doing, which then pulls him into my projects. And then there's him offering you a job as manager. He hasn't said it, but there're enough signals flashing that I know he's not sure I can handle Adair on my own someday."

"Give it time. I don't think him offering me a job had anything to do with your skill. He knows I'm awesome and wants a piece of it." I managed to say it with a straight face.

"Oh my God." She burst out laughing. "Your ego truly knows no bounds."

I chuckled. "Good thing I've got you around to keep it in check."

"Yes, good thing. Though this golf game isn't helping. What's the score?"

I arched my eyebrows. "Do you really want to know?"

"Probably not," she muttered.

"Let's forget the score. Play for something else instead."

"That sounds dangerous. What?"

"Tell you in a minute." I jerked my chin for her to take a putt.

The people behind us were getting closer and this was not something I needed them to overhear. So we finished that hole and as we moved to the next, putting distance between us and the other players, I moved in close enough that I could draw in the sweet, orange-blossom scent of her hair.

"If you beat me on one hole, you get a prize."

"I'm intrigued." Her chin lifted, not shying away as I inched closer. Her mouth was so damn close it took effort not to bend and take it. "What kind of prize?"

"An orgasm."

Her gasp, her eyes flaring, shot straight to my cock. Then her cheeks flushed as she glanced side to side, making sure no one was close.

She was never prettier than when her face was that pretty shade of pink. The same shade as her mouth.

"What are you . . . Do you mean . . ."

"No, not that."

I wanted her naked and spread out beneath me, but I wasn't taking her virginity until I was sure of where we stood. But we could have some fun in the meantime. If we ever took it all the way, I wanted to know every inch of her body first. I wanted her to crave me as much as I craved her.

She blinked too fast, her gaze shifting to my gray T-shirt, staring blankly at the Wildcats logo over my heart. "What do you get? If you win?"

I leaned in close, my nose brushing the shell of her ear. "To give you an orgasm."

Stevie did another quick intake of air, and I let the sound sink deep, let it stoke the heat in my veins.

"Have you ever had one?"

"Yes," she whispered.

"Has anyone ever given you one before?"

She whimpered as I dragged my mouth along her cheekbone. "No, um, not really. There was a guy who tried but I couldn't . . ."

Couldn't get out of her own head.

Whoever that guy was, he was an idiot. I'd gladly show him up. I'd show her what it felt like to have someone else's hands on your body, chasing away any other thought and blowing your damn mind.

She pulled her bottom lip between her teeth, worrying it for a moment.

I tugged it free with my thumb, taking a moment to get lost in the gold flecks of her eyes. They were on fire tonight, alight in the soft evening glow. "What do you say? Want to make the bet?"

She swallowed hard. "After last week, when you said you wanted to be friends and left, I didn't think . . . I didn't think you wanted that anymore. Anything, um, physical."

I snaked my arm around her waist, hauling her against me. And then I pressed my growing arousal against her hip. "Thought we covered that in the back seat of my truck."

Her eyelids drifted closed as her hand came to my bicep, using me to keep her balance. "I'm not . . . what will happen, specifically?"

Of course she'd want specifics. Something to stress over for the next eleven holes. Well, if this happened, it was going to be my way. We'd do what felt good in the heat of the moment.

"You'll have to take the bet to find out."

Not that I was going to tell her. I wanted her to give up

that control she loved so much. And surrender to a little bit of my chaos.

"Yes or no, Nadine?"

She let me go, taking a step back when the voices of the people behind us came closer. With a shaky hand, she tucked an errant strand of hair behind her ear and placed her ball. She glanced to me as she took position, readying her putter.

Her nod was so slight I barely caught it. But when her eyebrows furrowed, when she put on her game face, I knew it was a yes.

She inhaled. Exhaled. Then with perfect concentration and execution, with finesse, she sent the ball down the green, through the white plastic pipe that dropped it around a corner.

And into the cup.

Hole in one.

I smiled, so wide it pinched my cheeks. "Nice shot."

She closed her eyes, unable to hold back her own smile. "Maybe mini golf isn't so bad."

"My turn." I took her place, keeping my gaze on hers as I dropped the ball. When it stopped bouncing, I whacked it with my putter, sending it nowhere near the right direction. "Darn. I guess you win."

"Maverick," she whispered.

"Go and get your ball."

She hesitated for a moment. A pause that made me worry I'd gone too far. But then she whirled, collecting her ball while I did the same with mine.

When I met her at the start of the next hole, I took her hand and pulled her toward the hut.

"We're done?" she asked.

"With mini golf."

"Oh my God." She said it so softly I barely caught it.

"Thanks," I told the clerk, returning both balls and putters. Then I led Stevie through the exit.

The gravel lot was packed with vehicles, other couples and families out to enjoy a beautiful summer evening. A night like this, most would take a moment to appreciate the beauty that was Mission, Montana.

I'd catch it another time. Tonight, I wanted to lock myself inside a room and not come out until dawn.

She wiggled her hand as we got to the truck, trying to slip from my grip, but I walked her to her door, pressing her against the warm metal of my truck.

Then I crushed my mouth to hers, swallowing a mewl as my tongue swept inside and tangled with hers.

Her hands came to my shirt, fisting the hem, as she rose up on her toes.

I'd never kissed a woman the way I kissed Stevie. There was no holding back. No teasing or foreplay. No fragment that I didn't surrender to her entirely.

Everything I had, I gave this woman.

The sound of a car parking broke us apart. I took a steadying breath, a moment of composure to get my dick under control.

That moment was all it took for that lip to be worried between her teeth again.

"Hey." I hooked my finger under her chin, forcing her to meet my gaze. "One word and we forget the bet. Stops right here. Right now. It's your call."

She closed her eyes and shook her head. "Where should we go?"

That breathy whisper. I wanted it in my ear when I was buried inside of her.

"Is there anyone home at your place?"

"No. Jennsyn and Liz are both spending the night with their boyfriends."

Thank fuck. "Your place it is."

CHAPTER SIXTEEN

STEVIE

The drive from mini golf to my house was like a fever dream. Maverick drove with one hand on the wheel and the other in mine, his thumb circling over my knuckles, around and around and around.

That touch had pulled me into a trance. Buildings streaked past the windows. The tires whirred on the asphalt. My body would shift, left and right, with different turns. But I was so locked into those circles, I couldn't focus on anything else.

My mind was spinning in time with those loops. The pulse in my core had started as a weak flutter and steadily grown into a booming throb. The tingles from my knuckles surged through my nerves like endless ripples, crashing into each other as they built into stormy waves.

I'd never been this turned on. Never been so flustered and edgy. Not even when my anxiety would spike before a game. Not even when I was keyed up over an exam.

Maverick pushed buttons I hadn't even known existed.

At this point, I couldn't tell if I liked it, or if I should jump out of this truck at the next light and run away.

I was losing control. It slipped away, like water through my fingers, with each of those infuriating circles of Maverick's thumb.

And while I was having an internal fucking crisis, he'd become the epitome of calm and collected. He drove the speed limit. He came to a full stop at every sign. He took corners at a glacial pace.

This was not the same man who'd pressed me against his truck and frantically devoured my mouth.

Was he trying to torture me? If so, it was working.

I pressed my thighs together, craving some friction for the ache in my center. When he finally turned onto my street, my exhale was audible. My knees began to bounce in rhythm with my racing heart.

Then we were in my driveway and his hand was gone. The tingles stopped, and I'd never been so aware of my bare knuckles before.

Mav climbed out of the truck, spinning his keys on a finger as he took in the neighborhood, inspecting it like he'd never been here before.

All while I fumbled with the door's handle and hopped out onto wobbly legs.

I wasn't just in over my head.

I was drowning.

Maverick met me in front of his truck, and for a moment, I worried he'd say goodnight. That on the drive, he'd changed his mind about taking this any further. But when I met his eyes, the color wasn't his usual icy blue. They'd darkened to a silvery gray. His pupils were blown wide and inky black.

There was a promise in those eyes. A challenge.

Everything would change after this, wouldn't it? If I let him inside my house, my bedroom, there'd be no going back.

What were we doing?

This was going to get messy. This had the potential to end in a bloodbath. Didn't we have enough problems to deal with at the moment? The last thing we needed was to go up in flames.

We could just hit pause. Go back to the original agreement. Saturday dinners where he'd watch TV and I'd read a book. Fake smiles and feigned friendship in front of his parents.

That could work. Probably. Right?

"Mav, I—"

"Don't." His hand came to my chin, taking hold to gently pull me forward as he stepped closer. "Don't think."

"I don't . . ." I exhaled, shoulders sagging. "I don't know how to stop."

The corner of his mouth turned up. "I can help with that."

Then his lips were on mine, his hand still holding my chin as his tongue slipped past my teeth.

The worries vanished in a blink, like he'd shut off my brain. Maverick slanted his mouth over mine, groaning as that urgency from earlier returned. His kiss was rough. Hard. Wet.

I swayed, my head spinning, as his tongue circled mine, just like his thumb. Around and around and around.

Maverick growled, the vibration driving right to my center. Then he ripped his mouth away and grabbed my wrist, pulling me behind him as he stalked to the house.

"Keys." He held out his hand, waiting until I fished them

from my pocket and flipped through to the brass key that fit the lock.

Time seemed to warp as he opened the door. One moment, we were outside. The next, I was pressed against the wall of the entryway, the door closed and the keys landing with a sharp crash on the floor beside our feet. His hat had tumbled off his head, or maybe I'd pushed it free.

Mav swallowed my gasp as he hoisted me up by the back of the knees, wrapping me around his hips as he pressed into my center. His hands slid up my thighs as his frame kept me pinned. His fingertips dipped beneath the frayed hem of my shorts, squeezing my ass as he fluttered his tongue against mine.

He was everywhere, and not where I needed him most.

A noise came from my throat, a cross between a whimper, a moan and a plea. A sound I'd never made before. I clung to Mav's shoulders, meeting every stroke of his tongue with my own. My hands fisted his shirt, balling it up as I locked my ankles around his back, pulling my chest against his.

My nipples were hard and aching, my breasts heavy inside my bra. But no matter how tightly I pressed my body against his, how hard he ground into my core, the friction wasn't enough.

He tore his lips away, dragging them down the column of my throat, his teeth scratching at my skin. "Fuck, Stevie."

"Yes," I panted.

"Bedroom."

I flung out an arm toward the hallway. "That way."

He shifted an arm beneath my ass and another around my back, then he hauled me off the wall and carried me through the house, all while he sucked and nipped at my neck.

No one had carried me in years. Not since I was a kid. I wasn't a petite woman, but Mav carried me without effort, and God, I liked it. A lot. I liked feeling precious. I liked that he was tall and strong and that nothing about my own strength and height had ever intimidated him before.

When we walked through the door to my suite, he kicked it closed, the slam rattling through the house. The blinds were open, and the summer sun filtered through the glass.

"Let me get the shades." I unhooked my ankles, about to drop to my feet, but Maverick stalked for the bed, planting a knee in the mattress before we crashed, his weight settling over my body.

"Leave them open." His teeth skimmed my earlobe as his hand slid beneath my shirt. "I want to see you."

No way. I wouldn't be able to shut off my mind if it was this bright. I'd only ever imagined this in the dark. "Just let me—"

"Close your eyes, Nadine."

I shook my head. "Mav—"

His mouth sealed over mine, silencing any other protest.

Okay, so we'd do this in the light. I could handle it, right? I squeezed my eyes closed, focusing on the kiss. On that hand of his splayed over my ribs, inching toward the bottom of my bra.

What did I do with my legs? I raised a knee. Laid it flat. Bent it to the side. Pushed it straight.

I squirmed beneath Maverick, all while he kept kissing me, the slow, languid strokes of his tongue tasting every corner of my mouth before he moved to my neck again.

Another whimper escaped my lips, this one laced with

frustration as my hand fisted at my side. There was making out in the back of his truck, where it was so cramped all I could do was feel up his torso.

But this was a bed. My bed. Maverick Houston was in my bed and seemingly intent on giving me an orgasm. What did I do with my hands? Should I touch him too? Kissing was one thing, but this?

How did I do this? I didn't know how to do this.

I lifted an arm in the air, then let it fall to the mattress as my eyes popped open.

The ceiling had a thick texture beneath the white paint, like tiny mountain peaks. There was a spot that seemed more gray than white, like it was the drywall and the painters had missed it during construction. I'd never noticed that spot before.

Mav lifted off me, his hand sliding out of my shirt as he propped up on his elbows and stared down at me with those stormy eyes. "What's happening in your head?"

"Well, there's a spot on my ceiling I'll never be able to unsee. And I don't know what I'm doing," I blurted.

"So?"

"So, I don't like when I don't know what to do."

His eyes softened, a hand coming to my hair, pushing the strands away from my temple. "Does it feel good?"

I nodded.

"Then do whatever feels good. That's it. There's no secret. If it feels good, do it. If it doesn't, try something else."

"But what about you?"

"What about me? I just kissed Stevie Adair. In her bed. If I'm lucky, she'll let me touch her boobs. That's a thousand teenage fantasies come true. I'm good, honey."

Oh. My. God. "You had teenage fantasies about kissing me?"

"Have you *seen* you?"

My head had been spinning one direction and now it was whirling the opposite. "Mav."

His fingers dove deeper into my hair, gently tugging at the strands. "Say the word and we stop."

"I don't want to stop," I whispered, searching his eyes. "I just . . . I need you to tell me what to do."

"Close your eyes."

I closed them.

"Put your hand on my throat."

I gulped, sliding my arm between us to cup his throat. His Adam's apple bobbed beneath my palm. "Okay."

"Feel my pulse?"

"Yes." It raced beneath my fingers. Pounded. For me.

"You can touch me anywhere you want. Anywhere. Got it?"

"Got it."

"Good." He kissed the corner of my mouth, sweet and light.

My lips parted, my breaths shallow as he nuzzled his nose against mine.

"Don't move." He brushed his mouth across the line of my jaw, then he was gone, his weight lifting from the bed.

My eyes instantly opened as he stood at my feet.

There was a smirk on his face when he adjusted the bulge straining against his shorts. He reached for my shoes, pulling them off and tossing them to the floor. He toed off his own, then took me by the knees, and with a quick tug, pulled my ass to the end of the bed.

I gasped, lifting to an elbow.

"Lie back," he ordered, and I obeyed, my eyes lifting to the ceiling, to that spot, as his hands skirted up my bare thighs, trailing over my shorts to the button beneath my navel.

"Eyes on me." He waited until I looked down, then he flipped that button free. "Say the word and I stop."

I shook my head. "Don't stop."

"Good girl." His grin stretched as he took my hand, hauling me to a seat. Then his hands came to my shirt, lifting it over my ribs and off my head in a whoosh.

The air was cool against my skin, mingling with my nerves, and my nipples turned to pebbles, straining at the fabric of my bra. My hair tickled my bare shoulders and spine.

Maverick dropped to a knee, his eyes locked on mine as his hands spanned my ribs, his thumbs drawing the same circles he'd been drawing in the truck. "You're so fucking sexy. You don't even see it, do you?"

My hand lifted to his hair, diving into the thick strands, weaving them between my fingers. "Are you sure about this?"

"That's my line." He cupped my face, his thumb tracing over my mouth. "Are you?"

"Yes," I whispered. "I'm sure."

"Then fucking kiss me."

I leaned in to take his mouth, hesitant at first, not sure how to lead this, but like he'd told me, I did what felt good, and when he moaned, it was my reward.

Maverick lifted up, using his lips to press me back into the bed, and then he was kissing down my throat, to my sternum before trailing his tongue to my breast. He tugged the cup down on my bra and took a nipple into his hot mouth.

I sank into the bed as he toyed with it, licking and sucking, until my hands were splayed along the smooth, white cotton duvet. A stripe of sunlight hit my face, and for a brief moment, I gave the outside my attention. The green grass and blue sky and absolutely nothing stopping someone from peeking into my window.

But Mav was right about the light. It meant I could see him too. Watch as his long hands slid up my torso, cupping my breasts as he moved to the other side, yanking my bra away to give that nipple the same attention.

Damn, he was hot. The ache in my core was overpowering, that need for more and more.

His teeth grazed my nipple, a hint of pain mixing with the pleasure, as he let it free from his mouth. Then his trail of kisses went lower, across the sensitive skin of my ribs to my navel.

His fingers came to the hem of my shorts, dragging them over my hip bones.

My black lace panties came with them, inch by inch, exposing more of my body.

"Mav." My voice was shaky from the nerves. The lust. "I don't—"

"Do you trust me?" He spoke against my stomach, then lifted his chin, those stormy eyes finding mine.

"Yes."

"Then close your eyes."

My lids fluttered closed as he stripped the shorts from my legs, baring me completely. I could feel his gaze on my

DEVNEY PERRY

center, but I was too nervous to look, so I bit my bottom lip and waited.

"You're perfect." His hand came to my calf, his touch igniting a rush of tingles as he urged my leg to the side.

When I risked a glance, Maverick's broad shoulders were settling between my knees, forcing me to spread wider.

The first kiss on my inner thigh made me gasp. The second conjured a noise so wanton, so desperate, it took a moment for my ears to register it had come from me.

Maverick moved toward my center, his breath soft against my folds. When his tongue dragged through my slit, I tensed, every muscle in my body going taut. And then he did it again, and I melted. Into. A. Puddle.

"Oh God."

"You taste so good." He licked at me again, the tip of his tongue flicking my clit before he sucked it into his mouth and I came off my shoulders like a woman possessed. My body was no longer my own.

It was Maverick's and he seemed intent on making me come apart.

He kept lapping at my clit, licking until my hips began to rock against his face, my knees spread wide and my toes curled. When he brought his finger to my center, sliding one inside, my cry filled the room.

It was more sensation than I'd ever felt, so overpowering it was hard to breathe. "I'm . . . it's too much."

"You can take it." He kept going, not relenting for even a moment as he added a finger, finding that spot inside that made me begin to tremble, head to toe. "Come. Just let go."

He put those perfect lips on my clit, and with a quick suck, a flutter of his tongue, I shattered.

"Maverick." I arched beneath him, my hands fisting the duvet as fireworks exploded behind my eyes.

Every part of my body was shaking, like my bones themselves were rattling, as he kept at me, drawing out an orgasm unlike anything I'd ever felt in my life. I lost touch with reality for a moment, my mind so blank and empty I wasn't even sure of my own name.

I clenched around his fingers, my hips bucking against his mouth. Pulse after pulse, I kept quaking, riding out the release until, finally, the world returned in pieces. The chirp of birds outside. The scent of Maverick's cologne mingling with my fabric softener. The wetness between my thighs and the man sliding his fingers from my body.

Before I could risk a glance, he picked me up by the waist and lifted me higher into the pillows, his weight settling beside mine as he tugged the throw I kept at the foot of my bed over my body. Like he knew I wouldn't be able to look at him if I was naked.

I cracked an eye.

Maverick was stretched out beside me. A part of me had expected a cocky smirk on his face. Maybe another quip about his teenage fantasies. But he stared at me with so much affection my heart thumped so hard it hurt.

His hand came to my face, his thumb drawing a line across my cheek. "You good?"

"Yes." I nodded. "This should be weird."

"Yeah."

Maverick, my Maverick, had just gone down on me. He'd given me an orgasm that had blanked my mind. It should most definitely be awkward or embarrassing.

"But it's not, is it?"

"No, it's not."

All these years, what if it wasn't hate that had kept us from pushing and pulling?

What if there'd always been something more buried beneath our animosity? What if we'd spent years fighting a pull that we were both too stubborn to acknowledge?

Okay, now I really had something to think about.

Mav leaned down, kissing my forehead. "Want me to go? Or stay?"

I could hug him for giving me a choice. I had a feeling that he didn't do that for other women. He'd just leave. Or maybe that was my own wishful thinking.

"Stay."

"Got an extra toothbrush?" he asked.

"Yes.

"Um, what about that?" I let my eyes drop to his shorts. To the erection straining his zipper.

"It'll go away."

"Should I, um—"

"You'll have your chance." He winked, then rolled off the bed and ducked into my bathroom.

"Middle drawer," I called, hearing it open. Then the water turned on, and while he brushed his teeth, I took a minute to breathe.

When the faucet shut off, I flew off the bed, streaking naked past my open windows for my walk-in closet. I pulled on a fresh pair of panties and some baggy sweats with a Wildcats volleyball T-shirt, then padded into the room as Maverick stripped off his shirt, tossing it on the floor.

Holy. Abs. My mouth watered. I'd seen Maverick without a shirt, but he'd never been standing beside my bed before. I'd never been in a position to stare.

He pulled the covers down, fixing the pillows before he unclasped his shorts and let them fall to the floor.

The bulge in his black boxer briefs was hard and thick and prominent enough to make out the crown of his cock.

I'd just had the best orgasm of my life, but the throb of desire was immediate.

"Are you going to stand there and drool over me or get in this bed?"

"Drool," I said.

He smiled, his chiseled jaw sharpening. A dimple flashed, a dimple I hadn't seen in a long time.

His teenage fantasies might have been about my boobs, but I'd always wanted a guy with dimples like Maverick's. I just hadn't let myself consider they'd be his.

I crossed the room as he climbed into bed, pulling back the covers for me to slide beneath. It was still early, hours before I normally went to bed. But I didn't want to leave this room.

Maybe because I feared if we left, it would all go away. And tonight, I wanted to linger in this bubble. Eventually, it would pop. But not yet.

"Remember our last sleepover?" I said, turning sideways to stare at his profile, tucking my hands beneath my cheek.

"That time we made a fort in the basement?"

"No, after that. When we built that cardboard house in my backyard."

He smiled, linking his hands behind his head. "Then it rained and we were both too stubborn to go inside, so we stayed there all night, getting soaked. And we each got sick."

"Mom was so upset when we came in and our lips were blue. To this day, I can't ever remember being so cold."

"Same." He glanced over, his brilliant eyes catching the light.

"You said you missed me. I've missed you too."

He reached for me, banding an arm around my belly as he dragged me to the center of the bed. Then he curled his large frame around mine, his nose buried in my hair. "Goodnight, Adair."

"Goodnight, Houston."

CHAPTER SEVENTEEN

MAVERICK

R ush and I walked out of the fieldhouse, backpacks slung over our shoulders as we made our way through the parking lot.

"Heading home?" I asked.

"Yeah. Faye wants to swing by Dolly's later. I guess Dusty bought Rally a swing or something. We've got so much baby shit I can't even fathom what else we'd need but whatever. We're going out to the diner to pick it up."

"Rally already has a swing."

"I know. But I guess this one is for when he gets older. It's for jumping or something."

"Ah." I snapped my fingers. "A Jumperoo. Bodhi had one when he was a baby. They can jump and bounce around. If he ever gets plugged up, a few minutes in that thing, and it works all the poop out."

"Seriously?" Rush asked.

I shrugged. "That's what Mabel always said. Watch out for blowouts."

"Noted." Rush used the fob to unlock his Yukon, opening the back hatch to dump his gym bag inside. "No one ever tells you how much stuff comes with a baby. We're running out of room."

What didn't fit upstairs in the nursery or Faye and Rush's room had spilled into the common areas of the house. A bouncer. Blankets. There wasn't a single flat surface that didn't have a pacifier, but when you were actually looking for one to give him when he was crying, they'd magically vanish.

In less than a year, when we went our separate ways and moved out of that house, I was going to steal a few binkies to take as souvenirs. I'd miss all the baby clutter.

Too much was changing. Too much was on the horizon. Too much.

When I thought about the future, it only made me sick. So I didn't.

"That was a good workout," I said.

"Yeah." He nodded. "I was tired as fuck but I'm glad we came."

We'd come here at five this morning, like we had nearly every day since school had ended in May. We'd have a practice later with the team, but this one-on-one time with Rush was something I looked forward to each and every day. A chance to have some time with my best friend. A few hours to push my body to the extreme and shut out the world.

It usually wasn't hard to drag my ass out of bed.

Until today.

I'd been seconds away from canceling on Rush. My phone had been in my hand, fingers hovering over the screen, to tell him I wasn't going to make it so I could spend the morning curled around Stevie and sleep for a few more hours.

But then I'd worried it would be awkward when we woke up. That she'd stress over last night. So I'd crawled out of her warm, soft bed that smelled like her floral shampoo and left her a note that I'd gone to the gym.

Rush tossed his bag into the back of his SUV, then closed the door. "You good?"

After Thanksgiving, after Mom's announcement, Rush had been the person to stay by my side all night. He'd let me get angry. Sad. And when I'd finally broken down, he'd been a better friend than I probably deserved.

He worried. So did Faye.

"Yeah. Why?"

He shrugged. "You just seem a little distracted today. And you didn't come home last night. I was up pacing the living room with Rally, feeding him a bottle, and saw your room was empty. Not that it's my business or anything. It's just been a while since you did that."

Rush knew me better than anyone—well, except maybe Stevie. We'd been friends and roommates for years. He'd seen me bring countless girls home for a hookup. He'd watched me come in the house wearing last night's clothes on many occasions.

He probably thought I'd had a one-night stand.

I hadn't told him about Stevie, mostly because Rush was a relationship kind of guy. When he learned I had a girlfriend, he'd have questions. And when he learned that girlfriend was Stevie, he'd have even more. He knew our history.

It had been kind of nice to keep Stevie to myself, at least outside of our family. In our tiny circle, it seemed easier to put on the façade.

But was it a façade? Maybe before last night. Now it felt

real. Incredibly, deliciously real. Even if it had started for the wrong reasons.

"I've been seeing someone," I told him.

"Yeah?" His eyes widened. "Like a girlfriend?"

"A girlfriend." I nodded. "It's Stevie Adair."

His eyes bugged out. "As in the girl you've known since you were kids? That Stevie? The volleyball player?"

"That Stevie. Mom really wanted us to make up, so we've been going on a few dates. Trying to work through the past. It's, uh . . . nice. I was at her place last night."

Rush hummed, studying my face. "So it was your mom's idea."

That statement, right there, made my stomach twist. Yes, it had been Mom's idea. But it wasn't why it had continued. There was more to this than appeasing my dying mother, wasn't there? Maybe we wouldn't have made it to date number two or three or four without Mom's influence, but it was beyond that now.

"Yeah, it was Mom's idea."

"And Stevie knows that?"

"She does." For fuck's sake, did he think I was lying to Stevie? That I was leading her on at my mom's request? I didn't exactly blame him for asking, but it still annoyed the shit out of me.

Was it really so unbelievable that I could be a decent boyfriend?

"All right." He rubbed his jaw. "I, uh . . . hopefully we can meet her one of these days."

He didn't believe I had a girlfriend, did he? Well, she was my girlfriend. No matter how this had started, she was mine. And if he needed to see us together to prove that this was a real relationship, then I'd bring Stevie to the house.

Maybe that would help win her trust too.

She'd let me go down on her last night. Let me give her that orgasm. It was the best time I'd had in ages. But I was still worried she didn't want me enough.

If we did this, if we went all the way, I didn't want her to have regrets. I didn't want to see the skepticism I saw in Rush's gaze in Stevie's too.

"See you at home?" he asked.

"Later. I'm going to visit Mom for a while."

"Give her a hug for me."

"Will do." I jerked my chin and walked to my truck, still irked.

The problem with this whole situation was that there were too many people giving me their damn opinion. My parents. Stevie's. Mabel. Now Rush.

There were too many people meddling. Too many people with expectations.

I didn't know what would happen with Stevie. Did we really have to decide right now? The future wasn't something I wanted to think about at the moment.

All I knew was that I wasn't going to screw this up for Mom. I wouldn't disappoint her like that.

I drove across town, my mood shit, and by the time I got to Mom and Dad's, I had to force my jaw to stop clenching. I knocked, opening the door and calling into the house, "Please don't be naked."

"Maverick," Mom chided, her laughter drifting from inside.

That laughter helped. A lot. My molars stopped grinding.

I stepped out of my slides and headed to the living room, stopping short when I found her on the couch.

With Stevie.

"Oh. Hi."

"Hey," she said, her cheeks flushing. She hid the blush from Mom with a curtain of her hair as she stared at my mother's bare feet and the nail polish brush in her hand.

She'd come to paint my mom's toes. To spend time with her. Pamper her. Because she loved my mother.

Was that why Mom had pushed this reconciliation? So that she could say she knew my girlfriend? That she wouldn't feel like she'd missed out on that part of my life? That she could dream Stevie was the woman who'd someday become my wife?

It felt like a lie. For the first time in weeks, this felt like a lie. I fucking hated lying to my mom, but I wasn't going to stop.

Somehow, Stevie and I would stick this out. Until Mom . . .

My chest felt too tight, the air too thick. I cleared my throat and pointed to the kitchen. "I'm going to grab some water. Need anything?"

"I'm all set." Mom pointed over her shoulder to the tumbler on the end table.

"Stevie?"

"I'm good."

I escaped to the kitchen, dragging in a few deep breaths until that pressure in my chest was gone. Then I filled a glass with water and returned to the living room.

"Where's Dad?" I asked Mom, walking to the couch to drop a kiss on her forehead.

"The grocery store."

Of course. He'd go on a Sunday morning when it was quieter than a weeknight after work.

I took a seat on the floor, setting my water on the coffee table as I reached for my toes, stretching my hamstrings. My gaze shifted to Stevie but she was entirely locked on Mom's pedicure.

"How are you feeling today?" I asked Mom.

"Fine. Maybe a little tired." She finished that sentence on a yawn. "Did you go to the gym at the crack of dawn?"

"Yeah." I nodded. "Though it was hard to get out of bed this morning."

Stevie closed her eyes, pulling in her lips, her face still hidden from Mom by that silky hair.

It would be fun to tease her a bit, to hint at things only the two of us knew. Like when we were kids and had a thousand inside jokes.

Three more toes and Stevie returned the brush to the bottle, screwing it on tight. "Done. What do you think?"

Mom beamed at her feet. "Better than anyone who does it professionally. You've always been steady with a nail brush. We all probably should have pushed you to become a surgeon or something."

"I'm glad you like it." Stevie reached for the lotion on the end table, squirting a blob into her palm before she began to massage the soles of Mom's feet. "Is this okay?"

"It's great."

With Mom's system marinating in so many chemicals, she'd developed some neuropathy in her hands and feet. Every day, she'd get a hand and foot massage, mostly from Dad. But I'd given her my fair share. And her toenails were always painted. Always a new color. Today's was neon pink.

I hadn't really thought about the polish. I guess I'd just assumed it was Mabel or Dad. But it was Stevie, wasn't it? How often did she come over and do this?

That tightness in my chest returned, so I took a huge gulp of water.

Mom pulled the blanket she had draped on her lap closer to her chin and closed her eyes. It took less than ten minutes for her to fall asleep.

"You've been doing her nails," I said.

Stevie nodded. "I try to come over once a week."

"That's sweet. Thank you."

"I like doing it. Want me to paint yours too?" she teased.

"Sure." I scooted across the floor, lifting a foot up onto the armrest of the couch.

"Seriously?"

I shrugged. "Unless you need to leave."

"No, I was going to stay for a while."

"Then go for it." I lay flat out on the carpet, lacing my fingers beneath my head as I stared up at the ceiling. When her hands touched my feet, I closed my eyes, relaxing into the feel of Stevie's fingers on my skin.

The sound of the garage door opening echoed through the house as she was finishing up with my last two toes.

Dad came into the living room, eyebrows raised, as he took in my hot-pink nails. "Am I next?"

Stevie giggled, screwing on the top to the polish. "For you, I'd find a more masculine color, like fire-engine red."

Dad laughed. "How's everything going?"

"Fine." I jackknifed to a seat, then stood, careful not to wreck Stevie's work and get color on the carpet. "Need help with the groceries?"

"Nah. It was only a couple of bags." He pointed to Mom. "She okay?"

"Tired." Given the dark circles beneath Dad's eyes, he was tired too. "Why don't you go rest? We'll get out of here."

"Oh, don't leave," Dad said. "She'll want more time with you."

We all wanted more time.

"We'll go for a walk or something," I said. "Be back in a bit. Enough time for you to take a power nap."

Dad sighed. "That'll work."

Stevie carefully shifted out from beneath Mom's feet, covering them with the blanket after checking that the polish was dry. Then she squeezed Dad's arm as she passed by, heading for the entryway.

She stepped into the flip-flops I hadn't noticed earlier, then slipped outside, waiting for me on the sidewalk as I carefully put on my slides and closed the door behind us.

We set off down the block, falling into an easy pace through our childhood neighborhood.

There was always a heaviness, a fog, that lingered when I walked outside my parents' house. It lingered for a few minutes until the fresh air and sunshine chased it away.

A lawn mower hummed in the distance. The laughter of kids drifted from the community park ahead. This was the sidewalk where I'd learned to rollerblade. Where Stevie had crashed her bike and skinned both knees.

We passed familiar houses, some with familiar owners, some with people new to the neighborhood. When we passed a yard where a man was planting a tree, Stevie greeted him good morning as I waved.

"Where's your Jeep?" I turned, scanning the street behind us.

"Mom and Dad's. I stopped there first and walked over. Mom made a sourdough loaf for your parents."

Bread, plain, simple bread, was about the only thing

Mom would always eat, if not for the taste, just for some calories.

"Mav?"

"Nadine?"

"Do you want to work for my dad?"

I slowed, forehead furrowing as I stared at her. "I thought you didn't want me to work at Adair."

"I want my dad to believe in me. I want him to have faith that I could run the entire business without bringing on help. But when we made this deal, I didn't ask what *you* wanted. Do you want to come to work at Adair?"

There was genuine concern and curiosity in her voice. She felt guilty, didn't she? "You're not robbing me of a potential career. I don't want to work at Adair." I'd only entertained the idea to get a rise out of her.

"You're sure?"

"Quite."

"Then what do you want to do?" she asked. "I should probably know the answer to that question already, but I was thinking about it earlier. At dinners, we mostly talked about football and volleyball and Bodhi. Your mom. Everyone knew after graduation I'd go to work for Adair. The last time I remember anyone asking you what you wanted to do after college was years ago, and you said you weren't sure yet."

"I guess that answer still holds. I'm not sure yet."

As much as I loved my parents, I wasn't following in their career footsteps.

Mom had worked as a secretary at the Oaks for fifteen years. She'd smiled and waved any time I'd passed the office. She'd been beloved by the students and my friends. But she'd taken that job to be close to Mabel and me during our childhood, and for the tuition discount.

She'd loved her job at the Oaks, but I always wondered if she'd wanted a career that hadn't centered around her children.

Dad worked as an investment broker. He and a partner ran their own business, each managing their own portfolios. It was a great job now, but he'd put in a lot of years to get to this point. To bring on enough clients that they could afford for Mom to quit.

He'd offered to bring me into the business after graduation, to help me get my license and build out my own clientele. But I'd never had an interest in managing retirement money or insurance policies.

Just like I wasn't interested in managing a landscaping company.

I was getting a degree in business because it seemed like the most prudent choice. It would give me the most options when I finally made a decision.

"What about football? Will you miss it?" Stevie asked.

"Yes." I'd miss my teammates. I'd miss the coaches. I'd miss the game itself. But Stevie and I were alike in our collegiate careers.

Both would end at Treasure State University.

Rush had the talent to advance to the NFL, and if we had a stellar season this fall, if he made it through without an injury, chances were good he'd get drafted. I was a solid kicker and punter, but I had no delusions of a professional career.

"Would you want to get into coaching?" Stevie asked.

I shrugged, turning a corner to round a block. "I've thought about it."

A lot, if I was being honest with myself. I'd thought

about taking over as the coach at the Oaks. Maybe someday, going to work at Treasure State.

"For the record, I think you'd be a great coach." She tapped her elbow to mine. "I've seen you with Bodhi. You're patient. You're good at teaching, breaking things down. Keeping it fun while pushing him to do better."

I stopped, pressing a hand over my heart, feigning shock. "Had I known that all I needed to do to earn such high praise was give you an orgasm, I would have done it years ago."

"Maverick." She smacked my arm, and shot me a scowl, but there was no venom behind it. She knew I was just teasing. "Pig."

"I'm kidding." I slung an arm around her shoulders, hauling her close for a moment before letting her go and resuming our walk. "Thank you."

"Welcome."

"Honestly? I've thought about being a coach. But I feel guilty planning a future when Mom can't. I don't want to think about what happens next. So I just . . . don't." It was a truth I hadn't been brave enough to voice to anyone.

Stevie's hand slipped into mine. "She'd hate that."

"Yeah, she would." But it didn't change the reality. I couldn't plan a future knowing Mom wasn't in it. I couldn't process that reality in my mind.

We kept our hands linked as we rounded the block, slowly making a loop to head back to the house. When we passed the park, Stevie pulled me into the grass, leading me toward the playground.

"Returning to the scene of the crime, huh, A Cup?" I teased.

She reached up and flicked the tip of my nose. "Shithead."

"You know I'm sorry, right? For the stupid stuff I said when we were kids."

"I know." Her hand flexed in mine. "I'm sorry too."

"And you're sorry for telling Leah McAllister that I kissed Heather Olson?"

"Seriously?" She groaned. "Can we never talk about that—"

I slammed my mouth on hers, cutting her off.

She scrunched up her nose, holding my gaze, but didn't pull away. She rolled her eyes when I licked her bottom lip, and no matter how hard she tried to hide it, I could feel her smile stretching wider.

God, I loved teasing her. I loved the fire that sparked in those hazel eyes.

We could make it. We could figure out a way to stick this out for a while, right? Convince people it was real.

I pulled away, smirking down at her pink cheeks. Then I pulled her to the swings, each of us taking our own to kill some time so my parents could nap before we made our way home again.

"Will you come to dinner at my place tonight?" I asked.

"It's not Saturday."

"Nope." Maybe she only wanted to keep our once-a-week dates. Maybe that was the smartest idea. But damn it, I wanted her to come to my house, meet Rush and Faye and Rally.

Show them all I could be a boyfriend.

The five steps she took to think about it were agonizing. "Okay."

Thank fuck. "Six o'clock work okay? I'll make us all dinner."

"That's nice of you."

"I'm a nice guy."

"The jury's still out on that one," she teased.

It was only a joke. There was laughter in her voice. But if there was even a shred of doubt in her mind that I was the guy who hadn't been all that nice for the past decade, well . . . I guess I had some work to do.

CHAPTER EIGHTEEN

STEVIE

Maverick's house was not the football player's bachelor pad I'd expected. There was an apple orchard candle burning on the living room coffee table. There was a blue vase with white flowers on the bar that separated the U-shaped kitchen from the rest of the open-concept space.

The cushy beige sectional was situated in front of a massive TV, but the toss pillows and throws gave the over-sized furniture style.

There were no smelly cleats by the front door. No gym bags piled on chairs. No neon beer signs or NFL posters littering the walls.

Instead of sports memorabilia or man-cave pieces, the personal touches were for a baby. The bouncer in the corner. The baby blanket folded into a square on the couch. The stuffie, a plush wildcat with a Treasure State jersey, on the end table.

"Nice place," I told Maverick.

"Thanks." He kissed my cheek, then waved me past the entryway as he headed toward the kitchen.

When we'd finished our walk earlier, he'd escorted me to my parents' house before returning to his. I'd run some errands this morning and cleaned the house. Then I'd sat around, waiting until it was time to leave.

Part of me had almost said no. It would be easier if we kept this to Saturdays. If we stuck to the original agreement. But the other part wanted to pretend, for a night, that we were a real couple. That kissing counted. That what he'd done last night had been more than physical attraction.

At this point, I was practically begging for a broken heart.

Maverick had smothered my sense of self-preservation somewhere along the way.

"Make yourself at home," he said. "Rush and Faye should be down in a minute. Rally just had a blowout, so they had to do an emergency bath."

"Can I help with dinner?" I followed him to the kitchen, leaning my forearms on the bar.

"Nah. I've got it." He lifted the glass lid on a pot, letting a puff of steam escape with the scents of garlic and herbs and wild rice.

The sound of footsteps made me turn as Rush Ramsey, quarterback of the Treasure State Wildcats football team, came down the staircase with a baby boy tucked in his arm.

"Hey, Stevie." He crossed the space, lifting a hand to wave.

"Hi, Rush."

We'd crossed paths enough times at the fieldhouse that I knew Rush, but not the woman who came down behind him.

"Hi, I'm Faye." She smiled, tucking a lock of strawberry-blond hair behind an ear.

"Stevie." I shook her hand, then nodded to the little guy. "This is Rally?"

"The poop machine." Rush beamed at his son.

"Please tell me you washed your hands. Multiple times," Maverick said.

"Squeaky clean." Rush handed Rally to Faye, bending to drop a kiss on her hair. Then he joined Maverick in the kitchen, opening the fridge to take out a tray of steaks. "Dude. Are your toenails hot pink?"

Maverick glanced over his shoulder, grinning as our gazes met. "Yep. They sure are."

"Do I want to know why?" Rush arched his eyebrows. "Actually. You know what? Don't answer that. I don't need to know if you have a weird toe kink. I'll get the grill going."

Mav chuckled. "Twenty more minutes on the potatoes. Then we'll be ready."

"Cooking is their new thing. They're this adorable, domestic couple." Faye laughed, carrying the baby to the couch as Rush left to start the grill. She sat beside him, laying Rally on his back so he could wiggle and kick. "Maverick has made it his life's mission to find a sauce that I like."

"You don't like sauce?"

"No. He says I'm almost as picky as you. Not quite, but almost."

"I can't even deny it. I know what I like." And at the moment, I liked Maverick. More than I wanted to admit.

Faye tickled Rally's bare toes, then crisscrossed her legs, getting comfortable beside him. "How long have you guys been dating?"

"Not long. Since graduation."

There was something about her, something sweet and kind, that made me want to tell her the whole truth. That it had started as something fake. That for Maverick, he was doing this for his mom. While it had started to become real for me.

Yep, heartbreak was imminent. And yet here I was, fooling myself into thinking this was a dinner with my boyfriend and his roommates.

"Ah." Faye nodded. "I'll admit, when Rush came home earlier and said you were together, I was a bit surprised. He said you've known each other forever but weren't exactly friends. And Maverick is, well . . . Maverick."

"He's infuriating." And protective. And funny. And charming.

Faye laughed. "There was a point in time when I regularly contemplated murder."

I snorted. "Really? Is he hard to live with?"

"He used to be. There was a day I came home to a naked woman who was supposed to be in his bed but was in Rush's instead. And he didn't exactly welcome me with open arms. He'd decided that I was baby-trapping Rush and was this close to running me out of the house." She pinched her fingers together, leaving only a sliver of space between them. "But we worked it out. And now I kind of love him."

"That's good." I forced a smile, though I was stuck on the thought of a naked woman in Maverick's bed. In this house.

Eventually, I'd get over his past. I just wasn't sure how. Not yet. I was still locked in my own ridiculous jealousy.

Had other girls sat on Maverick's couch? Had they had a meal at this table?

"So you went to the Oaks?" Faye asked.

"Yeah. Maverick said you went to Mission High. I knew

most of the volleyball players on their team. I bet we've got some mutual acquaintances."

As the guys cooked, we chatted, sharing names from the past. Then she let me gush over how much I loved Dolly's, the diner where she worked. It was an older restaurant, one that had been in Mission for decades, but it had become a new favorite spot of mine. Jennsyn and I would go for a cheeseburger every month.

"Dinner's ready." Maverick carried our plates to the table, and once Rally was situated in his bouncer, we sat down to dive in.

Rush had grilled steaks. Maverick had made wild rice, potato wedges and roasted carrots. The skins on the potatoes were crispy and brown. I'd be skipping those. I loved potatoes, but only without the skin. I hated the weird, papery texture and the brown spots that made me think of dirt.

"Here." Maverick brought over one last bowl, setting it beside my plate.

Potato wedges. Without the skin.

My heart skipped.

"Thank you." So maybe it didn't matter that Maverick had brought other women to his bed. To this house. I doubted they got special potatoes.

"How's the volleyball team going to be this year?" Rush asked as he cut up his steak. "They lost a lot of seniors."

"They did." I nodded. "And Jennsyn will be impossible to replace. It might not be their best year, but some of the upcoming girls have a lot of talent."

"I heard Jennsyn is dating Coach Greely," he said.

"Yep." Dating seemed too tame a word. Those two were endgame. She might not have changed her address, but she lived at Toren's. And that man's entire world revolved around my friend.

I knew more about their relationship than anyone else, but it was that subject that could get Toren in trouble, so even with Maverick, I steered clear. Before I could change topics, the front door opened and Erik Manning, another guy from the football team and Maverick's other roommate, walked inside.

"Hey, guys." He held the door open for his girlfriend, Kalindi, to come inside.

"Hey," Mav said. "Hungry? There's plenty of food."

"No, we just stopped by to share some news." Erik beamed at Kalindi.

She beamed back.

Kalindi was friends with a couple girls from the volleyball team, and we'd all placed guesses on when the two would get engaged.

She was stunning, with perfect dark skin and a beautiful smile. People teased me for smiling all the time, but I'd never seen Kalindi without that smile. It was brighter than normal tonight.

Erik took her hand, lacing their fingers together. They shared a look, then he held up their hands, twisting so we could see a sparkling diamond ring. "We're engaged."

"Fuck, yes." Maverick shot out of his chair, walking over to hug them both.

Rush was right behind him with Faye.

"Congratulations," I told them both.

"Thanks." Kalindi leaned into Erik's side. "We're going downtown to celebrate. You guys should come after you're done eating."

"Sure." Maverick shrugged. "I'll text you later."

They shifted to leave, but before they could go, the door opened again, two girls coming inside. One, I didn't know. The other was Samantha, Dad's new assistant.

In the weeks we'd been working together, we still hadn't hit it off. I kept avoiding her whenever possible and simply hoped that she'd figure out a career that was more suited to her education and take her and her drama somewhere else.

"Okay, vehicles are situated and we are your faithful designated drivers. You two can go wild tonight," Samantha told Kalindi. When she glanced around, spotting me, she startled. "Stevie?"

"Hey, Samantha."

"I didn't, um . . . I didn't realize you knew these guys."

I shrugged. "Small world."

"That it is." Her gaze flicked to Maverick, lingering for just a moment too long.

Wait. Did they know each other? Had she been here before? There was too much familiarity in her gaze. Too much comfort in this house to waltz inside.

It wasn't because of Kalindi either, was it?

My stomach dropped.

"Hi, Maverick," she said, her gaze shifting between the two of us.

"Hey." His hand came to the small of my back. "How do you two know each other?"

"She's Dad's assistant at Adair."

Surprise flashed across his expression before he schooled it into blank neutrality.

My stomach just kept falling.

He made a point not to look at her. The same way he'd ignored that blond at the sports bar weeks ago.

Maverick and Samantha. It was that encounter with Megan at the grocery store all over again.

Except I didn't have to see Megan every weekday.

Oh God. Seriously? Why her? She was a gossip and a kiss-up. She wasn't particularly kind or sweet. But that didn't matter when he was searching for his next hookup. All he cared about was a pretty face and a *yes.*

Maverick's hand twitched on my lower back.

I took a step away.

"We'll let you guys get back to dinner." Erik moved for the door, holding it open for the ladies to go out first. "See you downtown?"

"Yeah, man," Maverick said. "Later."

There'd be no later, not for me.

I returned to my chair, diving into my meal with fervor, until my plate was clear. Then I took it to the kitchen, helping Faye load the dishwasher.

"You should go downtown," Faye told Rush. "Have a drink to celebrate with them."

"Are you sure? You'll have to do bedtime on your own."

"We'll have to get used to it at some point. When the season starts and you've got away games, it'll be just us."

Rush frowned, like it had only now occurred to him that he'd be gone a slew of nights starting in August, missing his son's bedtime routine.

"You're coming, right?" Mav asked me.

"Sure," I lied.

"Nadine."

I smiled, but it was weak. He saw right through it, but before he could stop me, I hurried to my purse, digging out my keys. "I'm going to run home and change. This isn't exactly downtown attire. Text me where you end up going. I'll meet you there."

They could all think that I didn't want to go to the bars in black joggers, gray slides and a green, drapey gray tank. "Nice to meet you, Faye."

"You too, Stevie." She had Rally in her arms. As I waved, she lifted his chubby arm and waved back.

Then I was gone, bolting to my Jeep.

"Stevie," Maverick called from the doorway, but I was already gone, ignoring him as I started the engine.

It didn't matter. It shouldn't bother me. His past was out of his control, and I'd promised not to hold it against him. And it wasn't really about him.

It was me.

This was my insecurity. It had a pretty face. Megan's. Samantha's.

God, I had to get over this. How? How did I stop?

I didn't change when I got home. Instead, I switched out my slides for a pair of running shoes and left the house, leaving my phone behind. It took five miles before the envy subsided. Before I didn't feel that unbridled jealousy swimming in my veins.

Five miles, and when I turned the corner for my block, drenched with sweat, there was a shiny truck in my driveway. And a pretend boyfriend sitting on my stoop.

Maverick was staring at his phone, forearms braced on his knees. He glanced up as I reached the driveway. "So much for changing."

"I needed to clear my head. I'm sorry."

He blew out a frustrated breath as he pushed to his feet. "This again? Is it going to happen every time?"

I lifted my hands, palms out in surrender. "For the record, I'm not mad at you. I'm mad at me."

"Um, okay," he drawled. "Better explain that."

"I'm jealous." The confession tasted like rotten eggs. "And I hate that I'm jealous. I hate that I can't be cool about this. I hate that it immediately bugs me and all I can picture is you kissing another woman. I don't want it to bother me, but I don't know how to make it stop."

In my head, I knew he didn't make Samantha special potatoes. I doubted he knew her last name. And he sure as hell wouldn't have let her paint his toenails.

"I've never been this person before," I said. "I don't know how to deal with it."

"You're jealous?"

I tipped my head to the sky, the sunlight still bright through these long Montana summer days. "Insanely jealous. I hate me."

Maverick's hand came to my chin, forcing me to look at him. "If we never knew each other, if you weren't my oldest friend, if my parents didn't know yours, if my mother hadn't guilted us into this mess, if your dad hadn't offered me a job. If I was just Maverick, if you were just Stevie, would you still be jealous? Would you want me?"

"Yes," I whispered without hesitation.

"Say it."

"I want you."

I was jealous because I wanted Maverick to be mine. Only mine.

He tugged at the end of my ponytail, shaking his head. "Then fucking kiss me."

CHAPTER NINETEEN

STEVIE

The time warp happened again. I was kissing Maverick in the driveway and then the door to my bedroom was kicked shut and I was on the mattress, trapped beneath his weight.

"I need to shower," I said as he kissed along my jaw. I couldn't be sweaty and gross for this.

"No." A hand dove into my hair, to the sweaty strands at my temples.

"I'll be fast." I wiggled out from beneath him, scurrying to my bathroom and easing the door closed.

The moment it clicked shut, I sagged against the surface, sucking in a breath. *Oh God.* This was happening. Was this happening? I wanted it, more than anything.

"Don't freak out," I whispered to myself, catching my reflection in the mirror. My cheeks were rosy, my lips the same pink shade. My hair was a mess, and my skin was sticky from the run.

But there was a light in my eyes. A smile on my lips.

I slapped a hand over my mouth, smothering a giggle, as I

went to the walk-in shower and turned it on. As steam filled the room, I stripped off my clothes and stepped beneath the spray, letting the glass door swing closed.

My skin felt too sensitive, my nipples hard beneath the rivulets slicking over my body. The ache in my center was dizzying.

I snagged my puff from its hook, soaping it up as I scrubbed with fury. Then I squirted too much shampoo into my palm but worked it into a quick lather. My hands were in my sudsy hair when the bathroom door opened.

"Maverick," I gasped, whirling. It was habit to cover myself, to cower against the tiled wall.

Even past the steam and water drops on the shower door, I caught his smirk as he reached behind his nape, fisted his shirt and tossed it to the floor. Then he stripped off his pants and boxers, baring himself completely.

His cock was long and thick, hanging heavy between his muscled thighs.

He held my reflection through the glass, his gaze roaming down my naked body as he fisted himself, stroking his shaft.

My pussy clenched, my knees wobbled. It was the sexiest, hottest thing I'd ever seen in my life.

He opened the shower door and stepped inside.

"What are you doing?" Were we doing this in here? How was that going to work?

"You're the one who wanted a shower," he said.

"Okay." I tried to meet his gaze, but I couldn't seem to look away from his cock, wishing it was my hand stroking, not his.

I had no comparison, but he seemed huge. His arousal was getting harder, thicker, and when he let himself go, his dick was jutting between us.

A clump of soap and bubbles dripped from my hair into my eye, stinging it instantly. I hissed, rinsing it away.

Maverick's hands joined mine in my hair as he tilted my head back to the spray. "Let me do it."

My hands fell from my hair as he turned me around to face the wall, tilting my head back so the water sluiced over my hair, down my spine. Once the shampoo was rinsed away, he shifted closer, the heat from his chest at my back, his broad frame against my shoulders.

My body moved of its own volition, leaning against him. The moment his cock nestled between my ass cheeks, I froze, my eyes popping open to stare at my tiled wall.

"Relax." Maverick wound his arms around me, pulling my slick body against his.

"I'm nervous." I wished I had the confidence to be sure in a moment like this. But I was trembling, my heart pounding too fast.

"I've got you." He kissed my temple. "Promise."

"Okay." I closed my eyes and leaned against him, letting my hands hang at my sides while his roamed over my body, moving from my breasts to my ribs to my hips.

When his exploration was over, Maverick banded an arm across my chest, ready to take all of my weight, as his other hand splayed across my ribs.

It moved, inch by tortuous inch, lower and lower, down my side and around my hip. Then he came to my center, his long fingers sliding through my slit, stroking through my folds until a fingertip came to my clit. One flick and I melted, letting my head fall back against his shoulder.

"Spread your legs for me, honey."

This voice was entirely new. Gravelly and dark. It sent a tingle down my spine.

I didn't like it when people told me what to do, but for that voice? I'd obey every time. I shifted my bare feet on the tiles, taking a wider stance.

"Fuck, you're so wet for me." He pushed a finger into my core, dipping it in and out.

"Yes." I rocked my hips against his hand as the throb in my core built. My legs began to shake, my breaths shallow.

He held me up with his arm, his cock pressed hard against my ass, as he fucked me with his finger.

I reached behind me, splaying my hand across his muscled thigh, my fingertips digging in to hold tight, to keep my balance. "More."

Maverick's mouth latched on to my pulse, giving it a hard suck as his fingers continued their torment. Every circle of my clit made my breath hitch.

It was ecstasy. It was intimate and freeing. Being trapped in this shower, closed away from the world, the water drowning out any noise, all I could do was feel. I relaxed into the way my body responded to Maverick's touch, letting every thought escape my mind as he took me higher and higher.

Until I was tilting my ass against his cock, rolling my hips in time with his fingers.

"You're so perfect." He kissed my shoulder, dragging his tongue along my skin. "Come on my fingers. Let go."

I moaned, moving my hips faster as he thrummed his finger on my clit. And then I came apart, my body shaking and quivering as I cried out. Stars broke behind my eyes, my muscles quaking as I shattered, hard and fast.

I sagged against Mav until the aftershocks faded, until I was able to take a deep breath and force open my eyes. "Wow."

Maverick's mouth was at my ear. "You are so fucking perfect."

I smiled, tipping my face to the water.

He was careful in letting me go, making sure I had my balance before he shut off the water and took my hand, helping me out of the shower. Then he snagged a towel from a shelf, running the gray cotton over my skin until I was dry. He did the same to himself, but used one hand. Like he was afraid if he stopped touching me, I'd disappear.

My hair was a nightmare of tangles, hanging in thick, wet strands down my back as he tossed the towel aside and pulled me to the bedroom.

The light outside was slowly beginning to fade. I expected Mav to leave the blinds open, to do this in the light like he had before, but he kept our hands locked as he moved around the room, closing each shade before guiding me to the bed, pulling back the covers.

The blue of Maverick's eyes swallowed me whole as we stood together, his hands lifting to my cheeks. He searched my face, then his mouth came down on mine in a kiss that stole my breath. Captured every heartbeat.

A kiss that could stop time. A kiss that claimed me as his. A kiss that promised me the world.

A kiss that I would never forget.

He held me to him like he never wanted to let go. Like the world beyond the walls and windows didn't exist.

We clung to each other, my arms around his back, fingers digging into the roped muscle of his shoulders as his tongue tangled with mine. As he slanted his mouth over mine, his tongue delving into the deepest corners of my mouth, that desire from the shower returned tenfold.

When he broke away, there was a vulnerability on his

handsome face, like he was about to tell me something I wasn't going to like.

"What?" I threaded my fingers through the dark strands of his wet hair, pushing it off his forehead.

"I don't have a condom. This isn't why I came here tonight."

"Oh." The disappointment was crushing. The lump in my throat was instant, the burn of tears.

"We should stop."

"I don't want to."

He closed his eyes, dropped his forehead to mine. "I've always used protection. Always. I haven't been with anyone in a while. I was at the doctor for my physical last month. But . . ."

"I'm on birth control." I'd been taking the pill for years to regulate my periods. "And I trust you."

There was an intensity to his expression when he leaned away. A frustration. "I want to do this right."

"It is right." More perfect than anything I could have imagined. This had nothing to do with my mission to lose my virginity. I only wanted Maverick.

Maybe I'd wanted him longer than I'd ever realized.

I lifted on my toes, kissing the corner of his mouth. "Please don't go."

He growled, taking my face again, and this time when he pressed his body into mine, it was to lay me on the bed, covering my body with his as he settled into the cradle of my hips.

I wrapped a leg around his as the head of his cock settled against my entrance.

Maverick froze and stared down at me, searching my face. His hand found mine, lacing our fingers together. "Do you have any idea how much I want you?"

"Yes." As much as I wanted him. As much as I wanted nothing between us tonight.

"Deep breath," he whispered.

I inhaled, holding it in my lungs.

He rocked his hips forward, thrusting inside with a smooth stroke.

There was a moment of pain, enough for me to tense and wince.

"I'm sorry." Maverick kissed my jaw, holding steady as my body stretched around him. "I'm sorry, honey."

My hand clutched his. "I'm okay."

"Sure?"

The pain was already beginning to fade, the desire returning to chase it away. "I'm sure."

He brought his mouth to mine, kissing me gently as he eased out and pushed inside again.

The stretch was incredible. I exhaled against his jaw, and as a wave of tingles spread through my limbs, any lingering discomfort melted away. "More."

He braced above me, one hand diving into my hair, and drove inside, making me gasp. "Fuck, you feel so good."

My eyelids fluttered closed, too heavy to do anything but fall as he worked us together, over and over, in perfect, rhythmic strokes.

He bent and took a nipple in his mouth, sucking hard before letting it go. Then he trailed his mouth along my throat, licking and sucking and worshipping my body until I was writhing beneath him.

I lifted a knee, the change in angle sending him deeper and I moaned as my inner walls began to flutter.

It was more intense than I could have expected. A million times stronger than when he'd gone down on me last night. His cock hit a spot inside that drove me to the edge, to the point where I knew nothing would ever be the same.

"Maverick."

"I've got you."

My fingers dug into his back, hard enough he hissed, pistoning his hips faster and faster. Our ragged breaths mingled.

His hold on my hair became a fist, enough for the slightest sting in my scalp. Then his mouth crashed onto mine again and it was sensation overload. I felt him everywhere, through every cell. That lingering taste of cinnamon gum clung to his tongue.

And he kept pounding inside, driving me higher and higher. Too high. It was too much. I was losing control, my body no longer responding to any mental commands. My toes were curled, my legs shaking.

It was too much. My eyes flew open, searching for that spot on the ceiling.

"Let go, Stevie." Maverick took my hand, bringing it to his mouth, holding my knuckles against his lips. "Trust me?"

I nodded, meeting his gaze.

"Then let go." He held my hand, so tight I couldn't let go, then he sealed his mouth over mine, kissing me, fucking me, until I cried out his name.

And let go.

I clenched and pulsed around him, my back arching off the bed, as I gave in to the release, letting it roll through my body, letting it rip through my bones and quake my muscles. Letting the fireworks explode behind my eyes until there were tears dripping toward my temples.

Maverick kept hold of my hand as I came, burying his face in my hair. And with a groan that only seemed to stretch out my orgasm, he poured inside me, his entire body tensing as he came.

We collapsed together in a tangle of limbs and thundering hearts. He breathed in my hair, wrapping his arms around me, snaking them between my back and the mattress.

With a quick spin, he shifted to his back, draping me on his chest as he broke our connection.

"Fucking hell." He dragged a hand over his face. "That was . . . fuck. You've ruined me."

I burrowed into his chest, hiding my smile in the crook of his neck.

His hand came to my ass, splaying wide over my bare skin. "You okay?"

"Great."

"Don't run away." He kissed my hair, then shifted me to the side, ducking into the bathroom. Drawers opened. The faucet turned on. Then he came back with a warm cloth to clean between my legs.

It was more intimate than the sex. I felt that prickle of tears again but blinked them away, forcing myself to breathe as he finished with the washcloth, then shut off the bathroom light before joining me in bed.

He hauled me into his arms, tossing a leg over mine to trap me against his chest. "Stevie?"

"Yeah?"

"Do you want me to stay or go?"

"Stay."

He wound a lock of my damp hair around his index finger. "Never cut your hair."

"Okay," I whispered. "Mav?"

He hummed, his finger twirling and twirling.

I pressed my lips to his throat. "Thank you."

I'd wondered what it would be like, the first time. I'd heard plenty of stories from friends about losing their virginity. Most had said it was a little bit painful and a lot awkward. I hadn't expected it to feel like this. To feel incredible. To feel right. Maverick had made tonight more than I ever could have hoped for.

He leaned away, staring down at me. There was so much tenderness in his gaze it was hard to breathe. "That's my line."

CHAPTER TWENTY

MAVERICK

C oach Greely was cutting his lawn when I pulled into Stevie's driveway. He shut off the mower as I climbed out of my truck, spinning his hat backward as he walked over. "Hey, Maverick."

"Coach. How's it going?"

"Not bad. Just doing a little yard work today. Then Jennsyn wants to go to Adair later to buy flowers before my annual Fourth of July party."

"Stevie's influence, no doubt."

"I think you're right," he said, glancing to the stoop.

It was crowded with hanging baskets and pots teeming with blooms. I'd come over every evening this past week, and usually, I'd find Stevie outside, situating some new purchase she'd brought home from work.

"Got plans for the Fourth?" he asked.

It was still two weeks away, but Mission loved Independence Day. There were flags on the streetlamps downtown. Houses in every neighborhood had added touches of red, white and blue. And the fireworks show was unbeatable.

"Probably a barbeque at my parents' place. My nephew loves fireworks. We usually set them off in the driveway."

Since Bodhi had been a little boy, Dad and I had always planned a night of fun. It had become an ordeal, a challenge, to see who could find the best stand in town. Doing it for Bodhi's amusement had just been our excuse to light shit on fire.

This year, we were going all out, and I'd already spent a small fortune at four different stands. Dad had done the same. I wasn't sure if we'd even get through them all at this point, but if it took all night, we'd try.

If Mom didn't see another Fourth, we'd make this year's the best.

Declan and Elle would probably come over. Stevie might too. Or maybe she'd stay here and spend the night with her friends. And I could come over when all of the festivities were done.

I'd spent every night at her place this week. Every night worshipping her body. It had been the best week I'd had in a long, long time.

"I'll let you get back to mowing," I told Coach. "Good luck flower shopping."

"I have a feeling I'll need it." He chuckled, waving as he retreated to the mower.

I started for the house but paused. Since Coach Greely was the defensive coordinator and I played on special teams, I didn't spend much time with him on or off the field. But I knew him well enough to know that he'd played at Treasure State in college, then moved into coaching. Rush looked to Coach Ellis as a mentor. He'd gone from the Wildcats to professional football. But I saw myself more like Coach Greely.

And maybe, his career path could be mine.

"Coach?" I called before he could start the mower's engine.

"Yeah?"

"Would it be okay if I stopped by your office Monday and talked to you a bit about coaching? About how you got into it?"

"Of course." Greely nodded. "Door's always open."

"Thanks." I waved goodbye, and as I stepped past Stevie's flowers, the buzz of his mower filled the air.

After Stevie had asked me about becoming a coach, I hadn't been able to get the idea out of my mind. I only had one more year of football left, then I'd be done and graduate. I'd be like Stevie, joining rec leagues and teams to play on for fun.

But that didn't seem like enough. I wasn't sure if I could deal with two big losses within the next year.

What if I didn't say goodbye to football? What if I coached? What if I didn't find some boring office job and instead built a career around something I loved?

Mom would like that. So would I.

Monday. I'd talk to Coach on Monday. Get Mom's take on it too.

After a quick knock on the door, I stepped inside, calling out, "Hey."

"I'm in the kitchen," Stevie hollered.

I kicked off my shoes and made my way past the empty living room. "No Liz or Jennsyn?"

"Nope. Just me. Liz is still at her boyfriend's house. Jennsyn came over after you left for the gym and we made a list of flowers she wants to buy for Toren's, but she just left to get a car wash."

"Ah." Every night this week, the house had been ours alone. Her roommates spent every night with their boyfriends, which was fine by me. It was nice to have Stevie's place to ourselves. To not worry about how loud we'd get in her bedroom.

I leaned against the counter, watching as Stevie took a large metal mixing bowl out from a cupboard and set it beside a stack of ingredients on the counter. Flour and sugar and a yellow bag of chocolate chips.

Hell yes. "Making me cookies, Nadine?"

A pretty smile stretched across her mouth. "These are for me."

"You're not sharing? Rude."

"I don't know." She shrugged, leaning her elbows on the counter. "Have you earned cookies?"

Flirting with her was the most fun I'd had in ages. "We both know the answer to that question."

Three orgasms last night meant I definitely got cookies. Plus my morning workout meant I was starved. But food could wait.

I'd gotten up early to meet Rush this morning, and while I'd been gone, she'd dressed in a pair of loose gray shorts and a matching tank. No bra. Her nipples were beginning to peak beneath the fabric, like they wanted my mouth.

I preferred her in nothing at all, but I liked this too. Relaxed and happy. Smiling for me and only me.

"I like this top." I tugged at the fabric, using it to pull her close.

"Yeah?" She lifted up on her toes, her mouth reaching for mine, but just before we touched, I breezed past her, walking to the oven to shut it off.

"Tease," she muttered.

Damn straight. Teasing her ranked right up there with flirting.

"If you want cookies, you'd better turn that oven back on."

I crossed the kitchen, taking the hem of my T-shirt in my hands and whipping it over my head. Then I threw it in her face, earning a laugh as I picked her up and set her on the counter, standing between her legs.

She tossed my shirt to the floor and settled her hands on my shoulders. Then she moved in for a kiss, but I shied away.

"Close your eyes. Don't open them."

She pouted. "You're not going to kiss me?"

"Not yet."

Stevie huffed but obeyed, dropping her hands to her lap.

Trailing my fingers up her bare arms, I circled them around her elbows, then up to her shoulders, tracing the skinny straps of the tank down to the swell of her breasts. Her breath hitched as I moved lower, finding her perfect nipples with my thumbs.

The moment I touched them, she arched into my touch, letting out a sexy moan.

Every day with Stevie felt like an adventure. A new exploration. I'd had years of meaningless sex, years of getting off and getting out. This wasn't just new for her. It was new for us both.

I wanted nothing more than to make her come apart. To make each orgasm an experience. So far, I'd kept it tame, not wanting to press too far, test too many boundaries.

It was time to play.

I bent to her mouth, dragging my lips across her cheeks and chin and nose. Every time she leaned in, I pulled back, denying her a kiss, all while I continued to pluck and pinch and roll her nipples.

She started to squirm on the counter, inching closer to the edge, her legs wrapping around my hips to draw me closer. Seeking some friction against her pussy.

"Would you come if I kept this up?" I asked.

"I don't know."

I pulled her shirt beneath her breast, exposing it to the air before I dropped to suck her nipple into my mouth.

"Yes." Her hands dove into my hair. As much as I loved her hair, she played with mine just as much if not more, weaving it between her knuckles, combing it through those delicate fingers.

I gave her nipple another suck, then let it pop from my mouth before righting her shirt.

A disappointed whimper came from her throat, but she kept her eyes closed.

"We're going to fuck. Hard. Then I'll kiss you. And then you can make me cookies."

Her eyes popped open, shock and desire making those hazel irises spark.

"You like that idea, don't you?"

She chewed on her bottom lip as she nodded.

"Good girl." I hoisted her off the counter, lifting her high enough that she was draped over my shoulder.

"Mav." She laughed, covering it with a hand as I smacked her ass and carried her to the bedroom. She caught the door, slamming it closed, right before I tossed her on the bed, her perfect body bouncing on the mattress.

I took her ankles, using them to spin her onto her belly.

She gasped, her hair covering her face until I looped an

arm around her middle, hauling her to her knees as I stood behind her.

Her shirt was gone in a flash, exposing the long line of her spine. Then I shimmied down her shorts and panties, waiting as she shifted side to side for me to slide them down her knees and off her calves.

One look at her heart-shaped ass, the exquisite curve of her hips, and I was rock-hard, straining against my boxer briefs and gym shorts. With a quick push at the waistbands, I kicked them free of my legs. Then I moved Stevie's hair aside, sealing my lips over the sensitive flesh below her ear.

I lifted her hands to her breasts, using her own fingers to play with her nipples as I stepped closer, letting my arousal press against her ass.

"Are you wet for me?" I kissed her shoulder, then pushed her forward to her hands and knees, taking in that slick pussy. "Fucking drenched."

"No more teasing." She leaned back, pressing against me as I lined up at her entrance and drove inside, burying myself to the root.

"Fuck." I clenched my jaw, fighting for control so this lasted more than five seconds. Then I eased out before thrusting forward again. "So damn tight."

She twisted enough to look back at me over her shoulder. Stevie moaned, her back arching as she bit her bottom lip. Her eyes were hooded, her cheeks flushed. Her hair tossed over a shoulder and her spine arched.

Sexy. Beautiful. Mine.

She looked like mine.

I reached for her jaw, using my thumb to pull that lip free from her teeth. Then I gripped her hips and did exactly as promised. I fucked her. Hard. We fucked until the sound of our skin slapping filled the room, mingling with our short breaths and groans. Until her breasts bounced, and when I thrust forward, she'd shift back, our bodies in exact rhythm until her inner walls began to clench.

I reached around her, sliding my finger to her clit and stroking it twice.

She cried out as she came, as she squeezed me like a vise, falling forward, letting the bedding muffle her lovely sounds.

I pounded into her, chasing my own release and that build at the base of my spine. When I came it was on a roar, my abs bunching as I kept driving my hips, pouring inside until I was spent.

"Fuck." I kept a hold of her waist as I let the stars clear from my eyes and the dizzy wave pass. Then I closed my eyes and tilted my face to the ceiling.

Ruined. Stevie had ruined me. And I couldn't find it in me to care.

When I pulled out, my come leaked down her thigh.

I caught it with a finger and smeared it over her pussy and that pink puckered hole.

She shot up, hair and eyes wild. Shock mingled with excitement and lust on her expression. A hint of curiosity that made my cock twitch.

If she didn't want to go there, I didn't care. But if she was up to try, if she'd let me have her in every possible way, I'd make it the best fucking night of her life.

I took her chin, holding it as I slammed my mouth on hers for the kiss she'd craved and damn well earned. As our tongues tangled, she spun on her knees, her arms looping over my shoulders, holding tight as I laid her down, working the covers over our bodies.

There were hours and hours of the day remaining, but all I wanted to do was hide away in this bed.

"I'm spending the night." Every night this week, I'd given her the choice if I stayed here or went home. Just in case she needed a night without me in her bed. Well, fuck that. I was staying. "I like your bed."

She curled closer to my side, looping a leg over mine. "Then I guess you'd better stay."

"I am."

"You can."

"I don't need your permission."

"Well, you have it."

This woman. With a quick spin, I rolled her to her back, pinning her beneath me. "Do you always have to have the last word?"

She giggled. "Yes."

I did my best to glare but she lifted a hand between us and flicked the tip of my nose.

"You like it," she said.

Yeah, I kind of did.

Not that I'd ever admit it.

Or that I was falling for Stevie Adair. My Stevie.

She'd always been my Stevie.

"Do you think this is what it could have been like?" I asked as we curled together.

"What do you mean?"

"If you hadn't hated me, and I hadn't hated you. If we had been doing this from the beginning."

She pressed a kiss to my throat. "No. Our parents wouldn't have let us within ten feet of each other. If my dad had thought you might be interested, he would have come to every family dinner with a shotgun."

"True." I chuckled.

Except it still felt like wasted time.

And we were running out of time.

We were all barreling toward an end I couldn't even fathom.

I shoved that thought aside and buried my face in Stevie's hair, myself in her body. Because when I was lost in her, I didn't have to think about anything else.

CHAPTER TWENTY-ONE

STEVIE

Maverick was propped against a stack of my pillows, the sculpted plane of his chest and those drool-worthy abs on display as the sheet covered his legs. His hands worked the muscle of my calf, massaging up and down, knee to ankle. "Better?"

The cramp was gone. The cramp he'd given me trying to bend me into a pretzel earlier. But I didn't want him to stop. I craved his hands on my skin. "No."

"Liar." He dragged his fingernail along the sole of my foot, making me jerk and laugh.

"Hey, that tickles." I took the pillow behind my own head and threw it at his face.

He chuckled, returning to his massage. "Heaven forbid, Stevie Adair get tickled."

"You know I hate it."

"I know. Remember that time you threw a massive tantrum because I tickled you on the bus?"

"That wasn't a tantrum, Houston. That was a protest." I pushed up on my elbows, clutching the sheet to my naked

DEVNEY PERRY

chest. "You wouldn't stop. You made me laugh so hard I almost peed my pants. It's your own fault that I didn't sit with you on the bus for a week."

"A week is a long time in fourth grade."

I gave him an exaggerated pout. "Poor Maverick."

He rolled his eyes, then pounced, abandoning the pillows in a flash as he ripped the covers from my body, covering my bare skin with his. My legs opened so he could fit himself into the cradle of my hips. And the second his tongue slid past my teeth, his cock sank into my body.

For the past two months, I'd lived in a haze of Maverick and sex. We fucked constantly, before I left for work in the morning. In the evening when I got home. At night, for hours and hours until we both crashed.

It wasn't enough. No matter how many times we were together, I wanted more and more. It was better than I could have ever dreamed.

Maybe there was a reason I'd waited so long to have sex. Maybe I'd been waiting for Maverick this whole time.

He was insatiable. Urgent. He seemed frantic to be together as often as possible, even on lazy Sunday mornings like this. Like it was easier to have sex, to drown in each other's bodies, than deal with reality.

I didn't blame him.

But I was starting to worry. Every time I asked if he was okay, he'd say yes. It was sounding more and more like a lie.

Those worries crept in for a second, taking me out of the moment, dulling the lust. Until Maverick must have felt my mind wandering and reached between us, finding my clit.

Worries gone. "Yes."

"Fuck, that's good," he hissed, driving inside, burying

himself to the root. His mouth dropped to my ear before he kissed along my neck.

"Mav." My fingers dug into his shoulders, a leg wrapping around his thigh, all while his finger and mouth and cock blanked my mind.

My orgasm came over me like a wave, not as hard and powerful as either of those he'd given me this morning, but no less satisfying. And as he took me over the edge, he came with me, pouring inside until he was spent.

We clung to each other until our bodies were limp, until the cramp in my calf was long forgotten, and my heartbeat thundered against his chest. Then he carried me to the shower, because whether we wanted to leave our bubble or not, there was a world beyond my bedroom walls.

And we were expected at Monty and Meredith's house by noon to celebrate a Wildcats victory.

Maverick and the football team had traveled to Utah for their first game of the season yesterday. A nonconference game where we'd won, thirty-five to thirty-one. Mav had kicked the game-winning field goal.

His parents hadn't traveled that far, for obvious reasons, but they wanted to do something to celebrate his kick. He wasn't usually the player who kicked field goals.

"Do you think they'll keep you as placekicker?" I asked Mav as I put on my makeup.

He stood at the second sink in the bathroom, his jaw covered in white shaving cream. "I don't know. I expect we'll talk about it Monday at practice."

School hadn't started yet, so the guys were still spending extra time at the fieldhouse practicing and having meetings.

"Would you rather stick as punter?"

"I mean, it's familiar." He shrugged. "But it was a rush, scoring those points yesterday."

He'd been riding such a high after their flight home. It had been nearly two in the morning when he'd finally made it to my house and he'd still been wound up.

We'd fucked so hard I'd practically blacked out afterward.

Maverick had spent years as punter for the Wildcats, focusing on distance. But their placekicker, the player who kicked extra points and field goals, had gotten cramps during the game. It had been in the nineties, and he'd been dehydrated. So Mav had stepped in to cover, since the backup, a sophomore without much gametime experience, hadn't traveled with the team.

Mav had been flawless on the field. If he'd had any nerves, they hadn't shown through on the TV. I'd watched the game alone in the living room after a long Saturday at Adair, and when he'd kicked that field goal, I'd shot off the couch and screamed.

I hoped they let him stay as placekicker this year. He needed that challenge. That personal win.

He wasn't sleeping as much as he should be. Part of that was my fault. We stayed up late to be with each other. But the other part was that he'd wake up, tossing and turning. The dark circles under his eyes had been there for weeks.

His gaze flicked to mine in the mirror. "What?"

"Nothing. I just like watching you shave."

He turned on the water, then dragged his razor along his cheek. That razor, along with a toothbrush, toothpaste and a stick of deodorant, now lived in the top right drawer of my bathroom. His shampoo and bodywash were lined up beside mine in the shower.

"Are you okay?" I asked.

"Yes." It was the answer he always gave. And each time, it sounded more and more like a lie.

"You can talk to me."

"I do."

No, he really didn't. He didn't talk to anyone. Maybe he wouldn't talk to me. But he should talk to someone.

"My mom mentioned the other day about getting a grief counselor."

Maverick flinched so hard he nicked his skin, red blood instantly welling on the surface.

"Shit. Sorry." I grabbed a square of toilet paper, handing it over.

His jaw clenched as he tore off a corner, pressing it to the wound. Then he went back to shaving, like I hadn't mentioned a thing about grief counseling. He kept his gaze locked on the mirror, not so much as blinking in my direction.

"Sorry," I said. "It was just an idea."

He rinsed his razor under the faucet. A coldness crept into the bathroom, chasing away the warmth from the shower.

I was two feet away, wrapped in a towel, my hair hanging damp down my shoulders, and there might as well have been a wall between us. So I bent for the bottom drawer and took out my hair dryer, going to work on my hair.

Maverick finished shaving and stalked from the bathroom, likely heading for the backpack he brought over every night with clothes.

I hadn't offered to let him leave any in the closet. The toiletries were one thing. Clothes felt like maybe we needed to have a conversation.

About how this fake relationship of ours wasn't fake and hadn't been for months. About how everyone in our family was counting on us staying together for Meredith's sake. About how Maverick and I had sex practically around the clock, but it had been nearly two months since we'd gone on a date.

And if I was actually his girlfriend, why wouldn't he talk to me?

When I brought up his mom's treatment, he'd wave it off and silence me with a kiss. When I asked if he was doing all right, he'd shrug and take off my shirt. When I offered to listen if he wanted to talk, he'd reach for the waistband of my pants.

Meredith's cancer wasn't only eating her alive.

It was killing him too.

I wanted to help. I wanted to be there to support him. Maybe what that meant right now was that I was there to take his mind off it. I was there to kiss him back. To curl close during those precious few hours of sleep he got each night. To give him my bed, a quiet space for him to breathe.

If that's all I could do, then so be it.

With my hair dry, I went to the closet and dressed in a sage-green romper. I added a gold necklace and stepped into a pair of white tennis shoes. When I went in search of Maverick, he was on the couch, elbows to knees, as his fingers flew over his phone.

"Ready," I said.

He stood, tucking his phone away, then with a tight smile, he rounded the coffee table and held out his hand.

"Sorry about your face."

"That sounds like a comeback from when we were kids."

I smiled. "Kind of does."

He pulled me close to kiss my hair. "Don't worry about it."

Except I was worried.

He wasn't the only one not sleeping all night long.

Maverick held my hand as we drove to his parents' house. The closer we got, the tighter his grip, like he was bracing for what we'd find.

We both visited Meredith as often as possible, but it was rarely together. I'd swing by on a lunch break from work or if I had a client in the area. I'd fix her nails and tell her about work. I was still shadowing Dad on the larger, commercial jobs, but from time to time, he'd give me a small residential project that I could manage.

The other designers were in full swing, and we all worked from sunrise to sunset, cramming in as much as possible for the short, Montana landscaping season.

There seemed to be a permanent layer of dirt in my cuticles from the hours I helped out in the nursery. Most days when I came home, I smelled like earth and wind and sweat, but I wouldn't have wanted it any other way.

If I could just convince Dad I was capable of running Adair, it would be the perfect job. Well, that and I'd have to fire Samantha.

She hadn't brought up her past with Maverick, but it lingered in the air whenever we were in the same room.

I made sure that was as infrequently as possible.

The driveway was full when we got to the Houstons'. Mabel's car was parked beside Mom's Escalade, so Maverick parked on the street, hopping out to go inside.

"Hey," he called, taking off his shoes.

I did the same, then followed him to the guest bathroom to wash my hands.

When we made it to the living room, my parents were each in a chair. Mabel was sitting on the stone ledge of the fireplace.

And Monty was on the couch beside Meredith.

She looked so small, so pale and gaunt, that I nearly tripped over my own feet as I walked into the room.

I hadn't stopped by since last Monday. What the hell had happened in a week that she looked so awful?

Cancer. Fucking cancer. That's what had happened.

I crossed the room and took a seat beside Mabel.

This was the place where we stacked gifts during Christmas. I'd thought, hoped, that Meredith would make it until after the holidays. A week ago, I would have counted on it. Now?

She wasn't going to make it, was she? The doctors hadn't given her a timeline—or maybe they had and she just hadn't shared it with us.

Meredith, the only aunt I'd ever really known, wasn't going to be here for Christmas. At this point, I wasn't sure if she'd even make it to Thanksgiving.

The lump in my throat was choking me, so I breathed through my nose, eyes aimed at the floor until I could swallow it down. God, this was hard.

"Hey, Mom." Maverick walked over to the couch and kissed her coral headscarf. If he was surprised by her appearance, he didn't let it show. After he squeezed her hand, he took the seat on his sister's other side on the fireplace.

Mabel had spent years between us, the unofficial buffer. Today, I really wished the Houstons had one more chair so I could be beside Maverick.

"Where's Bodhi?" he asked.

"Yes, Mabel. Where is my grandson?" Meredith asked.

Her voice was tinny but lit with humor. "We were just asking where he is today and, so far, your sister has dodged the question. Apparently Bodhi is *busy*."

"He is busy." Mabel frowned.

"Busy taking conference calls? Busy working manual labor? Busy practicing trick shots?" Maverick poked his sister in the ribs. "What does an eight-year-old do to stay so busy?"

Mabel swatted at his hand as she gave him a glare. "He's golfing, okay?"

"Oh." Maverick stared down at her, eyebrows raised. "Then why the secrecy?"

"Because he's golfing with Kai." Her voice trailed off so drastically, it was hard to hear that last word.

"Kai?" Mom asked. "Is that what you said?"

Mabel huffed and nodded. "Yes, Kai."

"And who exactly is Kai?" Maverick looked around the room, but we were all puzzled. Well, everyone except Meredith.

There were tears swimming in her eyes. A smile stretched across her chapped lips.

"The doctor," Meredith whispered.

Mabel nodded, giving her mother a shrug. "He wanted to take Bodhi on an outing. Just the two of them. So they went golfing."

"Wait. Is this Kai guy your boyfriend?" Maverick asked.

"Yeah." Mabel's face began to flush. "We've actually been dating for a few months. I didn't want to make a big deal out of it in case things didn't work out, but he's the best guy I've ever known, and he adores Bodhi. I, um . . . I kind of think I love him."

The room went quiet for a moment, then erupted with questions.

When do we get to meet him?

What kind of medicine does he practice?

How old is he?

Mabel answered them all, and it was like a dam had burst. She gushed about him, telling us about each of their dates and how he worked with kids and how he'd moved to Mission from Seattle, hoping to settle down in a place where he could grow roots.

"I'm trying not to get ahead of myself," she said. "It's only been a few months. But someday, maybe, I hope he'll be another guy Bodhi can look up to."

Bodhi's biological father was not in the picture. Hell, his name was basically taboo under this roof. But that kid would not be lacking in positive male role models.

"Then it seems like we've got multiple things to celebrate today." Dad pushed out of his chair, holding out a hand to help Mom from hers. "We'll get started on lunch. Burgers and dogs. Great kick, Maverick."

"Thanks, Declan." Mav smiled.

"I'll help." Mabel stood, finally freeing the space between us.

The moment she was gone, Maverick took my hand, his thumb circling my knuckle.

Meredith stared at us for a long moment, then she dropped her chin, tears spilling freely down her cheeks.

"Mom?"

She sniffled, waving it off. "Oh, I'm just a little more emotional than normal. Don't think anything of it. But I could use a fresh water. And there's a box of stuff in your old bedroom I went through this week for you to decide if you want to toss or keep. Maybe you could bring it down."

As in, she needed a moment alone.

240

I laced my fingers with Maverick's and stood, hauling him to his feet. "I'll get the water. You get the box."

He nodded, his throat bobbing as he swallowed hard. Then we left Meredith and Monty alone, giving them a few moments to breathe.

I forced a smile when I got to the kitchen, filling one of Meredith's tumblers with water as Mom, Dad and Mabel bustled around, taking out lunch fixings from the fridge and pantry.

When I decided I'd given Meredith enough time, I headed back toward the living room, about to round the corner when I overheard her talking to Monty.

"Now I can go," she said. "I didn't want to leave when they were alone. I'm just so tired, Monty."

"I know, dear. I know."

My heart broke into a thousand pieces. It hurt, more than anything had ever hurt. Almost more than I was able to bear.

But at least Maverick hadn't heard.

I sucked in a breath, blinked away my own tears, then straightened, about to take in her water. Except a creak in the floor behind me made me turn.

Maverick stood behind me, a plastic tub with a lime-green lid clutched between his hands. The color had drained from his face. There was so much sorrow in his gaze it smashed the broken pieces of my heart to dust.

He'd heard their conversation too.

I reached for him.

Except he was already gone, striding toward the door, setting that tub in the entryway. He stepped into his shoes, and before I could stop him, he was out the door, crossing the lawn for his truck.

I chased him outside. "Maverick, wait."

He didn't.

Without a backward glance, he climbed in his truck and drove away.

"Shit." I stood on the porch, staring as his taillights disappeared around a corner. Then I waited, hoping and wishing, that he just needed a few minutes alone.

But when the street stayed empty, I sighed and spun to go back inside.

I hadn't even noticed I wasn't alone on the porch.

"This is going to change him." Meredith had snuck up on me, looking like she'd used every ounce of her strength to come outside.

The same worry I'd seen in my own gaze this morning filled hers.

"I don't know what to do," I said.

"It will get worse before it gets better. I don't know if you two are still pretending or not on my behalf. If you are, you're doing a hell of a job, because it seems real."

It was real. At least, for me. That was another part of the conversation that Maverick and I should have but hadn't yet.

"Whether this turned into something real or it's still only for my sake, don't give up on him, Stevie. He's going to pull away. It's just who he is. And I doubt he'll be nice about it. But don't give up on him."

I held up my pinky. "Promise."

CHAPTER TWENTY-TWO

MAVERICK

I t was always quiet after a loss. The whole team was in a
shit mood.

Or maybe that was just me.

I'd been irritable and grumpy for a week, and my mood
only worsened with every worried or wary glance. Everyone
was tiptoeing around me; they had been for months. And it
was pissing me right the fuck off.

It wasn't a secret Mom had cancer. One of the guys had
asked me a few days ago in the locker room how she was
doing. It was none of their business, and instead of telling
him to fuck off, I'd made the mistake of answering, "Not
great."

The guy in the bus seat ahead of mine, a sophomore who
played defensive end, would give me a pitiful smile each
time he made eye contact. One more, and I might lose my
damn mind.

"Maverick." Rush touched his elbow to mine.

"What?" I snapped.

"I can hear your molars grinding." He was the only one

who didn't shy away from my shit mood. Even Stevie backed off when I was being an asshole.

I unclenched my jaw. "I hate losing."

"So do I. But it's nonconference and a money game."

We'd traveled to Oregon to get beat by an FBS school so they could have a win on their record and Treasure State could score a payday for athletics. Rationally, I knew it was a win-win. But tonight, I didn't feel all that rational.

I'd been on edge since Sunday, since I'd overheard Mom tell Dad she was ready to die.

Deep down, I understood how hard and draining it had to be for her to fight. But it felt a lot like giving up. She might be ready, but I sure as hell wasn't.

I needed her to make it to Christmas so I could buy her a fuzzy blanket and Mabel could get us all matching socks. I needed Mom to live until I had kids of my own so they could know their grandmother was a living, breathing angel on this earth.

Where the fuck was our miracle?

I couldn't lose her yet. I couldn't do this.

My molars started grinding again, radiating pain into my skull and making the headache I'd been nursing on the trip home worse.

Rush sighed, probably feeling the tension rolling off my body, but he let it go as we pulled into the fieldhouse parking lot.

The moment the bus's wheels stopped, I was out of my seat, blowing past everyone in the rows ahead to get out. I collected my bag from the storage compartment, and without stopping by my locker inside, I headed for my truck.

Tomorrow, I'd deal with my gear, but tonight, I needed to be done with football.

Not something I'd expected to feel, but it wasn't the distraction it had been weeks ago.

School had only started ten days ago, and it hadn't been enough to keep my mind off Mom either. The only time when it truly faded away was when I was with Stevie.

So I threw my shit in the back seat and made my way to her place. Parking in her driveway, I breathed a sigh of relief as, before I'd even shut off the truck, her front door opened.

Stevie stood on the threshold, her face clean and her hair pulled up into a messy knot. She had on a pair of sleep shorts and a long-sleeved thermal. For the first time in hours, my shoulders crept away from my ears. My jaw relaxed and I filled my lungs.

"Hi," she said when I made it to the door.

"Hey."

"Sorry."

I shrugged. "It was a nonconference game."

"So?" she huffed, moving to the side so I could come in. "Still sucks to lose."

This was why she was perfect. Because she knew exactly how I felt. With sports. With Mom.

I didn't have to explain anything. She already knew.

"Yeah, it does." I hauled her into my arms, breathing in that sweet scent of orange blossom and flowers and Stevie.

She held on to me for a few moments, her cheek resting over my heart. "Did you talk to your mom?"

"Yeah. I called her after the game."

She'd made light of the loss, saying it didn't matter. But if the last game she watched was us losing, I'd be angry for decades.

At least they'd let me stay as placekicker. I'd scored our only points. Two field goals. We'd lost six to thirty-five.

"Are you okay?" Stevie leaned away.

Not even a little bit. "Fine."

She saw right through the lie and gave me one of those sad smiles that made me want to scream. "Maverick."

"Don't start, okay? Not tonight," I snapped, regretting it instantly when her hands fell away from my waist.

She stepped back and crossed her arms over her chest.

"Sorry." I hooked a finger under her chin, then bent to give her a kiss on the lips. Except before I could take her mouth, she turned away. My lips landed on her cheek.

"I'm trying to talk to you, not just jump into bed."

"And I don't want to fucking talk, Stevie." I backed away, dragging a hand over my face. "I want to go to your bed and fuck until we both pass out. So do you want an orgasm tonight or not?"

The words came out of my mouth automatically, this bad mood seeping from me like poison. It was paired with a punishing regret that only made it all worse. What the fuck was wrong with me?

Stevie's nostrils flared, something I hadn't seen much lately. I didn't miss it. But she kept her cool, unlike me, even though I'd gone too far tonight.

She was going to make me pay for it. Rightly so. "You don't get to be an asshole to me. Not when I'm only worried about you. We don't have to talk. But you don't get to say shit that I know you'll regret."

Fuck. She was right. We both knew she was right.

I rubbed both hands over my face, wishing I could take it all back. Wishing I didn't feel like there was this gaping, raw wound inside my chest. Wishing it didn't hurt so bad all the damn time. Wishing I didn't feel like I was coming out of my skin.

Wishing I wasn't so angry.

It wasn't fair. It wasn't fucking fair. And there wasn't a thing I could do to fix it. So that fury simmered, boiling hotter and hotter. It was too close to the surface tonight, making me jittery and tense.

"I'm going home," I told her.

"Good idea." The way she said it, like she would have kicked me out herself, like I'd been dismissed, only made it worse.

"Want to come?" I asked even though I knew the answer. Even though I knew it would start a fight.

But I couldn't seem to stop that poison from spewing. I needed an outlet for this anger. Normally it was football or fucking. Without either, I was searching for a fight.

When she looked up, her forehead was furrowed. "What?"

"You never sleep at my place."

"And you know why," she gritted out. "Hard pass."

If she'd had as many men in her bed as I'd had women in mine, I'd have a damn hard time staying here too.

"Glad to see you've gotten over your jealousy," I deadpanned.

"Unbelievable." She scoffed. "You're seriously trying to pick a fight tonight, aren't you?"

I guess so. "Night, Steve."

Fire flashed in her hazel eyes as I stormed for the door.

But for once, I had the last word. It tasted bitter, like ash on my tongue.

It took a moment behind the wheel for me to start the truck. I knew the right thing to do was apologize. To go inside and sleep on the couch and wake up tomorrow to start over.

We couldn't break up until after Mom . . .

We couldn't break up.

But I didn't trust myself not to say more bullshit I'd immediately regret. So I drove away, winding through the lonely, dark streets of Mission until I was home.

Faye and Rush were on the couch when I walked through the door, Rally asleep on Rush's shoulder.

"Hey." I jerked up my chin.

"Thought you'd be at Stevie's," Rush said.

"Just left."

Faye and Rush shared a look as I passed the living room.

"It's so fucking annoying when you two have your silent conversations."

"Maverick," Rush warned.

Well, if I was picking fights, I might as well add my best friend along with my girlfriend. If Stevie was still my girlfriend after tonight.

Would Mom fight harder to stick around if Stevie and I broke up? Would she stop telling Dad she was ready to die?

God, I wanted to scream. Except if I screamed, it would piss off Rush and wake up Rally, which would piss off Faye. And with every step toward my bedroom, the anger was fading.

Bone-deep sorrow was taking its place.

"Mav." Faye's voice was soft. Gentle.

When I slowed and turned, she was in the hallway.

With Rally.

Before I could tell her it wasn't a good time, that I was in no mood to talk, she thrust her son into my arms and took a step away so I couldn't just hand him back.

I adjusted my hold, cradling him in my arms.

And when I exhaled, some of the pain faded away.

"You know I understand what you're going through," she said.

Her mother had died last year. They hadn't been close, not like me and my mom. But it had still been her mother. Faye had watched her die from cancer too.

"Yeah," I said, dropping my gaze to Rally.

He had Faye's red hair, but otherwise, I thought he looked like a mini version of Rush. His dark eyelashes were perfect crescents against his smooth cheeks.

Another exhale. Another bit of that sorrow blowing away.

"He's a good listener," she said. "Especially when he's asleep. Think you could watch him while Rush and I take a shower?"

I nodded, swaying side to side as I kept my eyes on this baby boy. "Yeah. I'd be happy to."

"Thanks." She touched her son's chubby hand, then disappeared down the hallway.

By the time I trudged to the couch and kicked off my shoes, settling Rally into the crook of my arm, the water turned on upstairs.

His crib would have been just fine for him if they wanted a little alone time. But tomorrow, I'd owe Faye a thanks. The pressure in my chest loosened with every minute this kid was in my arms.

"You have a good mom, bud. I have a good mom too." A tear dripped down my cheek before I could catch it.

I blinked the others away, sniffling through the sting in my nose. Then I shifted to dig my phone from my pocket and hit Stevie's name.

"Hi," she answered on the first ring.

"I'm sorry. I'm an asshole."

"Good thing I'm used to it."

I blew out a long breath. "Yeah."

"You're not the only one losing her, Mav," Stevie whispered.

No, I wasn't. "I'm sorry, Nadine."

"It's okay."

"Promise?"

"Yeah. Are you coming back?"

I should go back to her place. I should tell her I was sorry in person and ask how she was holding up. Instead, I shifted my hold on Rally, keeping him close.

He didn't ask hard questions. He didn't give me sad looks. He had no idea that I was coming apart at the seams and fought tears with every breath, every heartbeat.

"I think I'll just crash here. See you tomorrow?"

"Sure." There was disappointment in Stevie's voice.

"Stevie?"

"Yeah?"

I love you. It was there, on the tip of my tongue. But I couldn't say it, not like this. Not after a fight. Not over the phone. "Good night."

"Bye."

The silence was heavy when she hung up. It settled on my shoulders, almost as heavy as the dread resting on my heart.

I was pushing her away. I was putting everyone at arm's length. If I wasn't careful, I'd lose more than just my mother through this.

"How do I stop?" I asked Rally.

His only answer was a drop of drool on my shirt.

CHAPTER TWENTY-THREE

STEVIE

The Treasure State University football stadium was electrified. We were surrounded by smiling, laughing faces. The game hadn't started yet but people were already cheering, already clapping for their beloved Wildcats.

I'd only come to a handful of games when I'd been a student. The volleyball tournament schedule had usually been in conflict, either with an away game on the road or with an evening game at the fieldhouse.

Coach Quinn had certain expectations for game days, and screaming our lungs out at a football game before we had to play hadn't been a part of her regimen.

There'd only been one time that I'd disobeyed her orders and come to watch the football team anyway. Last year, Liz, Jennsyn and I had come to a game before our own, hiding in a sea of royal blue and silver.

Now that I didn't have volleyball, I couldn't think of a better way to spend my Saturdays than being here to cheer on Maverick for his last season.

And I wasn't the only one excited to be at the stadium today.

Mom and Dad had the seats beside mine. Monty, Mabel and Bodhi were in the row in front of us. Meredith was sandwiched between them in a foam stadium seat, wearing a silver headscarf and one of Maverick's old jerseys. It hung on her bony frame like a tent.

But her blue eyes had a sparkle I hadn't seen in weeks. Her smile was as bright as the afternoon sun.

The heat from August had bled into the first weekend of September, but she had a blanket on her lap to keep warm. There was a long-sleeved shirt beneath that jersey.

I was already sweating in a pair of denim shorts and a Wildcats T-shirt.

Meredith had insisted on coming to today's game. She'd waved off the mask that Monty had brought along, and though it broke my heart, this was her living her last days to the fullest. She was going to breathe the warm, fresh air. And watch her son like any other proud mother.

Maverick had scored us all tickets today, seating us in the first two rows at the forty-yard line.

I wasn't sure what he'd done to get these tickets. They were about as good as you could find in the stadium. If I'd asked, he wouldn't have told me anyway.

He hadn't talked to me much this past week, not since our fight after his away game. We weren't fighting, but the strain between us meant I constantly had this sinking feeling in my stomach.

He'd only spent the night twice, and both, he hadn't made a single move to do anything more than sleep.

Last night, on his coach's orders, he'd stayed home to rest up before the game. Maybe it was true and they expected players to chill. Maybe Maverick worried that Toren would see his truck parked next door.

Or maybe it was another excuse to push me away.

I was losing him. I could feel him slipping through my fingers like sand.

He wouldn't call it off, not while Meredith was still with us. But he was going to break my heart, wasn't he?

Was it better or worse to know it was coming? To know that after Meredith passed, he would leave me?

And I was helpless to stop it. All I could do was watch as he fell apart. As he withdrew from everyone, especially me.

The announcer's voice blasted through the sound system, drowning out the noise from the crowd. "All right, Wildcats fans, time to get to your feet!"

Cheers erupted around us, so loud I could feel the vibration against my skin. So loud I could barely hear my own voice.

We all stood, Monty helping Meredith up, and then thousands of fans began to clap in time with the blaring music, all eyes aimed at the doors where the team would leave the stadium's locker room for the field.

Two lines of cheerleaders and dance team members were on the field, forming a row for the players. Their pom-poms were raised and shaking. Between them were barrels for fireworks.

Meredith glanced over her shoulder, giving me a smile as she reached for my hand.

I took it, holding tight to her knuckles, to the paper-thin skin and frail bones, as the doors to the locker room opened. A cannon blasted, my heart seeming to beat just as loudly, as the Wildcats stalked toward the field.

Normally, they'd run down that column of cheerleaders,

but today, they marched, side by side, the fireworks beginning to pop and shoot around them.

Rush walked in the lead. Beside him was Maverick. Their faces were covered with their helmets, but I'd recognize Maverick's long, confident strides anywhere.

Meredith's grip tightened as she raised her other hand and waved.

Maverick was already looking our way. He held up his hand, waving at his mom the way he used to when we were kids. Wildly, with abandon, whenever he saw her in the office at the elementary school.

He'd never given a damn if the other kids teased him for being a mama's boy. He'd tell them his mom was awesome and they were losers.

Monty looped an arm around Meredith's waist as she let go of my hand and leaned into his side. She wasn't able to stay on her feet until every player emerged, and as her energy waned, she sank into her seat, righting the blanket over her legs.

Dad put his arm around me, bending low to speak in my ear. "You haven't said much today."

I shrugged. "There's not much to say."

Mom took my hand, holding it in both of hers. When I looked to her, there was an unwavering strength in her gaze. A surety that we'd all get through this together.

She'd been a rock. The pillar we could lean on. She and Meredith were sisters of the heart. Best friends. She wouldn't crumble, not until this was finished. She would tirelessly keep the rest of us moving, keep us breathing.

Before.

And after.

Someday, I wanted to be as strong as my mother.

She squeezed my hand, a silent reassurance that I could do this. And then we all faced the flag for the national anthem.

"There he goes," Dad said after the coin toss and Maverick jogged to the field for kickoff. "Did he say if they were leaving him as punter and placekicker today?"

"No." I shook my head. "I think they're taking it game by game."

I didn't want to admit that Maverick hadn't told me anything because all I'd gotten from him in the past two days were a couple of short texts.

Mabel cupped her hands to her mouth. "Let's go, Maverick!"

Monty lifted both arms in the air. "Go Big Blue!"

I laughed, cheering with them as the crowd around us began to jump and clap, to scream for this team.

Maverick placed the ball on its tee, then waited as the other players got into their formation. He stood yards back from the others, gaze locked on the football. He pointed to the left side, then the right, getting two nods. Then he jogged forward, picking up speed until he kicked the ball.

It sailed through the air, past the receiver on the other team, landing on the turf at the ten, rolling toward the end zone. The Wildcats special teams chased it down and surrounded the ball, not letting anyone touch it until it stopped moving at the three.

"Can't get much better than that." Dad clapped Monty on the shoulders before we all settled onto the bleachers as the offense jogged onto the field.

The coaches and players on the sideline all clapped Maverick on the shoulder as he tore off his helmet, flashing us a blinding smile.

It was the first real smile I'd seen from him in weeks.

"I'm glad we're here," Mom said, leaning her shoulder against mine. "Together."

"Me too."

It didn't take long for us to settle into the game. To cheer and clap and boo a bad call by the refs.

For the first time in months, it felt like us again. My family. The Houstons and the Adairs taking on an adventure.

The offense scored a touchdown, and when Maverick ran out to kick the extra point, we were all on our feet, even Meredith, screaming as the ball soared through the uprights.

We scored two more touchdowns before halftime while the other team had yet to score. As the clock ticked toward zero at the end of the second quarter, fans began streaming down the stadium stairs, making their way toward exits and the tailgates outside.

"Well, I think this calls for a cheeseburger," Meredith said once the players had headed into the locker room. "And a Coke."

It was the first time she'd asked for food in ages. There was a color to her cheeks that had been missing for months. Maybe the sunshine, the fresh air and Wildcats energy, was giving her a much-needed boost.

"I'll get them for you, Mom," Mabel said. "Bodhi's hungry too."

"I'll come with you." Meredith let Monty help her to her feet. "If you don't mind that I'm slow."

"Not at all." Mabel nodded for Bodhi to head down the row, then they set off for the concession stands, Mom going with them to get us some snacks as Dad and I stayed with our stuff.

"How's Maverick?" Dad asked.

"Not the best," I admitted.

"Understandable. It'll be good for him to focus on football, finish school. Then we'll get him on at Adair."

Dad hadn't mentioned Maverick coming to work at Adair in weeks. I'd thought it was because Mav had told him, definitively, that he wasn't taking the job. But maybe that conversation hadn't happened. Maybe Dad had simply been too busy.

We'd been slammed with the last hard push of the season, all of us pulling ten- to twelve-hour days while the weather held strong. We had a month, possibly six weeks, until it would get too cold. Once the ground froze, we'd shift gears to snow removal. Most of the designers would take a few months off, though I'd work year-round, like Dad.

"I don't think he's coming to Adair," I said.

"Really?" Dad pushed his sunglasses into his hair. He had a tan line in their exact shape, just like he did every year in September from a season spent in the sun. "He said he was interested."

"When?"

"Oh, it's been a while, I guess."

But Dad was still stuck on it. Even after I'd worked my ass off this summer, showing him I was capable. Yet he still didn't trust me enough to give me the chance.

"What if we break up?" I asked. "Would you still give him a job?"

Dad's eyebrows lifted. "Are you going to break up?"

"What if we do?"

He shifted his gaze toward the field, fitting his sunglasses over his eyes again. "None of us will be surprised when it happens. We all know how this started. Just wait, if you can."

Wait until Meredith was gone.

All this time together, they thought we were still doing this for her. Did anyone in our family believe it was real? Did Maverick?

Or was I the only person foolish enough to believe he wanted me?

That sinking feeling got worse, dread taking up permanent residence to twist my insides. I wouldn't be able to eat a burger if they brought one back from concessions.

The marching band began their performance on the turf, forming the letters T, S and U with their members. By the time everyone returned with the food, halftime was over and the players had returned to the field, without the fanfare this time around.

Maverick waved at us again, waved at Meredith as she nibbled on her cheeseburger. Then he went to a net to practice a few kicks, warming up his legs.

The roped muscles on his arms were on display. His pants molded to his strong thighs and the perfect globes of his ass.

He truly was breathtaking. I loved him and hated him all at the same time.

That jerk had made me fall in love with him.

How could I have let this happen? How could we have gotten to this point?

We were only supposed to do this for a little while. We were only placating his mother. But now, if this fell apart, how was I supposed to recover from Maverick Houston?

"Stevie, want some popcorn?" Bodhi thrust a red-and-white-striped box into my lap.

"No, thanks." I forced a smile, waving away the box to watch the third quarter.

The Wildcats scored another touchdown, swapping out the offense for defense. Rush and Maverick stood together with their helmets pushed up on their foreheads, watching and talking as the other team struggled to gain a yard.

That was the moment when Meredith slumped against Monty's side, her head resting on his shoulder.

It took us all a few minutes to realize she hadn't fallen asleep.

CHAPTER TWENTY-FOUR

MAVERICK

"It's good to see your mom here," Rush said.

We both glanced behind us to the stands, to my family and the Adairs.

Mom smiled and gave me a little finger wave. Dad had his arm around her shoulders as he talked to Bodhi. Mabel was taking a video on her phone. Elle and Declan were talking to each other, and between them was Stevie, her attention on the field, watching the play.

She looked beautiful today, her hair long and loose. Her Wildcats tee paired with my favorite frayed denim shorts.

I should have stayed at her place last night. I should have slept with my face buried in that hair and been there to watch her pull on those shorts this morning. Instead, I'd slept like shit, alone in my own bed.

She deserved better. I was a fucking asshole.

It had to stop. Tonight. After the game, I'd go to her place, and whether I liked it or not, it was time to talk. About us. About Mom. Everything.

It was time to stop being a fucking coward and tell her how I felt.

"It makes the game more fun when they're here to watch, doesn't it," Rush asked, stealing my attention.

"Yeah, it does." I followed his gaze toward the next section over, to where Faye had Rally strapped to her chest in a baby carrier, blue earmuffs on his ears.

Faye was with his parents, who'd come to town for the game. When she spotted us watching, she picked up Rally's hand in a wave.

Rush's smile widened before we both returned our focus to the game.

"Third and eight." Rush pulled his helmet over his face, then he rolled his shoulders.

"Ramsey." Coach Parks O'Haire, the offensive coordinator and quarterbacks coach, came to stand beside Rush. "I'll let you play through the third quarter. But unless this game gets away from us, I'm putting in second string."

"You got it," Rush said.

They wouldn't risk injuring their star quarterback when we were kicking the other team's ass.

"Same for you, Houston," O'Haire said. "Let's give the younger guys some playing time."

"Sure thing." I nodded.

All I cared about today was that Mom was here. She'd asked if there was any way she could get a ticket for today's game. I'd gone to Coach Ellis's office first thing Monday morning and begged for the best tickets he could find.

Coach hadn't let me down. First two rows, forty-yard line.

I owed him for this, big time.

The defense stopped the other team on third down.

261

They went for it on fourth and came up short, so Rush and the offense jogged onto the field.

We'd run the ball the rest of today. We'd bleed the clock down. Rush handed the ball to a running back who took off down the field, zigzagging through a hole in the line. He broke past the defenders, and, with legs pumping, tore off toward the end zone, not stopping until he scored another touchdown and the stadium went wild.

I laughed, pulling on my helmet, giving Rush a fist bump as he came off the field. "So much for running down the clock."

"Hey, it's not my fault their defense sucks."

I jogged past him, grinning, and got into position to kick the extra point.

Straight down the middle. "Hell yes."

I pumped a fist at my side as a few of the guys clapped me on the back. Then I got the nod from Coach as he sent the second-string punter to the field in my stead.

"Guess that's it for us today," Rush said when I joined him on the sideline again.

"Guess so. You guys going to dinner at Dolly's after the game?"

"That's the plan." He nodded. "You guys want to join us?"

"Maybe." I shrugged. "I'll see what Stevie wants to do tonight."

I turned to the stands, seeking her out again. Except the seats where everyone had been only minutes ago were empty. Everyone was gone.

Where was Dad? Where was Mom?

My stomach dropped.

No. Not yet.

An ambulance's siren broke through the noise of the crowd.

I tore off my helmet, searching for a familiar face. Maybe they'd just gone to grab some food. Gone to the bathroom.

A swish of dark hair caught my attention. Stevie stood at the rail, eyes wide.

Tears streaking down her face.

CHAPTER TWENTY-FIVE

STEVIE

M y hand was empty.

I flexed my fingers, my gaze dropping to my palm. My hand was empty. It shouldn't be empty.

Where was Maverick?

I spun around, searching every corner of the room at the hospital where a nurse had brought us after Meredith had . . .

Died.

She was gone.

Her heart had given out at the football game.

All this time, we'd known the end was coming, but it still felt as if someone had punched me in the stomach. Had stolen every bit of air from my lungs and I couldn't breathe. I was lightheaded, but there was this incredible weight shoving down on my shoulders.

And now my hand was empty.

I'd let go of Maverick's hand for just a minute when Mom had come over to give me a hug. I'd held on to her for only a moment, stealing a bit of her strength, before I'd let go.

Maverick was supposed to be in this room, holding my hand.

"W-where's Maverick?" My voice was hoarse from crying.

I'd tried not to break. To keep it all inside. To be strong and keep the tears from escaping. But when the doctor had come in here and explained what had happened, the tears had started and they hadn't really stopped. Every time I thought I was out of tears, they'd swell again and fall down my cheeks.

Maverick had held onto me, to my hand, and let me cry into his chest.

It was supposed to be the other way around. I was supposed to be the one comforting him. Letting him cry on my shoulder. And now he was gone.

I spun in another circle, making sure I hadn't missed him, but it was impossible to miss a six-foot-four man wearing a football uniform.

"I don't know." Mom's eyebrows came together as she looked around the room too. "The bathroom?"

"Maybe. I'll go check the hall." On the way to the door, I passed Monty and Mabel holding each other with Bodhi pressed between them, their faces tearstained.

Dad was talking on the phone in the corner, keeping his voice low.

My parents had made some sort of arrangement with the Houstons that they'd coordinate the funeral. Meredith hadn't wanted Monty to fuss over the details, so she'd delegated them to Mom and Dad.

The door creaked as I opened it and slipped from the room. It was noisy, chatter drifting this way from the nurses' station and the emergency rooms. Outside that waiting room,

265

the world was still spinning, oblivious to the loss it had suffered today. A nurse rolled an empty bed past me, giving me a sad smile. One of the wheels was rattling, the sound so loud it made me tense.

I checked left, then right, searching the hallways for Maverick.

When he'd spotted me at the game, he'd sprinted down the sideline, tearing off his helmet. I'd met him at the gate, and without a word, we'd both run for my Jeep in the parking lot at the fieldhouse.

We hadn't been far behind the ambulance that had brought Meredith. We'd parked beside Mom's Escalade. Met everyone in the lobby. We'd all come here together. So where was he?

He couldn't have gone far, right? He didn't have a truck. He was still in his cleats and pads.

I went to the closest men's bathroom, pushing the door open a crack. "Maverick?"

Nothing.

"Is anyone in there?"

Still nothing.

I went to the next bathroom and did the same, this time getting a reply from a man named Gary. When I couldn't find Mav, I headed for the lobby, scanning empty seats in the waiting area. Then I walked out of the double sets of sliding doors and outside.

It was dark already. Part of me felt like we'd only been here for minutes. The other part, decades.

We'd had to wait for news on Meredith. Then, after the doctor had come to tell us what had happened, we'd waited as Monty had gone into her room to say goodbye.

Mabel had wanted to go too, but he'd told her no. That

Meredith had left specific instructions that neither Mabel nor Maverick were to see her body.

Just Monty.

She wanted her children to remember her living and breathing.

I slapped a hand over my mouth as a new wave of tears filled my eyes, spilling down my cheeks. A sob was lodged in my throat, like a lump of burning coal. But I swallowed it down, burning the whole way, and wiped my face.

"Get it together, Stevie." I took a deep breath, then another.

Where the fuck was Maverick?

I looped the parking lot, checking every bench, wondering if he'd come outside for air. When I didn't find him, I lapped the entire building. The night air was cold, biting through my thin tee. My legs were pimpled with goose bumps by the time I finally retreated inside, making my way back to the family room. I pushed the door open, expecting to find him inside. But he was still gone.

"There you are," Mom said, touching my arm. "You're freezing."

"I can't find Maverick," I whispered, not wanting to worry Monty and Mabel, who were seated at the small table against the wall, filling out paperwork.

Once it was complete, we could go.

Monty's hand was visibly shaking as he held the pen. The sorrow on Mabel's face was heartbreaking, so I focused on Mom instead.

"He probably just needed a few moments alone," she said.

It was more than that. Something was wrong. I could feel it. Maverick wasn't here, in the waiting room. In the hospital.

"You're probably right. I'm going to see if I have a sweatshirt in the Jeep." I picked up my keys and phone from the side table where I'd left them, then I eased out of the room again, taking another hard look down both sides of the hall.

Would he have gone to see Meredith?

It was possible, but Monty had been adamant earlier. We'd all heard the steel in his voice. She did not want that, her wishes were perfectly clear, and I doubted Maverick would go against them. Not today.

I pulled up his name in my phone, pressing it to my ear.

"Hey, it's Mav. Leave a message."

"Damn it." I ended the call and took off for the Jeep. There was a sliver of hope that I'd find him by my vehicle, but when I reached our row in the lot, my Jeep and Mom's Escalade were alone.

The door's handle was cool beneath my fingers as I climbed inside, the seat cold against my legs. Noise and touch, it all felt sharper, like the world was fighting to keep me from going numb.

I fumbled for the ignition, my fingers shaking, and when the engine hummed to life, I couldn't seem to wrap my hands around the wheel.

There was a very real chance that I was being paranoid, that the stress from today had frayed my rationality. If he was still here, if he'd found a quiet corner of the hospital to mourn alone, then I was leaving him.

But that gut feeling was impossible to ignore.

Damn it. This was my fault. I'd let go of his hand.

And he'd floated away.

I cranked the heat, then pushed my doubts aside and drove away from the hospital, taking the dark roads that led toward the stadium. I scanned every sidewalk, every path, for a tall, heartbroken football player. But the sidewalks were empty on the quiet roads to the stadium.

The crush from earlier today was gone. The blockades they'd put up around the stadium had been taken down, stowed until next week's game. People had gone home. Most were likely eating dinner or spending time with their families.

The world kept on spinning, even when it should have stopped.

The streetlights blurred as my eyes flooded, but I kept driving, blinking away tears, both hands clutching the wheel.

It wasn't fair.

It wasn't fair that people just kept living while our family had been shattered tonight. That the man I loved was out here, alone, and I couldn't find him.

I fumbled with the phone in my lap, calling his number again.

Straight to voicemail. "Hey, it's Mav. Leave me a message."

"Maverick, where are you?" My voice cracked as I spoke. "Please call me."

He wasn't going to call me.

The parking lot outside the fieldhouse was mostly deserted, a sea of black asphalt and white lines. I drove up and down the lot twice, searching for Maverick's truck.

He would have parked here earlier, when he'd come to get ready for the game. I was certain of it. Which meant he'd either gotten a ride to campus from the hospital. Or he'd walked.

"Shit."

I fired off a text to Mom, telling her I'd left the hospital

269

and would call her tomorrow, then I drove toward the Houstons' house, hoping I'd find him there.

The windows were black, the house still. Like it was grieving too. Like it knew that half of its heart wouldn't be returning home tonight.

Mom and Dad wouldn't let Monty come here alone. Neither would Mabel. So I weaved through the neighborhood, making sure Maverick hadn't stopped at the park.

Where would he go?

"Think, Stevie," I told myself as I came to a stop sign.

Top Five places. He'd go to his Top Five.

I went to McDonald's next because it was on the way to his house. I parked in the pickup space and rushed inside. He wasn't in a booth or at a table, so I ran back to the Jeep, setting off toward his place.

His truck wasn't in the driveway beside Rush's Yukon, but I stopped and hurried to the front door anyway.

Rush answered before I could ring the bell, his gaze drifting over my head. Like he was expecting me to be with Maverick.

"He's not here, is he?" I asked.

Rush shook his head. "No. I haven't heard from him since he left the game. Did Meredith . . ."

I nodded, unable to say it out loud.

"Fuck. I'm so sorry, Stevie."

I bit the inside of my lower lip so I wouldn't start crying. Then I drew in a fortifying breath. "Maverick left the hospital and didn't tell anyone where he was going. Can I check his room?"

"Of course." He stepped out of the way, pointing toward the hallway past the kitchen.

I should have known the way to Maverick's bedroom. A

girlfriend would have gotten over herself and spent time in her boyfriend's room.

Instead I'd been too busy worrying about stupid shit, so I hadn't visited one of his Top Five.

Never again. I was never getting hung up on his past again. It didn't matter. None of it mattered. All that counted was finding Maverick.

The door was open. The scent of his soap and shampoo and cologne and Maverick was faint in the air. The lights were off. His bed was made.

Empty.

I called him again, wondering if I'd hear his phone ring or vibrate, but the room was silent.

"Hey, it's Mav. Leave me a message."

His voice fit in this room. If I closed my eyes, I could hear him laughing or talking. He had a picture of his mom on the nightstand beside his bed.

I skipped leaving another message and left before I could start crying again.

"If he comes home, would you call me?" I asked Rush.

"Sure." He dug his phone from his pocket. "What's your number?"

I rattled it off, receiving a text from him a moment later. Then I was out the door, driving back toward campus and the stadium that just hours ago had been so happy. Kicking myself that I hadn't checked when I'd come to the fieldhouse earlier.

If Maverick wasn't at home, then maybe he'd gone to a different Top Five place. After his house, the stadium seemed the next option to check.

After parking in an illegal space, the spot closest to the

field, I raced for the nearest gate, pressing my face against the chain link. "Maverick!"

Even if he was hiding out on the field and heard me, I wasn't sure he'd answer. But I shouted his name again and again and again until my voice was raw. Would Maverick ever be able to play here again?

It hurt to breathe, to think, and that weight on my shoulders seemed to get heavier with every passing minute. I tilted my face to the sky, to the stars, and closed my eyes.

"Where is he, Meredith?" My chin quivered, and I clenched my teeth together, my molars grinding as I fought to keep from crying.

His truck was in the Top Five, and if he was spending the night driving around Mission, I'd never find him. But before I gave up and went home, there was one more place to check. So I ran back to the Jeep, buckling my seat belt as I put it in drive and made my way to the mountains.

To a meadow bathed in frost and moonlight.

I let my headlights shine toward the trees, my stomach sinking as I stared into the night. Into nothingness.

Maverick wasn't here.

And I was out of options.

I'd let go of his hand and now he was alone. All I could do was wait until he found his way back to me instead. So I turned around and drove to town, taking the roads carefully and on constant alert for any deer that might jump into my path.

I called Maverick three more times on my way home, each call going to his voicemail.

Mom had left a message while I'd been in the mountains and out of service. She sounded worried, wondering if we were okay.

She assumed I was with Maverick.

She expected me to find him.

Meredith and Mom used to tell people the story of how our dads had lost Maverick when we were three. Dad and Monty had been doing a project in the garage and left the overhead door open. Mom and Meredith had taken Mabel and me upstairs for a bath, leaving Maverick with our dads. They'd been building the firepit and had been carrying cut bricks to the backyard while Mav had been banging some tools around in the garage.

Two minutes. They swore they left him alone for maybe two minutes. And during those two minutes, Maverick had taken off down the sidewalk. When our dads had realized he was gone, they'd searched everywhere, about to call the police. Until I'd run down the sidewalk, sprinting in the direction of the park.

Meredith had followed me, and we'd found Maverick on the slide in the playground.

I'd found him when we were three.

Why couldn't I find him tonight?

A choked sob, hopeless and hurting, escaped as I turned onto my street. I reached for the button to open my garage, only to pause, hand in midair, when I saw a truck in my driveway.

Maverick's truck.

The air whooshed from my lungs as I hit the garage door opener, parking and hurrying inside.

He'd used the keypad to get in the house but hadn't bothered with a light. It was so dark I nearly tripped on the jersey and pads and pants that littered my bedroom floor.

Maverick was on his half of the bed, lying on his side,

hands pressed beneath his cheek as he stared at my empty pillow.

I toed off my shoes and climbed into bed, taking his hand from beneath his face, threading our fingers together so mine wasn't empty.

He blinked, like the touch had pulled him from a fog. Pulled him back to reality. Pulled him back into the nightmare. His eyes flared with pain, then tears before he curled into my arms, pressing his face into my throat. "Stevie."

"I've got you."

His entire body began to shake.

Then, with my hand clamped around his so I wouldn't lose him again, I held him all night long as he broke apart.

CHAPTER TWENTY-SIX

MAVERICK

Stevie was asleep, curled on her side and burrowed under her blankets. She hadn't moved since I'd slipped out of bed a few hours ago. Since I'd pulled on my clothes, fully intending to sneak out of her house.

But instead, I'd sat on the floor, body propped against her bedroom wall, my forearms draped over my knees, and watched her sleep.

This was going to hurt.

I wasn't sure how much more hurt I could take at this point, but in the hours since I'd been sitting here, numbness had crept into my bones. A hollow, empty feeling, like all the love and joy and light had been sucked out of my body. It took mental reminders to breathe. To blink.

Mom wasn't the only person who was gone. The guy I'd been before, he'd died yesterday too.

Dad had been texting me all night, wondering where I was and when I'd left the hospital. I'd replied to him hours ago that I'd be over soon. But I couldn't seem to get up off the floor.

Last night, I'd walked all the way from the hospital to campus in my pads and uniform. My cleats. Even when I'd gotten to the fieldhouse, I hadn't bothered to change. I'd just snagged the keys and backpack from my locker and gotten in my truck.

The only place I'd wanted to go was Stevie's.

Somewhere along the way, her bed had become my favorite place. And Stevie Adair was the center of my universe. She always had been, whether we were lovers or friends or enemies. It had just taken me a while to realize she was the one.

Yeah, this was going to fucking hurt.

My pads and cleats and jersey were already in the back seat of my truck. I'd cleaned out my toothbrush and razor from her bathroom. All I needed was for her to wake up, then I'd be gone.

I could lean on her through this grief. She was so strong. She'd hold me up. All of the women in our family were strong—stronger than the men.

It was tempting to let Stevie be my crutch. My anchor. So damn tempting. But I knew what would happen next. Mom had pulled me aside a few weeks ago and told me not to become an asshole after she died.

I was going to become an asshole, despite her warning.

This numbness wouldn't last. It would fade, sooner or later, and when it was gone, the grief would become this monster of rage. It would tear through every bone, every muscle, every breath. I could feel it, deep inside, dormant and waiting.

It would destroy us. *I* would destroy us.

This sadness, this black, endless pit, would swallow us whole. I would be awful to her simply because she was there.

Because she wouldn't leave my side. Because she'd let me be awful to her.

I loved her too much to ruin us. To risk breaking her apart under the weight of my heavy heart.

Rush would call me a fucking idiot. Mabel would tell me to pull my head out of my ass. Dad would worry. The energy he'd given Mom would be transferred to his children.

The only person who might actually understand why I was doing this was Stevie.

And Mom.

Mom would have understood.

Mom and Stevie always knew me best.

Like she could hear her name in my thoughts, Stevie's eyes fluttered open.

She rolled to look over her shoulder, and when she found my half of the bed empty, she sat up with a jolt, searching the room. Then her gaze dropped to her hand, the hand that had held mine when I'd broken apart last night.

She stared at her empty palm almost like she was surprised I'd wiggled free.

"Hey." My voice was dry, my throat ragged from crying.

Stevie's attention swung to where I sat on the floor, then she pressed a hand to her chest, breathing a sigh. "There you are. I thought you'd left."

"Not yet."

"Where are you going?"

"See my dad."

She whipped the covers from her legs. "Give me five to get dressed and I'll go with you."

"No." I shifted to stand, my legs stiff and ass half asleep. "I'm going on my own. It's, uh . . . it's better if you stay away."

She studied me for a long moment. "Maverick. What are you doing?"

"I can't . . ." The urge to dissolve into tears came on so fast it choked me, cutting off the rest of what I needed to say. I swallowed hard, then cleared my throat. "I can't do this. I can't stay with you. We were always going to call this off. It's time to be done."

A moment of shock, of pain, crossed her expression. Then those beautiful hazel eyes narrowed and she crossed her arms over her chest. "Don't say something you'll regret."

"That's why I'm doing this," I whispered. "I'm going to fall apart, Nadine. And you'll try to pick up the pieces. Hell, I'll probably let you. But I don't trust myself, and I don't want to hurt you."

She opened her mouth, probably to argue, but then a sadness washed over her face that was a knife to my chest. "Okay."

"I have to go." Before I changed my mind. Before I fell to my knees and never left this room.

Every step through the house was difficult, like my legs and feet and knees were fighting my decision, but I trudged on anyway.

Stevie followed, her hair a wild mess, her eyes swimming in tears as she watched me pull on the shoes I'd left beside the front door.

"Mom loved you," I said, barely breathing through the burn in my throat. "I'm sorry."

Stevie shook her head, swiping at a tear that streaked down her cheek. "You're apologizing to me when *your* mom died?"

"We both lost her."

She nodded. "And now I'm losing you too."

I put my hand to her cheek, my thumb catching another tear. "Take care of yourself."

"That's my line."

I leaned in and pressed a kiss to her forehead, giving myself one last inhale of her hair. Then I tore myself away and walked out the door while I still had the strength.

I was almost to my truck when she called my name.

"Maverick?"

I turned, my chest so tight I could barely breathe.

Stevie stood on the edge of her stoop, in the exact place where we'd had our first kiss, and held up her pinky. "I'll be here. When you're ready."

"Don't wait for me."

"Don't tell me what to do." She went inside, slamming the door.

Fuck, it hurt. So much I almost went to the grass and puked. Probably would have if there was anything in my system. I waited until the nausea passed, then climbed in my truck and drove away.

Dad and Mabel would be at the house. They'd be waiting for me. But I couldn't bring myself to go home, not yet. Not when Mom wouldn't be there. So I shut off my brain and, just like I had last night, let my body steer me to where I needed to be.

Rush's Yukon was at the fieldhouse. I pulled into the empty space beside it, then hauled my pads and gear inside. None of the guys were in the locker room, but the sound of music and clinking metal drifted in from the weight room.

The chatter, the conversation, the movement, all came to a stop when I walked through the door. Everyone stared, face after face twisted in pity, until the only sound was the music through the sound system.

"Houston." Coach Ellis walked over, his face sheened with sweat.

Sunday workouts were optional, though I didn't know a single guy on the team who didn't make it a point to show up.

Since Coach Ellis had taken over as head coach last year, he'd joined us for these workouts. Coach Greely usually did too. They both made it a point to be here, with us. They were available for more than whatever was happening in football. They cared about what was happening off the field as much as on.

They were the best coaches I'd ever had in my life.

Coach Greely walked over too, a towel in hand and sweat at the band of the hat he had on backward. "Maverick, you don't need to be here today."

Yes, actually. I did need to be here.

Rush appeared at my side, concern etched on his face. He put his hand on my shoulder and squeezed.

They were going to send me home, weren't they? They'd make me walk out of here and face everything I didn't want to face.

I'd have to go see Dad. I'd have to watch him cry and worry. I'd hear Mabel sniffle and see the sadness in Bodhi's face.

I wasn't ready yet.

If I left here, I'd have to say goodbye. I'd have to start the first day of my life without a mother.

I wasn't ready to leave.

Please, don't make me leave.

Damn it, I missed Stevie already. She'd understand why I couldn't go home yet.

"I'm good," I said, lying through my fucking teeth.

They all stared at me until Coach Ellis jerked his chin toward the nearest weight rack. "Rush, spot Maverick today."

The air whooshed from my lungs as Rush clapped me on the back.

"You got it, Coach."

CHAPTER TWENTY-SEVEN

STEVIE

I hated Fridays. Almost as much as I hated Saturdays.

I'd run out of work to do this week, and there were still three hours left in the day before I had to go home to a quiet, empty, lonely house. Maybe tonight I'd rent a movie. Maybe I'd make myself a fancy dinner for one. Maybe I'd put on a pair of old sweats and stare at the wall.

Whatever activity I didn't do tonight would be there for tomorrow.

I'd kill for a big project to tackle. Something that would occupy my mind for countless hours. I needed work. Desperately. Work was the only thing that had kept me going over the past seven weeks. It had been a distraction through the grief. And we were limping into our slowest time of year.

My office was clean, the scent of orange and lemon thick in the air from the solution I'd used to dust and polish my desk. The window was so streak- and spot-free that the pane was basically invisible. A person could eat off the hardwood floor. I'd even used an air sprayer on my keyboard to clean out the dust and crumbs.

Maybe my cleaning spree could continue at home. I'd started following a cleaning fanatic on TikTok the other day. She'd posted a video about deep cleaning a washing machine that I'd wanted to try out. Last night, I'd used her method to scrub my baseboards.

Maybe cleaning could become my new hobby, at home and work.

Most of the fall cleanup for Adair was complete. The inventory in the nursery had been safely stowed in our greenhouse. The prep work for rose propagation was finished. All of our equipment was parked in the shop, where our mechanic would ensure it was all in excellent working order before next spring. And the seasonal employees were off to enjoy their winters. Most of the younger crew members would be working at the local ski areas, manning chairlifts and hitting the slopes as soon as we had our first big storm.

The weather was cold, but we hadn't gotten more than a skiff yet. Nothing for the plowing crew to fret over. Though even if we got dumped on, it wasn't like I'd be out clearing parking lots and sidewalks.

No, I'd be stuck in this office, trapped within these walls, begging for something—anything—to pass the time.

I missed school. I missed volleyball. I missed Meredith.

And mostly, I missed Maverick.

I missed him so much there were times when it was hard to breathe. So I did everything in my power not to think about him. Not to worry and wonder.

Was he okay? How was he coping? Did he miss me too?

"Nope." I shut down that line of thinking and stood from my chair, walking out of my office. Maybe Dad had something I could do. Maybe I'd clean his office next. The coffeepot in the break room could use a vinegar wash.

I was halfway down the hallway when Samantha's voice carried from the reception desk.

"I'm so sorry, Mr. Jefferies."

Jefferies. Jefferies was my client. What was she apologizing for?

"I'll talk to Declan and get this straightened out immediately. And I'll find out if we can assign another designer with more experience to your account."

I stopped before I reached Dad's office doorway, breath lodged in my throat. What the hell was happening?

"You know how it is," she said, an eye roll in her voice. "Boss's daughter."

Wait. Had she just insinuated to my client that my only qualification was being Declan Adair's daughter? No fucking way.

"Declan will want to fix this. Don't worry," she said. "I'll talk to him right now, and we'll get back to you before the end of the day. I'm so sorry this happened. But thanks for calling and bringing it to my attention."

To *her* attention? When had she decided she was running this place? And what the hell was that comment about being the boss's daughter?

My lip curled as my heart began to pound, angry, harsh beats.

Her phone clicked into its cradle, then came the rolling of wheels on the floor as she left her desk. Samantha came up short when she saw me standing in the hallway.

"What was that about?" I crossed my arms over my chest.

She straightened, raising her chin. "Mr. Jefferies said he was overcharged, and he's pretty mad about it."

"He wasn't overcharged." I'd prepared and sent that invoice myself, having triple-checked every line.

Jefferies was a huge pain in the ass. He was demanding and rude. He changed his mind every thirty seconds and routinely forgot his own decisions, forcing me to backtrack and rework the design plan—every iteration of which I'd done for free. He'd been charged a single design fee despite endless revisions, plus the labor and materials.

"That's not what he said." She shrugged and waltzed into Dad's office without knocking.

I followed, my jaw clenched so hard I'd have a headache before the end of this meeting. But I stayed quiet, standing in the threshold, as Samantha explained the situation to Dad.

He didn't so much as glance at me for an explanation. He just hummed and put on his glasses before shaking the mouse on his computer to pull up the Jefferies account. He clicked a few times, then leaned closer to read the screen. "Well, I'll give him a call to smooth this over. We can refund the design fee or something. I'll take care of it."

"Thanks, Declan." Samantha wore a smug grin when she turned. "Excuse me."

It took everything I had to keep my mouth shut as I shifted out of the way so she could leave. Then I closed the door. "There's nothing wrong with that invoice."

"It's no big deal. Small project. We'll waive the design fee and make the customer happy."

"I've already waived six revision fees."

Dad's eyebrows came together. "Oh. Really?"

I opened my mouth, about to launch into the details of the project, but stopped myself before I could speak.

Did it matter? He knew I'd been standing here this whole time. And his first inclination was to believe Samantha. To waive a fee. To fix a mistake that didn't exist.

Why was it so hard to talk to my dad at work? He was my dad. But since I'd started at Adair this spring, our relationship had slowly changed. He was a boss who didn't seem to trust me.

"Why didn't you ask me about the invoice?"

He took off his glasses, setting them aside. "What do you mean? We're talking about it right now."

"After you listened to everything Samantha had to say, while I was standing here, and you didn't ask me a single question. Is that how you handle customer complaints for other designers? Or is that just for me?"

"Hey, I'm just trying to calm the waters." He leaned his elbows on his desk, nodding to one of the guest chairs.

I ignored them both, too pissed off to sit.

Dad frowned. "I know you don't like Samantha much. She told me there's some history there with Maverick. I'm staying out of it. But you two will have to figure it out."

"It's not about Maverick."

Did I like Samantha? No. Not even a little bit. Did it bother me to think about her with Mav? Yes. Whenever I let thoughts of them together slip into my mind, the jealousy was so strong it made me sick to my stomach. But my dislike of Samantha was mostly because of how she acted at Adair.

"We're never going to 'figure it out,' " I told him, air quotes flying. "I just heard her tell Mr. Jefferies that the reason I screwed up was because I'm the boss's daughter. Because I'm incompetent and the only reason I have this job is nepotism. She's not a team player, Dad. She's been stirring up drama since her first day."

He sighed, pinching the bridge of his nose. "I'll talk to her about it."

"And if it doesn't change?"

"Then I'll let her go." He lowered his voice. "But, Steve, no matter what, you are my child. For a while, people are going to think you're only here because you're my daughter. And they wouldn't be wrong."

No, I guess not. But I wouldn't have come to work at Adair if I'd been someone else's daughter. The reason I loved it here was because of him. Because when I'd been a kid, my favorite days had been when he brought me along to work.

What career would I have wanted if there hadn't been Adair? I hadn't ever let myself ask that question.

"That invoice is correct," I said. "I'll deal with Jefferies. Samantha never should have taken that phone call. She should have transferred him to me."

Dad nodded. "You're right."

I stood a little taller. "Thank you."

"Now will you sit down?" He motioned to the chair. "I'd like to talk about the garden center expansion proposal."

I was too angry to talk about that proposal. I wanted to go back to my office, call Jefferies and tell him off. Except no good would come from me losing my temper with a customer. Maybe some time to cool off was a good idea. And if Dad let me run with the proposal, well . . . maybe I'd have something other than cleaning to do on a Friday night. So I took the chair, sitting on its edge with my hands in my lap.

The garden center proposal was one I'd drafted a week ago, not because he'd asked me to put something together, but because I'd needed to keep busy. And no matter why I was here, Adair was my future.

Dad had promised to read my ideas and then we'd

discuss, but that had been days ago. After a week, I'd all but convinced myself that he hated every word. That I'd wasted countless hours researching other garden centers in Montana, and Adair would remain a landscaping company with a small greenhouse for retail sales.

He pulled out the green folder I'd left on his desk—Dad hadn't yet embraced going paperless. "It's good."

My smile wobbled as I exhaled. "Thanks."

He opened the folder. "I made some notes in the margins."

"All right. I can review them tonight and this weekend."

"Unless you changed your mind about the game?"

"Oh, um . . . I can't. I've got some stuff to do around the house tomorrow," I lied.

Dad and Mom were going to the Wildcats game tomorrow with the Houstons. Since Meredith, they hadn't missed a single home game. They bought me a ticket each and every time, but I couldn't bring myself to go. I wasn't ready to see Maverick yet.

"Okay." Dad didn't press about the game. Just like he hadn't asked what had happened with Maverick. In seven weeks, our relationship hadn't come up once. How he knew we'd broken up was a mystery. Mav had probably told Monty, who'd passed it along to Dad.

Or maybe they'd all expected it to happen. Now that Meredith was gone, our fake relationship was over.

Any tears I cried I blamed on losing Meredith, not a broken heart.

Dad flipped to the third page of my proposal. "We'll have to work up more detailed financial projections."

"Sure." I nodded. "I only included rough numbers as a starting point. I can—"

"We'll let Maverick tackle it when he starts," Dad said before I could finish my sentence.

Um . . . "What? Are you serious?"

"He's going to work here over winter break." Dad rubbed the back of his neck. "Just a few hours a week. Nothing major. I think he's just trying to keep busy, and since he won't have school, he'll have extra time outside of football. I offered him a short-term position and this could be the perfect project for him to tackle."

I opened my mouth but there were no words. All I felt was this soul-crushing ache. An all-consuming disappointment in my father.

Deep down, I knew he was just trying to help Maverick. That his heart was in the right place. But had he even considered what this would do to me? Not just to give Maverick the garden center project, something I'd spearheaded to this point. But also how much it would hurt to have Maverick in this office?

Adding Samantha into the mix would be insult to injury.

Dad knew we weren't together. Details aside, he knew Maverick and I weren't spending time together.

In the seven weeks, the nearly two months since the morning he'd left my house after Meredith had died, I'd only seen Maverick once.

The day we'd taken her ashes to the mountains.

Meredith had gotten her wish. We'd taken her ashes to the meadow and scattered them into the wind. It had been family only—the Houstons and the Adairs.

Maverick hadn't looked at me once. He hadn't spoken a word. But when Meredith's ashes were gone, when there'd been nothing to do but leave her behind, I'd walked over and looped my pinky through his.

He'd held tight.

In my heart of hearts, I knew the reason Maverick had left that morning. That he'd been falling apart. He was the kind of person who needed space to sort out his feelings. And if I'd pushed him, it would have ripped us apart.

He wasn't coming back, was he?

Seven weeks I'd waited. Wondered. Not a phone call. Not a text.

Instead, he'd taken Dad up on a job offer—an offer Dad shouldn't have made in the first place.

"What am I doing here?" I asked, my frame deflating.

"Huh?"

"What about me isn't enough?"

"Hey." Dad's mouth turned down, his forehead furrowing. "That's not what this is about. I told you this spring, I don't want all of Adair resting on your shoulders."

"Isn't that my choice to make?"

"Can't you just trust me on this, Steve?"

"Stevie," I corrected. "I hate being called Steve."

He blinked, forehead furrowing. "You do?"

"If I was a boy, would we be having this conversation? Would you have offered Maverick a job?"

Dad didn't have an answer to that question. He stared at me, seemingly lost for words.

"I don't know if this was a good idea," I said.

"What was a good idea?"

"Me, working here."

"Oh." He pressed a hand to his heart.

But when I stood and walked to the door, he let me leave.

To hell with Fridays. If I didn't have anything else to do, I'd go home. Alone.

It took only a moment for me to grab my coat and purse, then I was out the back door and marching to the Jeep.

I bit the inside of my cheek, refusing to cry. I'd spent enough time crying over the past seven weeks. A job didn't seem like enough of a reason to ruin my makeup.

But maybe a damaged relationship with my father was enough.

Tears flooded, and before I could stop them, they tracked down my face, taking smears of mascara and foundation with them. By the time I got home and risked a glance in the bedroom mirror, my eyes were puffy and my cheeks splotchy.

"Grr." I wiped my face dry.

I was so tired of crying. Of feeling sad. Of feeling stuck.

The only good thing about living alone was that no one was here to see me upset. I'd cried in the kitchen. The living room. The dining room. The garage.

I'd cried endless tears in this house.

All by myself.

Now that Jennsyn and Toren were engaged, she'd moved into his house next door. Liz's boyfriend had taken a job in Washington, and he'd asked her to move in with him.

So it was just me in this house. A house my dad had chosen. A house he'd picked out because it was so close to Adair.

It was mine now. I was making payments to the bank after buying it from my parents. But what if I didn't want this house? What if working at Adair was a huge mistake?

What if it was time to let go?

It wasn't the first time I'd had the thought of making a big change. I'd had a real estate website bookmarked for weeks.

But each time I'd decide it was worth a call, I'd tell myself to sleep on it. By morning, I'd have chickened out.

I fished my phone out of my pocket, and before I could let myself think, I pulled up the website. I hit the number and closed my eyes as I pressed the phone to my ear.

"Mission Realty. This is Anna."

"Hi, Anna. I'd like to get some information about listing my house for sale."

"Sure, we can help you with that. Are you moving?"

I spun in a slow circle, staring at my bed.

Maverick wasn't coming back. Seven weeks. It was time to stop waiting. "Yeah. I think so."

CHAPTER TWENTY-EIGHT

MAVERICK

My breath billowed around me in white puffs as I shifted from foot to foot. It was cold as fuck today, and all I could do was keep moving to stay warm. Or maybe it was just my nerves making me bounce around.

There was no reason to be nervous. I checked the scoreboard, stared at it for a few moments longer than necessary to make sure I wasn't imagining the numbers.

Treasure State Wildcats, forty-five.

University of Montana Grizzlies, three.

The rivalry between our schools was legendary. We hated the Griz, and I didn't give a shit if that sentiment was returned.

This football game was always the pinnacle of the season. It was usually our last regular-season game, and while everyone on the team loved making the playoffs, as long as we beat the Griz, the year was a win.

We weren't just beating them today.

It was a goddamn slaughter.

The defense was on the field, absolutely punishing their

quarterback. He'd been sacked four times, and they'd all been hard hits—slamming into the frozen turf had to hurt like hell. I almost felt bad for the guy. Almost.

"This is getting embarrassing." Rush came to stand at my side, cupping his hands in front of his mouth and blowing hot air into his palms.

"Think Coach will put in second string?"

"Not against the Griz. Not after that interview."

I grinned. "Good."

Earlier this week, the arrogant head coach for the Griz had gone on a radio show and absolutely raked the Wildcats, calling us lucky and lacking true talent. Then he'd gone on a rant about Coach Ellis, saying that Coach was unqualified and his success in the NFL had been a fluke.

If the dickhead had intended to piss off everyone in a Wildcats uniform, it had definitely worked.

Maybe next year, he'd think twice before running his damn mouth.

Maybe next year, I'd be on this sideline not as a player, but as a coach.

The original plan for my fifth year at Treasure State had been to mail it in. To go light on credits, enough to maintain eligibility to play football, but coast through my class load. That plan had gone up in flames.

On the last possible day to add or drop classes, the Monday after Mom had died, I'd piled on two extra courses, both geared toward sports administration and management. After sitting down and talking about my future with Coach Ellis and Coach Greely, they'd both encouraged me to graduate. Not to change my major this late in the game, but to supplement my business classes with a couple that would give me a lift into the world of coaching.

I had six classes, twenty credits, and it was more than I'd taken on in all my years as a college student. If I wasn't at practice, I was studying. If I wasn't studying, I was coaching.

I'd spent the fall as the assistant coach for Bodhi's flag football team. Their games were on Saturdays, so I'd missed all of those, but I'd been there for every practice. Their season was over now, and he'd immediately started basketball.

I was the assistant coach for that team too so that three nights a week—Monday, Wednesday and Friday—I could spend time with my nephew and his friends.

On Tuesdays and Thursdays, I spent my evenings at the Oaks, helping one of my former teachers with a new winter soccer program. We ran conditioning and footwork drills. I wasn't great at soccer, but I was pretty good at kicking a ball. Plus the kids were mostly little, kindergarteners through third grade. Uncoordinated and adorable and if they weren't laughing, then I was doing something wrong.

My grief counselor said that burying myself in tasks wasn't a long-term solution. That eventually I'd have to stop and face my feelings. She wasn't wrong.

But if I stopped, it hurt.

So I didn't stop.

I packed every single day with an activity, filling each spare moment.

On Sundays, I studied. I'd visit Dad and we'd pretend that the house didn't feel empty without Mom. We'd have lunch together; sometimes Mabel would join us. Then I'd go home to hang with Rush, Faye and Rally in the afternoons before my weekly appointment with my grief counselor.

And on Saturdays, I missed Stevie.

Even with the distraction of a football game, I missed her so much it hurt.

Not just Saturdays. Every day. But Saturdays were the worst.

I'd had seven without her. Seven weeks of wondering if I'd made the biggest mistake of my life.

Yes. Without question.

But I'd said some shit over the past seven weeks I regretted, and all I could be thankful for was that it hadn't been aimed at her. Those first few weeks, before I'd started counseling, I'd been the worst version of myself.

I'd called my sister a fucking bitch when she'd told me she was going to help Dad clean out Mom's closet. I'd told Dad he was a fucking coward when he'd sold Mom's car. I'd told Rush to fuck off whenever he asked if I was okay. And when Faye had marched into my bedroom to tell me I needed help, I'd told her to go back to her precious diner and wash dishes.

The next day, when I'd realized just how much of a fucking asshole I was being, I'd made my apologies, then looked up a counselor and made the call.

There was a long road ahead. There'd always be this missing piece in my heart, but I was learning to accept it. Live with it.

To be the man my mother had raised me to be.

I tipped my head to the blue sky, to the sunshine that streamed through the guard on my helmet.

"How about this game, Mom?" I whispered. It helped to talk to her. To think that she was watching. Listening.

"What did you say?" Rush asked.

"Nothing." I waved it off, then turned toward the stands

at my back. My family was sitting about ten rows up from the railing on the thirty-yard line.

Dad was wearing a pair of Carhartt bibs and his ski coat. Mabel had a fleece scarf wrapped around her face and a stocking hat with a blue-and-silver pom-pom on top. She'd brought Kai along, and each time I turned, his arm was around her shoulders, keeping her close.

That day I'd called her a fucking bitch? He'd been at the house too. And he'd told me that if I ever spoke to her like that again, we were going to have a big problem.

I liked Kai. For Mabel. For Bodhi. For our family. I liked him a lot.

Bodhi was bundled up in a thousand layers, the outermost an old jersey of mine. And beside him, Elle and Declan were dressed for winter too.

None of them had missed a game since Mom had died.

I hadn't expected them to want to return here, not so soon. But if I was here, so were they, cheering and clapping like the rest of the Wildcats fans.

The only person who hadn't come was Stevie.

A cheer rose up from the crowd, forcing my attention to the field. The defense had just sacked the Griz quarterback again for a loss of six yards.

"Yes." I laughed, grinning at Rush.

"If the season ended right here, if this was my last game, I'd be happy."

"Same." It wasn't my last game. We'd have the playoffs. But no matter what happened, I would have no regrets when it came time to walk away from football.

Whether I became a coach or not, I'd given my all to this team. To the Wildcats.

I was ready to let it go when it was time.

Rush rubbed his hands together, stealing a glance toward where Faye was standing with his parents. She had Rally strapped to her chest in a carrier, and he looked like a baby marshmallow in his snowsuit. There were headphones over his ears to quiet the noise, and clearly, they'd worked. He was fast asleep, his head lulled to the side.

"I guess this game is boring your son," I teased. "Try to do something exciting on this possession, will you?"

Rush chuckled as special teams players swapped out with the defense for a punt return. "Fuckwad."

I shrugged, taking another look toward my family.

A woman with long, dark hair in a loose braid walked along the railing, and for a moment, my heart skipped, hoping it was Stevie. But then she turned and started up a staircase, showing her face.

"She didn't come today," Rush said.

"No."

"Have you talked to her?"

"No."

"Wow. Normally when I ask you that, you tell me to fuck off."

I wished he were joking, but I'd been a shithead for weeks. "Caught me in a good mood."

Rush took a step forward, ready to get on the field after we called for a fair catch. But before he could leave, he paused, turning back. "I didn't want to say this, not after your mom. But, Maverick?"

Definitely wasn't going to like this. "Yeah?"

"Pull your head out of your ass."

"Fuck off," I said, but he was already jogging onto the field with the rest of the offense.

I knew he was right. I'd screwed up. I'd known that since

the moment I'd walked out of her house. But right or wrong, I'd needed some time to myself. To figure myself out.

A part of me had feared that our relationship was too centered on Mom's dying wish. That only the pressure of our families had been keeping us together.

I wanted Stevie to love me on my own merit.

Because I loved her. I was in love with Stevie Adair and had been my entire life.

Maybe I was afraid to go back because she wouldn't feel the same. Maybe I was terrified that she'd break my already-broken heart.

All doubts I'd played and replayed for seven weeks.

How ironic that I'd become a chronic overthinker? Stevie had rubbed off, in more ways than one.

The center snapped the ball into Rush's waiting hands. He dropped back in the pocket, searching for an open receiver. Everyone was covered, so he tucked the ball into his arm and took off running, darting through a slit between the other players. Then he was gone, legs pumping as he sprinted for the end zone.

"Yes!" I threw a fist in the air, laughing when he scored a touchdown, turned to face me and pointed the tip of the football at my face.

I tilted my face to the sky as the stadium roared. "Okay, Mom. Message received."

It was time to make the most of it.

CHAPTER TWENTY-NINE

STEVIE

I couldn't get the fastener on my earring. I'd been trying to put on the damn thing for five minutes, but I couldn't stop my fingers from shaking.

"You know what?" I set the stud on the countertop, talking to myself in the bathroom mirror. "I don't even need earrings."

I shouldn't even be going tonight.

Why had I agreed to this?

Jennsyn had texted me this morning and invited me to go with her and Toren to the Wildcats volleyball game. I'd said *yes* too fast when I should have asked for more details. Because she'd also invited a guy from work, and though she'd promised it wasn't a blind date, it felt a lot like a blind date.

Jennsyn was working at the local YMCA as their sports director, and apparently there was a guy in her office, one of the donor liaisons, who was allegedly cute.

I wasn't really interested in an allegedly cute donor liaison. But I *was* interested in getting out of this house, so even though I didn't feel like going on a blind-ish date, I hadn't changed my mind about the game.

It was just something else that was twisting my insides in a knot. The biggest culprit was the sign now staked in my front yard.

Anna from Mission Realty had wasted no time. I hadn't signed the listing agreement yet. We hadn't landed on an asking price or taken photos. But one of her associates had arrived this morning and put a sign in my front yard.

When I'd texted her about it, she'd replied, *Just getting a jump on things! You can always change your mind.*

Apparently, the lack of inventory in Mission's real estate market meant she was doing everything to lock this in. Maybe she'd sensed my hesitation on our phone call yesterday. Maybe this was her way of nudging me into the decision she wanted.

Part of me wanted to tell her to take that damn sign out of my yard and stop being so pushy. The other part figured that if I was going to sell it, why not?

The guilt had been eating me alive for almost twenty-four hours. It had been a rash, impulsive decision, and I had little to no experience with rash and impulsive. Spontaneity was Maverick's style, not mine.

Though it had felt good in the moment. It had felt like exactly the right thing to do.

Last night.

Except by this morning, I'd reverted back to my regularly scheduled programming of overthinking. That ridiculous green-and-gold sign wasn't helping.

Was it a mistake to list this house? Or was it exactly what I needed?

This could be a fresh start, the change I craved. I hated

the idea of moving, of telling my parents I was leaving the house they'd picked out. I didn't want to disappoint them or seem ungrateful. But if I moved, I could pick a house for myself.

I wanted a big bedroom, like I had here. A kitchen adjacent to the dining room, like I had here. An extra bedroom I could convert to a home office, like I had here.

Why was I worried about moving? Because of a not-so-fun conversation with Dad? Maybe the problem here wasn't my address. Maybe the problem was my employment.

I loved transforming a space with landscaping. I loved plants and flowers and dirt beneath my fingernails. I loved lush, green yards and beautiful flower beds. But my relationship with Dad was more important than a business. It was becoming uncomfortable at Adair, and if it continued, I was scared it would fester. That I'd begin to resent my father.

What if I went to work for another company for a few years? I could gain some experience. Earn a reputation based on my skills, not my last name.

Dad would hate it. God, he'd be angry, and that resentment I was trying to avoid would be unavoidable. Maybe it had always been inevitable. I could go to work somewhere else and hope I'd gain Dad's confidence—or have my own wither away a little bit every day.

A breakup could be exactly what we needed.

Maybe Maverick had been onto something, all this time.

Or maybe he was the same massive jerkface he'd been when we were ten, and I was destined to hate him forever.

Enough feeling sorry for myself. Enough nursing this broken heart. Enough Saturday nights home alone. It was time to move forward.

Starting tonight with a blind-ish date.

"Ugh."

At least there'd be volleyball.

Even if this guy from the YMCA turned out to be a dud, I could endure a few hours to cheer on my former teammates in their rivalry game against the Griz.

The football team had won against the Grizzlies today in an absolute slaughter. I hadn't watched the game, but the temptation had been too much this afternoon, and I'd checked the final score a few hours ago.

Hopefully the volleyball team would have as much luck.

The doorbell's chime echoed through the house.

I did one last fluff of my hair, taking in my outfit in the bathroom mirror. My distressed blue Wildcats crewneck draped over a shoulder, leaving it bare. My jeans were cuffed at the hems and I had on my favorite pair of white tennis shoes.

The last time I'd worried about dressing cute had been a Saturday with Maverick.

It felt wrong, a betrayal, getting ready for this game. For a date.

I walked away from the mirror before I could change my mind and cancel this entire thing. When I made it to the front door, I snagged my coat from a hook in the entryway and opened the door.

"You could have just come in—" It wasn't Jennsyn on my doorstep.

It was Dad.

"Oh. Hey, Dad." *Shit.*

That sign in the yard might as well have been a strobe light for how it seemed to flash from over his shoulder.

That guilt from earlier came roaring back as Dad stared at me, twin worry lines between his eyebrows. Okay, so I

303

probably should have slept on this moving idea. Screw spontaneity. I wasn't built for hasty decisions.

"Hi." Dad was still dressed in his winter gear, what he must have worn to the game today. His gray-and-brown hair was covered in the Wildcats beanie I'd bought him for his birthday a few years ago.

"Want to come in?" I shifted to the side.

"Um, sure. You look nice. Are you going somewhere?"

"The volleyball game with Jennsyn."

"Ah. Well, I won't keep you." He stepped inside just as Jennsyn appeared behind him, having walked over from next door.

"Hey." She smiled and waved to Dad. "Hi, Declan."

"Hi, Jennsyn. Heard you guys are going to the game?"

"That's the plan."

"You guys go ahead," I told her. "I'll meet you there."

"We can wait."

"No, really. It's fine. I'll be right behind you." And if I had my own vehicle, I could bail.

She pointed at my nose. "Don't bail."

"I'm not going to bail." Probably. It was tempting. Which was likely why she'd arranged this ride with her and Toren, so I wouldn't have the chance to ditch her colleague and this awkward setup.

"Fine," she said. "See you at Upshaw?"

"I'll be there."

"Good. Also, we'll be talking about that." She twisted and gave the realtor's sign a pointed glare.

I cringed. Well, she'd have to get in line. Dad was here first, and I was guessing that his impromptu visit meant someone around town had told him about that sign.

News traveled fast in Mission. It wasn't as small of a

town as it had been once. As the university had expanded, bringing in larger and larger classes each year, so had the population. But we'd lived here a long time and Dad was very well-known around town.

He had spies everywhere.

I closed the door as Jennsyn headed back to her house, shutting out the cold night, then I steeled my spine and faced Dad. "I listed the house for sale."

"I fired Samantha."

We spoke in unison.

He wasn't surprised, obviously.

Me? I stared at him with my mouth agape. "Y-you what?"

"Yesterday, after you left, I brought Samantha in and told her she was going on a performance improvement plan. She's overstepped more than once and if she can't stop, then she's not a good fit. She didn't like that much. She said a few things, made it personal, so I let her go."

"Wow." Did I want to know what she'd said? Probably not.

"She isn't a good fit for the team. And you were right, she never should have interfered with your client. I shouldn't have either."

"Okay." This was not at all the conversation I'd been expecting. What was the catch? Was there a catch?

Dad put his hand on my shoulder, giving it a squeeze. "Why didn't you ever tell me you didn't like to be called Steve?"

I shrugged, my cheeks flushing. "I didn't want to hurt your feelings."

"But I've been hurting yours." He swallowed hard as tears made his eyes watery. "You know, I've been waiting for so long to have you come to Adair. There were so many years I missed something of yours because I was at work. I thought it would be our chance to spend time together before I retired. And now I'm worried that this job is going to be what causes a rift with my daughter I won't be able to repair."

"I don't want that either."

He blinked too fast, forcing a smile. "Our family has lost enough this year. I'm not willing to lose you over Adair."

"But you love Adair."

"I love you more."

My whole body seemed to exhale. "I love you too, Dad."

"I'm sorry." He pulled me into a hug, squeezing tight. "You are enough. I never wanted you to think I didn't believe in you. I just don't want you to be stuck to something that I built. To feel trapped by this company because of your loyalty to me."

"I don't feel trapped by Adair." And I didn't want to find a new job, not when I already had the one I wanted.

He let me go, sniffling. "Monday morning, we'll talk about a transition plan. You need more experience in the field and in the office. That's not a critique. I just don't want you to be unprepared to take over. I'm not going anywhere for a bit, but it's never too soon to start."

"I'd really like that."

"We'll talk about the garden center too. It'll be yours. You might as well set it up the way you want."

"Okay." Was this really happening?

"I told Maverick he could have a job over winter break, but I'll rescind that offer. It was wrong of me to force you into that. I know things between you two have been tense."

Tense would require we be around each other. Things between us were nothing.

We were nothing.

"If you want to hire a business manager someday, that's your call," Dad said. "For now, we'll tackle everything together. You and me."

Hell, I was going to cry and ruin my makeup. "Thank you."

"Don't quit." He gave me a sad smile. "If you need to sell this house, move someplace else, I understand. But don't quit Adair, not unless you want to do something different."

I nodded. "All right."

He hugged me again, resting his cheek against my hair. "I love you."

"Love you too."

We hadn't hugged enough in the past seven weeks. When we were at the office, he was my boss. We'd both been stifled under the weight of professionalism. But that was asinine. He was my dad, first and foremost. Adair was a family business. So come Monday, if I wanted to hug my dad, I was going to hug my dad. I doubted anyone would care or notice.

"You'd better get to the game," he said, letting me go.

"Yeah, I suppose." I waited until he was gone, then I hustled to the garage, a smile on my face for the first time today.

Even if this game, this blind-ish date, was a nightmare, tonight was already better than I'd expected.

The fieldhouse parking lot was packed when I arrived, this game almost always sold out every year. Jennsyn and Toren were waiting for me in the hallway outside Upshaw.

And so was my date.

"Hi, I'm Taylor." He smiled as he shook my hand.

"Stevie."

"Nice to meet you. Shall we?" He nodded toward the doors.

I let him and Toren go first, falling into step with the crowd shuffling into the gymnasium.

"Cute, right?" Jennsyn asked, lowering her voice as we walked together.

"Yes."

Taylor had blond hair and brown eyes. He was tall and fit, his navy, long-sleeved thermal molding around muscled arms and broad shoulders. And he had a swagger that reminded me a lot of Maverick's.

Except he wasn't Maverick. Not even close.

And it took everything I had not to turn around and leave the gym. I wasn't ready to be on a date. I didn't want anyone else.

"Want anything from concessions?" Taylor asked as we reached our seats, third row up from the floor.

"No, thanks." I took the seat next to his, close but not so close that we were touching.

Jennsyn sat on my other side, cuddled into Toren's side. She looped her arm with his as he splayed his hand over her knee.

They were adorable together. The perfect match. If I didn't adore them together, I'd be jealous.

More people crowded in around us, forcing Taylor and me closer.

"Sorry," he said as his leg pressed against mine. "Not exactly roomy in here."

"It's fine." I waved it off. "So you work at the YMCA?"

"I do. Jennsyn tells me you run a landscaping company."

"Well, it's not my company. It's my dad's. But someday, I hope to take over."

"Impressive."

"Thanks."

Taylor stared at my profile, a warm and handsome smile on his face. He really was good-looking, well beyond cute.

A guy I could see myself dating.

Except I didn't want him. And I hated that his cologne was so familiar.

He smelled so much like Maverick it made it hard to breathe.

A knee knocked into my shoulder, jostling me forward. The nudge was hard enough that Taylor and I both twisted in unison to scowl at the person behind me.

"Sorry." The man held up his hands in apology, but there was an arrogant smirk on his face.

He wasn't sorry. Not even a little bit.

"Hey, Adair," he drawled.

I hated the way my heart flipped. "Houston."

CHAPTER THIRTY

STEVIE

Sweat beaded at my temples and my armpits felt sticky. My shoulders were pinned, my spine stiff, and after sitting like this for nearly an hour, my muscles were screaming.

Perfect posture was incredibly painful. My entire frame was tense, and no matter how hard I tried to ignore Maverick behind me, he might as well be perched on my lap for how he pulled my focus.

Every few minutes, his knees nudged against my shoulders. There were the occasional, light tugs at the ends of my hair like his fingers would brush the strands. And his cologne. Damn him for always smelling so good. Every inhale was a reminder that he was right here, right behind me.

Why was he here? Was he interested in one of the girls on the team? Maybe he'd rekindled his thing with Megan.

That idea, combined with my nerves, made me want to puke on Taylor's shoes.

"That new freshman is good," Jennsyn said, nodding to the hitter that had taken her place on the team.

"Yeah." I nodded. "Definitely."

Was she good? I had no fucking clue and would have to take Jennsyn's word for it. Because despite staring straight ahead, pretending like my attention was locked on the gym floor, I didn't have a clue what was happening on the court.

"I'll admit I don't know much about volleyball," Taylor said, leaning close so I could hear him over the noise.

The moment his arm touched mine, Maverick's knee bumped my shoulder blade.

I gritted my teeth, fighting the urge to turn and pretend like I hadn't felt a thing.

"It's fairly straightforward," I told Taylor in yet another short answer to one of his questions.

To his credit, Taylor had tried for an hour to make easy conversation. He'd asked me about my job at Adair. About where I'd grown up. About my plans for Thanksgiving and if I had a favorite restaurant in town.

I'd tried to engage. I'd smiled and answered his questions, with albeit short replies, and asked a few of my own in return. But it was so hard to concentrate and relax.

At this point, I just wanted to go home.

"How many sets will they play?" Taylor asked.

But before I could answer, Maverick's knees were at my back again, pressed firm as he leaned forward. "Best out of five," he said, answering Taylor's question.

His voice was so close I could smell the hint of his cinnamon gum.

I closed my eyes, swallowing hard.

There was a pack of cinnamon gum in my purse. I

chewed it to torture myself. To remember what his mouth tasted like.

"First to win three sets," Maverick explained. "They play to twenty-five. Have to win by two."

Now he was a volleyball expert? Had Megan been giving him lessons after their hookups? God, I was going to be sick.

"Thanks," Taylor muttered, dismissing Maverick with a quick glance. Then he leaned in closer, like he was trying to block Maverick out.

Except there was no blocking him out. He was in my head. Impossible to ignore or forget.

I jammed my elbow backward, hitting his shin, but it only made Maverick inch closer.

"Stevie played setter when she was on the team." He pushed an arm between Taylor and me, pointing to the girl who'd taken my place.

"Do you mind?" Taylor asked, giving Maverick a glare.

"Just trying to explain the game." Mav held up a hand and leaned away. But those knees never left my back.

"How do you two know each other?" Taylor asked me.

"Our parents are good friends." I spoke loud enough for Maverick to hear. "I've hated him since we were ten."

The outside hitter, the girl Jennsyn had mentioned was good, delivered a kill and the crowd shot to their feet, the third set finished and a win for the Wildcats.

It was two to one, Wildcats leading the Griz. One more set and we'd be the winners.

Except I didn't think I could stand another set. The air was too thick and stuffy, the heat becoming unbearable.

"I'm going to get a water," I told Taylor. "Be back in a few."

He nodded, his hand touching my elbow before I shifted toward Jennsyn and Toren.

"You okay?" she asked, eyes darting to the row behind us.

No. No, I wasn't okay. "Just need some water."

"Sure." She gave me a sad smile as I shuffled past her and Toren.

When I reached the stairs, I jogged to the floor and hurried out of the gym. The noise from the game grew dimmer and dimmer as I made my way along the familiar fieldhouse hallways, passing the concession stand and the bathrooms. I didn't stop until I was outside, finally filling my lungs with the crisp night air.

The cold should have chased the dizziness away. It should have cleared my head and settled my stomach. But my knees felt weak and the twist of my insides only tightened.

I couldn't stay. I couldn't watch another game with Maverick here. Especially if he was here to watch Megan.

After gulping down another cool inhale, I started for the parking lot, digging out my phone to text Jennsyn as I weaved between cars for where I'd parked the Jeep.

Tell Taylor I'm sorry.

She replied instantly with three hearts.

Jennsyn was the only person who knew about what had really happened with Maverick.

I fished out my keys, hitting the fob to unlock the doors. Except before I could reach the row where my taillights flashed, footsteps sounded at my back.

"Go away," I said, not bothering to turn. I'd learned the sound of Maverick chasing after me a long time ago.

"Why is there a for-sale sign in front of your house?" he called.

"Because I'm moving." I whirled, crossing my arms over my chest so he wouldn't see my shaking fingers as he came to a stop in front of me.

"You're not moving."

"Yes, actually. I am moving."

His jaw worked. "Since when?"

"Since yesterday. It was a whim. Me being spontaneous."

"You're not spontaneous."

"I am now." I pointed over his shoulder to the fieldhouse. "You're going to miss the rest of the game. Better hurry on back so you can catch Megan in action."

"I'm not here for Megan."

My racing heart climbed into my throat, and even if I knew what to say, speaking was impossible.

"Ask me why I'm here." Maverick moved even closer until I could feel the heat from his chest.

I shook my head.

"It's Saturday," he said. "I hate Saturdays without you. And if the only way I can spend them with you is by crashing your fucking date with another guy, so be it."

It wasn't a date, not really, but I couldn't bring myself to correct him. He could suffer for a few minutes.

I'd been suffering for seven weeks.

His fingers came to my hair, pushing it away from my temple. "I'm sorry, Stevie. And if I have to spend the rest of my life groveling and begging for you to give me a second chance, then I'll do it every day and twice on Saturdays."

He didn't have to grovel. I'd promised him I'd be here when he was ready.

Except I still couldn't find my voice. My heart was

314

lodged in my throat, and if I opened my mouth, I'd probably start to cry.

"My grief counselor thinks I'll be lucky if you take me back."

I blinked, replaying that statement. He was going to a grief counselor? Since when?

"But I told her that we'd make it. That there wasn't a person on this earth who knows me the way you do. That you knew, before I did, that I'd need time to sort myself out. That we might have started this thing as fake, but it's real. We've got merit. And we'll make it because I love you. Because I've always loved you, Nadine."

A tear dripped down my cheek before I could stop it.

Maverick caught it with his thumb.

"It's been seven weeks," I whispered, finally finding my voice. "I'm so fucking mad at you."

"I'm mad at me too."

I swiped at my eye before another tear could fall. "Did you tell my dad you'd take a job at Adair?"

"Yes." The corner of his mouth twitched. "I knew it would piss you off. And you're beautiful when you're mad."

"Then I guess I've never looked better." I took a step away, glaring up at him.

It only made him smile. "How long do you think you'll be mad?"

"Awhile. I'm good at grudges."

"I'll wait." He stepped forward and took my face in his hands. "I love you."

I should push him away. Get in my Jeep and go home. Except I didn't want to go home alone.

My house, a space I'd once loved, had considered a sanctuary, was no longer in my own Top Five favorite places. Not without Maverick.

Maybe we both needed to make up a new Top Five. Together.

"Are you okay?" Despite my anger, despite my stubbornness to make him pay for a few more moments, I'd spent seven weeks worrying. And even though he never told me how he was feeling, I had to ask anyway.

"No, I'm not okay." He leaned back to give me a sad smile. "I'm sad. I miss Mom. I've been a dick to my family more often than not. I'm wearing myself thin trying to fill every moment of every day so that I don't have time to hurt. School is harder than I'd planned for my last year. Football is almost over, and I'm not sure who I'll be without it. Mabel is eventually going to marry Kai, and I'm pretty sure Bodhi likes spending time with him over me, which makes me insanely jealous and glad at the same time. Rush is going to get drafted this spring and then he'll leave Montana and take Faye and Rally, so I'll be all by myself. I miss you so much it's hard to breathe. Oh, and you went on a date tonight and your house is for sale. So no, I'm not okay."

I stared at him, eyes wide. "That's . . ."

"Real."

"Yeah." I nodded.

"I'm not good at real. But I'll try to be real with you." His hand cupped my face. "Are you okay?"

I shook my head. "I'm on a blind-ish date when I'd rather be at home in my sweats. I made a spontaneous decision to sell my house, my realtor is pushy, and I've been overthinking it ever since. It's exhausting trying to avoid you while always thinking about you. I miss your mom. I hate my bed. I love you, and I kind of want to strangle you too."

Maverick reached for me, but before he could say anything, Taylor's voice drifted across the lot as he walked our way.

"Stevie? Are you all right?"

Maverick twisted to scowl over his shoulder. "Date's over, man. She's taken."

"Maver—"

His mouth crushed mine, and my protest was lost with the swirl of his tongue, the taste of cinnamon gum.

Time warped as his lips fused with mine. One moment, it was just the two of us in the parking lot. The next, the crowd from inside was streaming outside, people getting in cars.

A car behind us turned on their headlights, forcing us apart and out of the way.

Maverick hauled me into his arms, breathing in my hair. Then he tipped his face to the night sky and let out a laugh. "She loves me, Mom. I think we're going to be okay."

Yeah. We were going to be just fine.

CHAPTER THIRTY-ONE

MAVERICK

Six months later ...

Stevie handed me my to-go cup of coffee. "You're nervous, aren't you?"

It would have been easy to deny it. To pretend I hadn't tossed and turned all night. That my stomach wasn't in knots and that my hands weren't shaking so badly I'd nicked myself shaving.

Except she slept beside me and knew when I was restless. She'd watched me pick at breakfast this morning and she'd seen the cut on my jaw.

She'd let me get away with a small lie, but I'd made myself a promise this fall, after Mom had died all those months ago.

Real. No matter what, with Stevie, I'd always be real.

"So fucking nervous." I set the cup on the counter and hauled her into my arms, breathing in her hair, letting it calm some of my anxiety. "I'm not qualified for this."

"If that were true, they wouldn't have hired you." She

leaned away, rising up on her toes to plant a kiss on the corner of my mouth. "You're going to do great."

I took her face in my hands, dropping my forehead to hers. "I love you."

"I love you too." Her arms snaked around my waist, and this time when she kissed me, it lingered, soft and sweet.

Part of me wanted to carry her into the bedroom. To lose myself inside her body because it was the only way to shut off the noise in my head, to quiet the doubts. But I didn't want to be the guy who showed up late for his first day of work.

She dragged a thumb across my mouth after she broke the kiss, wiping away her lip gloss. "Call me later if you can sneak away for lunch. I have a couple meetings this morning, but I'm free the rest of the afternoon."

"All right."

Her schedule had been slammed for months, and she'd been spending long days at Adair, even before the snow had completely melted in the valley. Declan had fully embraced the transition plan they'd put together, and though it meant she had long days at work, she was loving the challenge.

I'd never seen a person so excited to go to work each day.

I loved how she had that.

Maybe after I got over these nerves, I would too.

"Okay. Here goes nothing." I grabbed my cup, phone and keys from the counter, then followed her to the garage, where both our vehicles were parked.

My truck was in the stall that Jennsyn used to park in when she'd lived here.

The morning after we'd gotten back together, after we'd left the volleyball game and spent hours wrapped around each other beneath her sheets, Stevie had called the realtor and told her to come and pick up the sign.

I'd given her props for the spontaneity, then told her she'd better leave that to me from now on.

She promised to stick to overthinking for the rest of our lives.

If she wanted to move eventually, I'd gladly pack up our stuff and follow her around the world. This building wasn't my home. Stevie was my home.

Still, I liked this house. I liked mowing the lawn on Sundays. I liked going for evening runs in the neighborhood. I liked that we had friends living next door. And I liked that this house was our beginning. That this was where we'd had so many of our big moments.

Our first kiss. Our first night together.

My graduation party. Rush and Faye's send-off after he'd been drafted by the Cardinals.

Tonight, I hoped to add another big moment to the list.

There was a ring hidden in my toolbox inside the garage. It had been there for a week. I'd had lunch with Declan yesterday, and he'd given me permission to marry his daughter.

My nerves for today weren't just about my new job.

"Good luck." Stevie blew me a kiss before she climbed into the Jeep.

I winked. "Bye, honey."

Our garage doors closed in tandem, and as she turned right at the end of the block, I took a left, driving to the Oaks.

The parking lot of my former school had been repaved recently, the lines a stark yellow against the black asphalt. I picked the middle row, then sucked in a fortifying breath as I got out of my truck.

"I'm nervous, Mom," I whispered, then headed for the entrance. My hands were trembling so badly that I tucked them into the pockets of my gray slacks as I walked to the office.

Without question, I wasn't qualified for this. I had no professional experience, and my degree wasn't for sports administration or exercise science or even teaching. But when Elle had sent me the posting and Dad had told me it was at least worth a shot, I'd filled out the online application, expecting never to hear from them again.

Certainly not to get a job interview.

But apparently I'd made a name for myself with the winter soccer league. With coaching Bodhi's various teams.

That, and no one else had applied.

I'd jumped through countless hoops since the superintendent had offered me the job, completing a certification program and getting my educator license. All to be a football coach and physical education teacher at the Oaks.

"Maverick." Principal Davies was waiting inside the lobby, her gray hair twisted into a tight bun. "Welcome."

"Thanks." I shook her hand and glanced to the empty chair at the front desk.

Mom's chair.

I could still picture her there, smiling at students as they passed. If I closed my eyes, I could hear her happy laugh echoing off the walls.

"Let me show you to your office." Davies motioned toward the hall that took us to the gym.

I'd spent plenty of time at the Oaks in the past six months helping with the sports programs, but most of my time had been in the gym. I hadn't ventured this way, taking the hallways I'd walked as a student, past lockers and classrooms.

It felt smaller than I remembered, but it smelled the same, wood and disinfectant wipes and a hint of dry-erase markers.

We rounded a corner to a hallway lined with huge frames, each packed with photo collages.

"These are new. They didn't have them when I went to school here." I slowed, taking in the frames. Each had a small, golden plaque above it with the year that must correlate to the photos.

It was like a hallway of yearbooks.

"We added this just last fall. We wanted a way for current students to connect with those who came here first."

I took in one frame, then the next, giving the pictures a cursory glance. I was about to pick up my pace when a familiar face caught my eye, and I stopped, leaning in close.

She was seated at the front desk, a bright, white smile on her face.

"Hey, Mom," I whispered to the glass.

This was my new favorite hallway. I'd get to say hi to Mom every day as I walked from the gym to the teachers' lounge beside the office.

I shifted down a couple more frames, finding the one from my senior year.

Except I didn't look for my face in the pictures. Instead, I found Stevie in a photo of the volleyball team. "There she is."

"Who's that?" Davies asked.

"That's my Stevie." I smiled at the picture, then joined my new boss as we continued to the gym.

"High school sweethearts?" Davies asked.

I grinned. "Something like that."

EPILOGUE

MAVERICK

Two years later . . .

"You're nervous." Stevie pointed at the eggs she'd scrambled with her spatula. "Too nervous to eat?"

"Yeah. I think I'd better skip breakfast." My insides were too knotted to eat. "Tell me this isn't a huge mistake."

"It's not a huge mistake." Spatula aside, stove flipped off, Stevie moved in close, her hands on my waist. "You're going to do great."

She'd said the same thing two years ago, in this same kitchen, on my first day as a coach at the Oaks.

Now we were having the same conversation all over again, on the first day of my new job.

As the special teams coach for the Treasure State Wildcats.

I'd hoped one day I'd get to work for my alma mater. But I sure as hell hadn't expected it to happen so soon. I'd planned to be at the Oaks for years. Then Ford Ellis had called a month ago and asked if I'd be up for a challenge.

The former special teams coach, *my* former coach, was

retiring. Coach Ellis—he'd told me I had to start calling him Ford, but it was taking a while to mentally make that switch —wanted to bring in the next coach to make it a smooth transition.

"It's weird though, right? I played with some of the guys still on the team."

"So?" Stevie shrugged. "You were a player. Now you're their coach."

"It still feels weird." If these nerves didn't stop, I was going to puke. When was the last time I'd puked? That was Stevie's specialty lately, not mine.

She was four months pregnant with our baby boy. It had taken the entire first trimester for her to keep breakfast down.

"Maverick." Stevie took my face in her hands, forcing me to lock in on her face. "Breathe."

"I'm not qualified."

"You've been head coach at the Oaks for two years. You made it to the state championship last year."

"The kids are good."

"And so are you." She kissed me again, then let me go to finish making her breakfast. "Maybe call your dad on the way to work."

"Okay." I nodded. "Good idea."

For most of my life, Mom had been the person I'd call when I couldn't sort the mess in my head. Stevie was that person now. But Dad had gotten damn good at providing backup.

We were all finding our way after Mom. Creating new dynamics. Dad worked a lot. He golfed a lot too, mostly with Kai and Bodhi. He was arguably more excited than anyone to have a new grandson to spoil soon.

"I'd better go." I sighed and pulled her in for a hug. "Don't work too hard today."

"It's June, Mav."

Meaning she'd work too hard. It was peak season at Adair, and the season meant I had limited time with my wife.

Declan still worked as a landscape designer, not quite ready to retire fully yet. But she ran the place these days. He was there to be her backup, taking on some projects and offering his expertise.

"No lifting anything heavy."

"I won't," she said, her hand finding mine to loop our pinky fingers together. "I love you."

"Love you too." I kissed her forehead, then forced myself out of the kitchen, calling Dad before I'd even climbed in my truck.

"Hey, Dad."

"Hey. What's up?"

"I'm nervous."

"You'll be fine, Maverick."

"But what if—"

"This is a good decision. You can do this job."

His reassurances were the same as Stevie's. Either they were both telling me the truth.

Or she'd prepped him for this call.

"Thanks."

He chuckled. "Call me later. I want to hear how it went."

"Will do. Still on for dinner?"

"I'll be over with pizza at seven."

"Okay. Don't forget—"

"I know, I know. I'll get Stevie's special pizza. Good luck."

"Bye." It helped. But not enough. When I pulled into the parking lot of the fieldhouse, I still wanted to puke.

Two years of working at the Oaks, it almost felt like a betrayal to walk into a different office. But my replacement at the high school was perfectly capable. He'd just moved to Mission, looking for a smaller town to raise his kids after a successful coaching career in Las Vegas.

But I'd miss my students. I'd miss the familiar routine. I'd miss seeing Mom's picture in the hall every day.

Stevie had anticipated that one. She'd packed a framed picture of Mom and me to put on the corner of my desk. It was in my backpack along with a picture from our wedding day.

We'd gotten married in December, on New Year's Eve, a year and a half ago. She'd been flawless in a chiffon gown with a ruffled skirt. We'd had a huge party under twinkle lights with champagne and cake.

There'd been no need for reassuring phone calls that day. I'd known, in my bones, that Stevie and I belonged together. What the hell did it mean that I couldn't seem to open my door and start my new job?

"Is this a mistake, Mom?" I asked, staring at the fieldhouse.

I'd spent a lot of time talking to Mom over the years. If I listened hard enough, she always found a way to respond.

The engine was still running when a figure appeared at the hood of my truck.

Ford stared at me, eyebrows raised. Then he jerked his chin for me to get out.

So I got out.

"Morning," he said. "Strange to be here?"

"A little," I admitted.

"Felt that way on my first day too." He clapped me on the shoulder, almost giving me a shove like he knew I needed it to put one foot in front of the other.

The next few hours went by in a blur of human resources paperwork and re-introductions to people I already knew and faces I'd seen as a student. Then Ford was leading me to my new office, flipping on the light.

"We've got a coaches meeting in thirty in the conference room. I'll let you get settled in here. See you in a bit."

"Thanks, Coach."

"Ford," he corrected.

"That's going to take me a while."

He chuckled, then ducked out.

I didn't have much to unpack, but I set out my pictures and settled into my chair, seeing how it felt as a coach of the Treasure State University Wildcats.

Fuck me. I was a Wildcats coach.

I smiled so wide it pinched my cheeks.

"Coach." A knock came at the door before a stream of guys filled my office.

"Hey." I stood from my chair, grinning at the players who'd once been my teammates. Guys who'd been freshmen and sophomores.

One of them, the starting punter, began a slow clap. "Coach. Coach. Coach. Coach."

The chanting got louder. Faster. Until all of them were practically yelling as they cheered.

"Coach! Coach! Coach! Coach!"

I laughed. I laughed until my sides ached.

All right, Mom. I hear you.

Loud and clear.

———

TWO YEARS LATER ...

"Maverick." Stevie's nails bit into my shoulders as she wrapped her legs around my waist, her pussy fluttering around my cock.

No matter how many times I heard my name in that breathy gasp, how many times I lost myself inside her body, it would never be enough.

"You feel so damn good." I pounded inside of her, my hips rolling with every stroke.

"Harder."

Fuck. Yes. When my wife gave me an order in the bedroom, I listened.

She raised her arms, pressing her palms flat against the headboard as I pistoned harder. Faster.

"I'm going to come." She whimpered her warning, then shattered, her back arching as she cried out and pulsed around my length.

I only managed a few more thrusts before the build at the base of my spine was too much, until every muscle was clenched, stars burst behind my eyes, and I came on a roar, pouring inside of her as I came apart.

We collapsed in a heap of sweaty limbs and pounding hearts.

The pillows were gone, scattered somewhere on the floor. So were the blankets. It didn't matter. She curled into my side, tangling her naked body with mine.

"Three times?" I panted, tracing a circle on her lower back. "Something you need to tell me?"

"I don't know." She bit her lip, lifting to stare at me.

"Do you have one?"

She nodded.

"Then go pee on a stick." I swatted her bare ass.

She giggled, untangling our legs so she could scramble out of bed. She pushed her long hair off her forehead as she tiptoed into the bathroom, closing the door.

The last time she'd wanted sex three times in one night, she'd been pregnant with Swayze.

I rolled for the nightstand, clicking on the baby monitor. My boy was sound asleep in his crib, bundled in a sleep sack with his tiny fists raised above his head.

He slept like his mother.

And he looked like me.

Maybe that would change in time. He was only eighteen months old. But he had my eyes and my mouth. Dad had found some old baby pictures, and when you put Swayze's against mine, they were almost identical.

Maybe our next would take after Stevie.

God, I hoped she was pregnant. It wasn't something we'd planned, and though the idea was just minutes old, I wanted it.

I jackknifed to a seat, getting out of the bed. When I opened the door to the bathroom, Stevie was tying a robe around her waist.

"Should we set a timer?" I pulled her back into my chest, staring at the white stick on the counter.

"Probably."

But neither of us moved. We stood there, staring at that stick.

"If it's a girl, we're naming her Meredith," Stevie said.

She'd said the same when she was pregnant with Swayze.

When we'd been in this same bathroom, staring at a different white stick. Waiting until the tiny screen showed a single word.

Pregnant.

———

EIGHT MONTHS LATER . . .

"Are you sure you're okay?" I asked Stevie.

"I'm fine." She frowned. "Go. Coach. And for the love of all things, stop hovering."

That was never going to happen. Certainly not when she was nine months pregnant, two days past her due date and hadn't been feeling well all day. "Are you sure you're—"

"If you ask me one more time if I'm sure I'm okay, I'm going to scream."

"Do you think it's contractions?"

"Maverick." Her nostrils flared.

I'd learned a long time ago nothing good happened when Stevie's nostrils flared.

"Okay." I backed away from my very pregnant, very irritable wife, and held up my hands. "I love you."

She sighed, rubbing her belly. "I love you too. Now, go away."

I risked a kiss on her cheek, then bolted before I could piss her off. Again.

"Uncle Mav." Bodhi tossed me his basketball, getting into position for a layup drill.

I bounce-passed it to him, then took position beneath the

basket for any stray rebounds as the rest of his team lined up to shoot before the game.

Basketball wasn't my best sport, but I'd been the assistant coach to Bodhi's club team for years. Ever since Mom had died. The head coach just kept asking if I'd help, and since it was special time with Bodhi, I always said yes. Even when I didn't have much free time, I loved this team of middle schoolers.

Bodhi would be playing for the Oaks as soon as he was in high school, and I wouldn't be on the bench with him any longer. I'd be in the stands with Mabel and Kai and Stevie and Dad, cheering him on from afar.

But not this year. Not yet.

Stevie was sitting in the second row of the bleachers, beside Mabel. She was smiling and talking, but there was a strain to her features. She kept rubbing her side. Swayze was with Dad on the opposite side of the gym, running the length of the baseline, laughing and squealing when Dad would give chase.

Everything was probably fine. Stevie would tell me if there was a problem.

Except that niggling worry only seemed to get worse through the first quarter. Each time I glanced to the crowd, Stevie looked worse. Her face was pale, her jaw tight like she was in pain.

We were crushing the other team. The score was twenty to zero. But one of their guards dribbled down the court as the clock ticked toward zero, and right as the buzzer blared, he launched the basketball from the three-point line.

Swish.

Their side of the stands erupted. One of the grandparents raised an airhorn above her head and let it rip, the sound so loud she received glares from everyone, her side and ours alike.

But that horn was like a slap to the face.

"All right, Mom," I said under my breath. "I hear you."

It took only a minute for me to let the head coach know I was taking Stevie to the hospital. I squeezed Bodhi's shoulders, told him good job, then jogged across the gym.

"Come on," I told Stevie.

She didn't argue. "Swayze."

He was still chasing around the gym with Dad.

"We've got him," Mabel said. "Call me."

I nodded, helping Stevie down the stairs. Then we were rushing out the doors for the parking lot.

"Something doesn't feel right." She stared at me, those beautiful hazel eyes full of worry.

"It'll be okay." I kissed her hand, keeping it locked in mine as we strode for our new SUV.

I hit the locks, opened the door, just as Stevie gasped. "What?"

Her eyes blew wide, then pointed to her legs.

To the water seeping through her leggings.

"Okay, so maybe I'm having contractions."

"You think?" I exhaled, a bit of fear vanishing as I hauled her in for a quick kiss.

Then I drove my wife to the hospital.

And eight hours later, I sat in a chair while Stevie rested. Holding my daughter, Meredith Mae Houston, in my arms.

———

FIVE MONTHS LATER...

There were three people and four stuffed animals in my

bed. Swayze had brought all of his *pets* with him when he'd joined us around midnight. Meredith was too little for stuffies, but my baby girl had a sixth sense for when her parents fell asleep.

It wasn't easy to sleep when a squirmy two-year-old pressed his feet into your spine, but somehow, I'd managed to drift off after Swayze had finally settled in the middle of our bed.

Meredith's cries had rung through the monitor moments later.

I should have stayed in her room, rocked her back to sleep. But I'd been so damn tired I'd brought her to our bed too and let her sleep on my chest.

Stevie had her now, tucked into a crook of her arm. Swayze was sideways, taking up the majority of the king-size mattress.

I shifted him around, making sure all his pets were close as he drooled on my pillow. Then I rounded the bed and brushed a kiss to Stevie's forehead.

She hummed, not opening her eyes. "Are you leaving?"

"Yeah. Be back in a bit."

"Love you."

"I love you too, honey." I kissed her again, then smoothed Meredith's chocolate hair—her mother's hair—off her face.

On silent feet, I made my way through the dark house to the garage.

It was four thirty in the morning, but the long summer days of Montana meant the soft yellow light of dawn was already cresting the mountain horizon. The streets of Mission were quiet, like they usually were on Saturday mornings at this hour. I yawned every few minutes on my drive to the fieldhouse, and when I pulled into the lot, there was only one other vehicle waiting.

Rush was just closing his door when I parked.

"Hey." I slung my backpack over my shoulder and fell in step beside him as we walked for the door.

"Morning." He yawned. "I'm beat."

"Same."

It would be easy to turn around, go home and go back to bed. But we kept walking, into the gym and weight room, where we spent an hour working out together, just like we had all those years ago when we'd lived together. Played together.

Now we worked together.

Rush had just moved back to Mission after retiring from the NFL. He'd joined the coaching staff, and now I got to work with my oldest friend each day.

Yeah, we could have just worked out over lunch. But this was what Rush and I did. We met at dawn, at this fieldhouse, and though we didn't talk much while we worked out, we showed up for each other.

And by the time we left, we were both wide awake.

"What are you guys up to today?" he asked, putting on a pair of shades.

"I don't know. Stevie's swamped at Adair, so she mentioned maybe going into the office for a while this afternoon to catch up. I need to mow the lawn. I'll probably take the kids to the grocery store. You?"

"Faye was talking about heading into the mountains. Going for a drive or something. Find a spot for a picnic where the kids can chase around and get dirty."

"That sounds nice."

"Yeah," he said. "Tomorrow?"

"I'll be here."

We shared a wave, then went our separate directions.

I needed a shower. I had my own list of stuff to do. But my truck seemed to steer itself into the drive-through at McDonald's. And when I got home, I didn't take the food inside. I found Stevie in the living room, cartoons playing for Swayze as she fed Meredith a bottle.

"I want to do something this morning," I told her, shutting off the TV. "Will you come with me?"

"Sure." She gave me a strange glance but didn't ask questions. She just pulled on a sweatshirt and shoes, then helped me load up the kids. Helped Swayze with his breakfast as we drove through town.

Stevie might not be great at spontaneity, but she rolled with mine.

And she realized, soon enough, where we were going.

The minute I turned off the highway, onto a gravel road that wound into the mountains, her hand stretched across the console, reaching for mine.

She held tight all the way to Mom's meadow.

I hadn't been here since we'd scattered her ashes years ago. And if asked, I wouldn't be able to explain why I wanted to visit today. It just seemed . . . important.

"Where dis, Daddy?" Swayze asked as I took him out of his car seat, letting him look around.

I crouched in front of him, brushing a crumb from his breakfast off his cheek. "This is one of my Top Five favorite spots."

He took my hand as I led him toward the meadow, but he didn't hang on for long, letting go to explore.

Yellow and white flowers dotted the green grass. The scents of pine and wind and earth filled my nose.

It took him less than a minute to find a rock he could throw. "Wook it, Mommy!"

He tossed it forward, the rock landing a couple feet ahead. Then he picked up a stick with one hand and frowned at the mud the rock had left behind on the other.

Stevie came to my side, carrying Meredith.

I stole my daughter, holding her in one arm as the other wrapped around Stevie's shoulders.

"You okay?" she asked.

I rested my chin on the top of her head as I looked across the meadow. To the cloudless blue sky. "Never better."

———

SEVEN YEARS LATER...

The field at the stadium was teeming with kids. More kids than I'd ever seen at the annual Wildcats coaches' flag football game.

Between all of us coaches and our families, we had enough people for four teams, not just two. Especially now that most of the kids were getting older.

We used to have a few babysitters on hand to watch the little ones, but there weren't any babies, not anymore.

All of the kids were dressed, coated in sunscreen and ready to play.

Coach Ford Ellis's End Zoners versus Coach Toren Greely's Grid Irons.

This game had remained unchanged for over a decade. There were enough changes on the horizon for the Wildcats football program, it was comforting to leave this tradition untouched.

We'd pick teams, wives and kids always getting priority.

Then we'd play for a couple hours before an afternoon barbeque under the brilliant blue Montana sky.

This game had become a favorite tradition for my family. Stevie was sitting on the turf beside Jennsyn, stretching as they talked. Swayze was playing catch with Rally, both boys counting as they made catches without a drop. And Meredith was dancing around with the other girls, singing along to the music blasting through the sound system.

"I forgot the first-aid kit in my office," Rush said, coming to stand at my side. "Think we'll need it?"

"Hope not."

"Well, I guess if we do, I'll run back and get it." He surveyed the crowd, eyes crinkling at the sides as he smiled. "I love this game."

"So do I." Of all the games we'd played, coached, this was always my favorite every year.

It should be a fun time for all of us, except Ford and Toren were standing together, expressions too serious. They'd both been off since we'd arrived with tight smiles and hushed conversations.

"What's that about?" I asked Rush.

"No idea."

Ford and Toren spotted us, then shared a look that made my stomach sink before they walked our way.

We'd all worked together for years. We'd become friends. A family of our own.

I knew when news wasn't the good kind.

"Before we start today, we wanted to talk to you both," Ford said. "We, uh, wanted to ask you both to take over today. As captains."

"Absolutely not." I crossed my arms over my chest.

Rush hooked his thumb my way. "What he said."

"Hold up. Don't just say no," Ford said. "Let us explain."

"It's time to have someone else take over this game," Toren said. "With my change in jobs, Ford's retirement, we thought it best you both step in as leads. Carry on the tradition."

Ford had one more month left on his contract, then he'd no longer be the head coach of the Wildcats football program. He wanted to have his weekends free to watch his boys play their own football games. His daughter, Joey, was getting married in the fall.

He was ready for Saturdays to be his own. To cheer on Rush, as he took over as head coach, and me, as I filled Toren's shoes as defensive coordinator.

Millie, Ford's wife, was taking over as the athletics director, overseeing the entire program. And she'd asked Toren to step in to her former role, helping make sure every sport at Treasure State had the resources needed to succeed.

I still hadn't wrapped my brain around it all. I couldn't imagine standing on the sidelines without Ford and Toren nearby.

So I sure as hell didn't see the need to fuck with the annual coaches game.

"Hard pass," I said at the same time Rush told them, "No, thanks."

Ford frowned. "At some point, someone else needs to take my place."

"Not this year." Rush clapped him on the shoulder, then left our huddle, walking over to where Faye was taking a picture of the kids playing.

"Mav." Toren held out a whistle. It was pink, the same color as the T-shirts for his team.

Ford's team wore yellow.

"That belongs around your neck." I winked, then walked away to find Stevie.

She was rifling through the backpack we'd brought, fishing out a bottle of sunscreen.

I wrapped her up, copping a feel of her ass through the shorts she'd worn today.

"What was that about?" she asked, pointing to where Ford and Toren were, begrudgingly, putting on their whistles, though both were trying to hide a smile.

"Ford and Toren are trying to have Rush and me take over as captains for today."

"And?"

"I said no."

"Good." She lifted on her toes to kiss the corner of my mouth. "I love you."

"Love you too." I held her tight for a long moment, keeping her close. Then I let her go so she could douse our children with a second coat of sunscreen before the game.

I watched her walk away, hair swishing down her spine, a breathtaking smile on her face. And then I tipped my face to the sky.

"Thanks, Mom," I whispered.

Maybe Stevie and I would have found our way to each other without my mother's interference. But I loved giving my mom credit for the gifts in my life.

For my beautiful wife. My incredible children.

For a Saturday at the Treasure State Wildcats stadium, playing football with my friends. My family.

"Ready, Daddy?" Meredith came over, slipping her hand in mine.

I smiled down at her, at the girl who looked so much like her namesake. "Let's make the most of it, baby girl."

ACKNOWLEDGMENTS

Thank you for reading *Merit*! It's bittersweet to say farewell to the Treasure State Wildcats. This series has been one of my absolute favorites to write. Thanks for reading Maverick and Stevie's story!

A massive thanks to my editor, Elizabeth Nover. My proofreaders, Julie Deaton and Judy Zweifel. My cover designer, Sarah Hansen. My agent and publicist, Georgana Grinstead. Without you, there would be no book for Maverick Houston. And lastly, to my assistant, Logan Chisholm, for your support each and every day. I'm so blessed to have you all on my team.

Thanks to the influencers who read and promote my books. To my friends and family for your all-around awesomeness. And lastly, to you, my dear reader, for trusting me with your precious reading time. I hope this series has been the wonderful escape from reality for you that it has been for me. Go Wildcats!

ABOUT THE AUTHOR

Devney Perry is a *Wall Street Journal, USA Today* and #1 Amazon bestselling author of over forty romance novels. After working in the technology industry for a decade, she abandoned conference calls and project schedules to pursue her passion for writing. She was born and raised in Montana and now lives in Washington with her husband and two sons.

Don't miss out on the latest book news.
Subscribe to her newsletter!
www.devneyperry.com

Made in the USA
Las Vegas, NV
07 March 2025

19192479R00204